---- ★ ----

I looked about the dim porch and realized that I wasn't alone. At least thirteen cats were there, all moving about in jittery silence.

The open doorway led into a kitchen, the kind I dimly remembered from childhood, with a Formica table that had once been yellow and mugs hanging on hooks above the sink. The floor, it seemed, had long ago had a design on it, a jolly daisy pattern that had faded over the decades to a barely distinguishable gray. And lying face down on it, circled by her worried brood, was the cat lady. Even before I touched her outstretched hand, so still and so cold, the mass of blood that darkened her gray curls told me she was dead.

---- ★ ----

Clea Simon

MEW

is for murder

W❖RLDWIDE®

TORONTO • NEW YORK • LONDON
AMSTERDAM • PARIS • SYDNEY • HAMBURG
STOCKHOLM • ATHENS • TOKYO • MILAN
MADRID • WARSAW • BUDAPEST • AUCKLAND

For Jon

MEW IS FOR MURDER

A Worldwide Mystery/November 2007

First published by Poisoned Pen Press.

ISBN-13: 978-0-373-26619-7
ISBN-10:   0-373-26619-7

Acknowledgments

This book would not have come about at all if Kate Mattes of Kate's Mystery Books in Cambridge had not said to me, "You should write a mystery." So thanks go first and foremost to Kate! Beyond that, a warm and supportive crew of family and friends helped me make the transition from nonfiction to fiction. Brett Milano now says he always thought I'd write one of these, Karen Schlosberg read numerous revisions and improved each one, and Caroline Leavitt wouldn't give up cheering. The talented and careful editor Barbara Peters and the staff at Poisoned Pen Press never stopped believing in this project. Much credit goes to my indefatigable agent, Ann Collette of the Helen Reese Literary Agency, for her sharp eye and sharp business sense, and to Joan Lockhart of *GumboArts.com,* who created the adorable cover. Thanks as well to Iris Simon, Anne Trumbore, Eric Ruben, Vicki Croke, Lisa Susser, Ann Porter, the good folks at the Cambridge Animal Control office, Readerville, and the Cat Writers Association for support, advice, facts to back up my fiction, and more, and to Frank Garelick, Sophie Garelick, and Lisa Jones for unending enthusiastic encouragement. And finally—as always—to my husband, Jon S. Garelick, who still makes me purr.

PROLOGUE

Witness

FIRST THERE WAS a rustling, a scraping like metal on wood. Then the scream, though whether it was of rage or fright the few late-night listeners couldn't tell. Then the scuffle and the thud. As she dragged herself forward, each movement slower than the one before, silence washed over her like the dark. Only the circling eyes, pairs of yellow and green and gold, bore witness until at last the woman on the floor lay still.

ONE

"YOU EVER HEAR the one about the cat lady who died alone with her precious pussies? By the time they found her, the cats—" Ralph's voice boomed across the open room.

"That's an urban myth, Ralph," I snapped back. I couldn't help but see his broad grin. "And you know it." I was sorting through a stack of mail on a big, empty desk in a big, almost empty newsroom, but I heard him hoot with pleasure. He'd gotten to me.

"They're heartless beasts, you know." He swiveled his bulky bottom in the ergonometrically correct desk chair and called back over his shoulder. "No point in loving them."

"Well, you're not any kind of winner," I muttered. "Not with that attitude." Head turned away, he didn't hear me, and I saw him swivel back toward his desk, the only exercise he apparently ever got. He reached into the mountain of paper and cardboard mailers, cleared a space to reveal a computer keyboard, and pushed his Discman headphones back up on his head. As his tiny ponytail began to bob, I knew I'd been dismissed. Still peeved, I was tempted to grab that thin grey queue, as I'd never grab a cat's tail. To pull him on his rolling chair through the city room would be pure fun.

But that kind of fun was too expensive for me. I was a free-lancer, an interloper in this newsroom, even if I preferred to call myself talent for hire. An outsider, despite having labored as a paid employee here for the better part of a decade. Ralph was a staff writer—the *Morning Mail*'s senior rock critic—which made him a fixture while my kind came and went. And I'd just sold my former boss on a story that I cared about. Better not to ruffle any feathers—or fur for that matter. Despite the itch in my palm as I walked by that paltry bobbing lock, I resisted. Instead, I dumped the junk mail that had accumulated in my mailbox, tucked a long reporter's note pad in my bag, and walked toward the escalators that would lead me out.

Sunlight, one of the first real days of spring. I fished my dark glasses from the big, flat courier bag that held my life, pushed an unruly red curl back out of my eyes, and enjoyed the view through the paper's glass front. The trees were budding, the strip of earth that rimmed the building glowed with a faint green that would soon be lawn. Next week, or maybe in two, either the heat would kick in with all its wonderful bugs and mugginess, or it would turn frigid again. In Boston, you could never quite tell. But on one glorious May Monday, it was spring.

After years of using the grim employee's entrance in the back, I stepped out through the big, glass doors of the *Mail* and enjoyed the damp, fresh scent of the season. The first hint of lilac, salt from the nearby bay: it smelled to me of freedom. Which, considering I'm thirty-three, was coming just in time. Thirty-three, the "Jesus year," which my friend Bunny, a lapsed-Catholic-turned-Wiccan, had assured me would be a year of changes and decisions. Professionally, at least, she'd been right. Sure, my income had plummeted when I'd left the copy desk a few months back, giving up nights of spelling checks and correcting grammar for financial instability and freedom. But now I could tell anyone who asked that I was Theda Krakow, writer, and not want to correct myself, to tack on "part time" or even "hopeful." I had three months' rent in the bank, a reasonably sound Toyota, and I was doing what I loved most, finally, with no restrictive clause attached.

Thinking of claws, I tried to remember my cat food situation. The *Mail* was located right by a huge supermarket with a well-stocked pet department. It was just a moment's thought, but suddenly the bright sky turned misty. For a moment there, I'd forgotten this year's most devastating change: James was no more. The huge gray former stray who'd been my loyal feline companion for twelve years had succumbed three weeks before to kidney failure and an intestinal blockage that the vets had decided, too late, was cancer. Twenty-three days ago, actually. The bright sun no longer warmed me.

Time to work, I reminded myself. After several weeks of never leaving James' side and nearly daily vet visits, I'd thrown myself back into my career, such as it was. My closest friends, I knew, were a little worried about me. Their attempts to drag me out hadn't met with much success, even after James was gone, and when they did they noted the weight that had dropped from my normally healthy five-foot-nine frame, the rings that almost matched my dark eyes. At least one of my girlfriends had asked if I needed more time to mourn, or at least be with people, before diving back into a full work schedule. But I'd made the step out of my secure little job and toward a dream, and no matter how much I was hurting I wasn't going to let that become a mistake. Editors didn't understand delays, didn't understand anything but deadlines and word counts. The freelancer who was late might have the best excuse in the world, but she wouldn't get the call next time that editor wanted a thousand words by Thursday. Putting grief aside, I'd typed up fresh story pitches, Xeroxed my best clippings, and gone looking for assignments.

It wasn't just the money. I found the rhythms of reporting and writing to be mercifully seductive, particularly when my one-bedroom apartment had become so still and quiet. This kind of work was the perfect distraction—how can your own story bring you down when you're trying to get inside someone else's? I'd head home just long enough to make some phone calls, set up interviews, and immediately head out again. No point in crying or sitting around staring at the empty plush cat bed on the filing cabinet by my computer. There was always a source to be called or a fact to be checked. A story was in the offing, and it was time to hunt it down and pounce.

The story that was waiting for me this afternoon was one I'd been pushing for, one that sprang out of my adopted home town. Since coming to the area for college, I'd lived in Cambridge. This smaller city, across the river from the paper's Boston base, had been dubbed "Boston's Left Bank" and "The People's Republic" with varying degrees of affection by the academics, immigrants, and aging hippies I called neighbors. Of course, the presence of staff and students from Harvard, M.I.T., and a dozen smaller schools hadn't always blended easily with the area's solid working-class base, a mix of old Portuguese families and newer arrivals from Africa, Asia, and the Caribbean, but that's what kept things interesting. With the final demise of the Tasty, the old diner's linoleum counter giving way to a chi-chi chain store that peddled overpriced swim trunks, some said the real Cambridge was dead. What kind of town was it where you couldn't get an honest hot dog for under two dollars anymore, not to mention a lime rickey? But outside of Harvard Square, the balance still held. We still had more independent bookstores and coffeehouses than McDonald's, and for that I was grateful.

My area, at least, was resisting gentrification. Stuck between the universities and the river, Cambridgeport wedged town and gown together too tightly for anyone to take on airs. Even the architectures lived cheek by jowl. Right around my block, with the rusty brick buildings where I'd found a rent-controlled apartment a couple of years back, was a row of old

Victorians. Despite the wear, the graying clapboard, they had grace, not to mention the wrap-around porches and high ceilings I'd always longed for, and they gave the area character and a sense of warmth. You could wave at someone lounging on a swing on one of those sprawling porches, and he or she would wave back, regardless of color, language, or income level. The next time you saw that person, waiting in line at the drugstore or walking along the sidewalk, you'd both smile, like you knew each other. In a way, you did, thanks to the forced proximity of the neighborhood.

I'd made a habit of strolling through these tree-lined blocks as the dirty snow receded into the gutters these past few weeks. Deep in the heart of the riverside city they sat like a warm oasis. The neighborhood was definitely urban: traffic lined up on Putnam, the main cut-through, with loud salsa competing against NPR from the car windows as commuters sought a short cut to or from the turnpike. And in the mornings a definite sweet smell often filled the air—sometimes mint-flavored, sometimes pure sugar—from the confectionery factory that shadowed the area. I'd had roommates who said it made them gag, but Cambridgeport was home to me. I loved the mix of languages and people as well as the filigree touches that embellished an old arch, the detailing on top of a painted wooden column. And until I could afford one of those magnificent old houses, I was happy enough to live in a big brick box nearby as long as I could walk by those aging beauties and pay my respects.

It was on one of my morning walks, just two days earlier, that I'd found my story. It had found me, actually. Or she had, a small black and white kitten who'd barreled into me, nearly tripping me as I strolled unaware, eyes up on a particularly well preserved bit of masonry detail.

"Yow!" I'd exclaimed, catching myself from a stumble

and seeing, at last, the black and white dumpling who'd woven between my ankles. "What's up, little kitty?" But she took off, not deigning to answer, and I followed. Partly, I'll admit, because she was adorable, those tiny white boots kicking up behind her, but partly too because she looked awfully young, with fur that still clumped like wool and a little spiky tail that seemed too short for her round body. I hadn't spied a collar, but if I found one on her I'd make sure to deliver her right back to her mama's door.

She was too fast for me, however, and ducked under an overgrown holly bush before I could scoop her up. I could see two light green eyes staring back at me from beneath the dark green cave, but the thorny leaves that came almost to ground level made access challenging.

"Okay, little girl. Maybe you're home." I've always spoken to cats. Who knows how much they understand? More than we knew, I'd venture. At any rate, she didn't respond, and I stood to straighten my back. Suddenly I was aware that I wasn't alone. Standing up had brought me eye level with the elevated porch of one of those Victorians—and face-to-face with three of the largest cats I had ever seen. Two tabbies and a long-haired gray stared at me, and as I stepped back—an involuntary response to their pure size and majesty—another, somewhat smaller, joined them.

"Hello." It couldn't hurt to be polite. They didn't respond, but a fifth walked up, a bright orange tiger, coming, I could see now, from the opened window that let out onto the sagging, paintless porch. She (or he, I couldn't really see) was joined by another, basically white and frankly a little grimy, with a black spot like an eyepatch on her right side. "Meh!" she said, summing me up rather quickly, and flopped on the boards beside her colleagues.

Six cats, seven counting my kitten. I was beginning to

wonder who lived here. Forgetting my original intention of simply perambulating toward groceries, I walked up the pitted driveway that ran up alongside the house and was nearly tripped again as a door opened inward and four more kittens—adolescents, really—charged out, all long legs and skinny tails as they batted each other and wrestled their way around me to disappear in the weeds of the lawn.

"Do you have a kitten?" I looked up at the sound of a voice so faint it could have been the rustle of the leaves. "Did you bring me a kitten?"

I was momentarily dumbfounded as I looked up into a small round face surrounded by white curls. Despite the day's growing heat, she wore a blue-gray cardigan, which I couldn't help noticing was misbuttoned. And on her shoulder sat another cat, a small one, brown and sleek with at least a little Siamese in its background.

"Did you?" Her voice had grown a bit louder. Was she expecting tribute? Then I remembered how I'd first noticed her brood.

"There was a kitten, a little black and white one. I thought she might be lost." My answer sounded feeble. Clearly, I realized, this kitten was part of a much larger pride. How many cats did this woman have?

"Ah, Musetta. My little flirt. No, she's fine. We're all fine here," she said turning back into the house. On her shoulder the almond-shaped blue eyes of the Siamese turned back to watch me and blinked once. "We're doing fine." The door closed behind her and I was once more alone in the sun. The cats on the porch had disappeared, as had the adolescents play fighting in the long grass. All that remained were my questions and the memory of one roly-poly kitten, too young to be out on her own and destined, I feared, for trouble.

"Excuse me. Excuse me!" The sharp voice that broke my

reverie didn't seem to be begging anyone's indulgence, but I looked up automatically. Was I blocking someone's way? I'd begun to wander away from the cat lady's house, my mind lost in a vision of cats' eyes, and stood at the end of her driveway, where an overgrown lilac had begun to show its first dark-purple buds. "Excuse me!" A thin thirtyish woman in a bright turquoise suit was waving to me from the steps next door, one of the nicer houses on the block. "Are you with animal control?"

"No, I just thought there was a lost kitten…" I began to reply, raising my voice to match her volume, when she cut me off with a wave of her manicured hand. I caught a glimpse of a gold bracelet, the obvious mate to the heavy gold chain around her neck. At her gesture, I approached.

"Kittens! There are always kittens there." She said it as if it were a bad thing. "People are always bringing them by to her. I don't know what to do."

"Do you think she's a hoarder?" Ever since I'd seen those cats assembled on the porch, I'd wondered. While true cat hoarders—the kind who take in so many stray felines that both their health and the well-being of their pets is endangered—might be uncommon, the number of cats that I'd seen, plus their caretaker's unwillingness to chat, had set off a small alarm in the back of my head. Cat hoarders, or collectors, tended to avoid outside contacts. We are all the enemy in their eyes, since we often come around to remove the animals that we see as endangered and they see as family. I'd heard of hoarders who lost almost all connection with reality, as their isolation fed the wild stories that grew around them and they were ostracized by their neighbors. This woman had seemed to recognize the kitten I'd described, so she wasn't too out of it. But why had she brushed me off like that? How many more cats were sheltered inside the rundown house? Sure, the old lady might just be a bit reclusive, a private person or shy. But

I'd thought of this as a friendly block. Here was her neighbor, a woman who obviously had a life—and a well-financed one at that—willing to talk with a perfect stranger.

"Hoarder? She's a freak, that's what she is." Her clipped tones accented the word dismissively, leaving no room for discussion. "A freak. But everyone brings their cats to her. Never mind what they do to our yard or to the songbirds in our trees."

"Do they look healthy and well fed?" I asked, knowing full well that some hoarders will feed their cats before they put dinner on their own tables.

"The cats? They make this area look like a ghetto!" She spit out the word. It didn't answer my question, but her own gesticulations brought her attention to the thin gold watch that lay beside the bracelet. "My ten-thirty!" She disappeared inside. Just as I turned to walk on, her glossy dark-green door opened again.

"If she's a friend of yours, you tell her that I'm calling animal control again. You tell her." She ducked back in before I could reply, but there was no doubt in my mind who the nicely dressed woman was talking about. All I questioned now was my own readiness to believe appearances.

TWO

"A CAT WHAT? Is this another pet story?" My editor Tim hadn't really been listening when I'd brought him my idea for an article later that day. It was a state of inattention I'd grown used to. The key, I'd discovered, was to make my pitch in fewer than twenty-five words. Words that, ideally, included "family," "trend," or something that he called a "youth angle." Trying to sell him on a feature about an older woman who apparently lived alone was going to be a stretch.

"Cat hoarder," I repeated, slowly and clearly, as he paced around his glass-fronted office. "A person, usually a woman, who quote-unquote collects cats, so many that the animal control people have to clear them out."

"Is this a trend?"

"No, not really." I hedged. "Some researchers think it's a form of mental illness, a variation on obsessive-compulsive disorder. They're treating it with antidepressants, like Paxil."

Anti-depressants were hot, even if hoarders weren't. Tim sat down and, picking up a pen, began to twirl it between his fingers. He was listening.

I perched gingerly on the office's one guest chair and made my pitch. "Do you remember the movie *Grey Gardens,* about the rich old sisters who had cats all over the place? Well, they're an example. There was another outside San Francisco recently where they cleared out a hundred ninety-six cats before all was done. And I think it's possible that we may have one right here in Cambridge."

"So she's a crazy cat lady, that's what you're saying?"

He seemed interested, but inwardly I winced. "Well, it's more extreme than that." I didn't add that I'd been called a crazy cat lady in my day, usually when I had trusted James' opinion of someone, usually some man, over anyone else's. Unlike me, my wise old cat had tended to be right about which ones were keepers and which I should've thrown back. "It's sad for the hoarder and can be really tragic for the animals. These people don't realize what they're doing. They think they're saving the animals, that the cats are their family. But in reality shelter workers find cats dead and dying, some-times even cannibalizing each other out of desperate hunger."

"Disgusting." Tim paused for a moment, thinking of his budget of upcoming stories. Or maybe his upcoming lunch. "Disgusting animals." He tossed the pen into an open drawer, dug through some papers, pushed some others aside. "Can you turn it around by next week? Stop by photo and see if they can send someone over."

I nodded and fled before he could reconsider. I had the assignment.

The truth was, I didn't know if the old woman was a hoarder. She might simply be a pet lover, fully in control of herself and her feline charges. I'd read enough on the subject to know that it's the care and capability of the cat lover, not the number of animals, that makes a hoarder. Someone who can keep the litter boxes clean, the kitties and herself fed, and the heat turned on is doing fine, whether she has three cats or thirty, though personally I'd have added the requirement that anyone who sees herself as a savior of cats should also have the sense to have them neutered. But I'd been fascinated by the phenomenon ever since I'd read about that San Francisco case, and my neighbor would be a good focal point, whether she was a hoarder or simply an indulgent pet lover. If everything was copacetic, I'd have a happier story, one that explored cat-love and discussed the prejudices and the stereotypes. If she was a hoarder, well, maybe I'd save some cats.

Before I began making judgments, however, I knew I needed to do more research. This being the computer age, that meant dropping by the *Mail*'s library on my way to photo. Since I was actually on assignment, I had every right to ask any of the staff librarians for help. But I was still happy to see Bunny in her carrel, surrounded by photos of her pets. Some of the librarians prioritized us freelancers at somewhere below "don't bother," and not only was Bunny—Barbara only to complete strangers—a computer whiz and a cat lover, she was also a longtime friend.

"How you doing, hon?" The concern in her voice was real, but I couldn't face the searching gaze behind the cats'-eyes glasses. Not at work.

"I'm okay," I muttered. "I need some research, if you can help me." The built-in desk attached to the carrel was piled high with request forms. Bunny was the best, and everyone at the *Mail* knew it. "I'm looking for kittens in the news. Cat shelters in the area, unofficial or private."

Her round face brightened up and the rhinestones on her tortoiseshell frames positively sparkled. "Another cat? I know just the one for you. There's a new rescue group…"

"It's for a story," I interrupted. "There's a possible cat hoarder in my neighborhood. I'm going to focus on her, but I want to get some background, you know, no-kill shelters, the myth of the 'crazy cat lady,' adoption statistics, kitten dumps. See if anyone has filed any complaints about strays in the Cambridgeport area."

"I'll get right on it, hon." Despite the mass of prior requests,

I knew she would. "Anything I find I'll e-mail you at home."
She looked like she wanted to say more, but held herself back.

"Thanks, Bunny." I squeezed her ample shoulder and gave
her a peck on the cheek, more for what she didn't say than
for what she did. "Love to Cal."

"Oh, *him*," she harrumphed, shaking her brown curls dismissively, and I made my exit smiling. Clearly we'd have
something else to talk about next time we chatted.

Back up in the newsroom, I'd told Ralph about my assignment as a way of thinking it over. His cracks didn't help, but
vocalizing the idea did. Somehow talking about a story could
make it all more clear. I was mulling over the angles, the
follow-up interviews I'd want to do to give the story sub-
stance. Vets, shelters. I made a mental note to look up some
of the national animal protection agencies as well, as I sorted
through the unread mail that had piled up since I'd last come
in. Since I'd had James put to sleep, I realized, tossing an invitation to a party three weeks past. It was good to be out,
good to not rely merely on e-mailed articles and electronic
submissions to keep my name alive in the public's mind and
pay my bills. It was even good to chew over a pending story
with a colleague, or so I had thought until Bunny's concern
got me smarting and then Ralph had followed up with that
crack about cat ladies. Clearly, I wasn't completely ready to
be out in society yet. Not human society, anyway. I remembered the fleece-like wool on that little black-and-white kitten
and her perfectly round green eyes, and headed for my car.

THE NEXT MORNING I woke up ready to work on the story, if
not exactly refreshed. The afternoon had proved fruitful. I'd
spent some of it working on one of my money gigs, a story
for a glossy bridal magazine that would cover next month's
rent and most of my utilities, too. And by the time I had my

adjectives in order—sixteen ways to describe the season's new bouquet styles, including four different words for "flower"—Bunny had e-mailed me a load of articles, some from competing papers, about the problem of stray cats, feral animals of all sorts, and the latest research on the mysterious condition of hoarding. I'd printed out all the pages on my rickety little DeskJet and lain down on the sofa to study and take notes. Since I was reading, and not writing, I could queue up the stereo, a good-quality sound system that had been one of the perks of the *Mail* job. A little soup and some microwaved leftover lo mein accompanied by Professor Longhair's rollicking piano, and I was back at it till the wee hours, reading in my PJs until my blurring vision cued me to put the papers down and kill the music, pull the woolly throw off the back of the sofa, curl up, and nod off.

Sleeping on the couch wasn't great for my back, but it was simple. It made the work-to-unconsciousness transition smoother and had become a habit. Not having James around had made going to sleep on my perfectly good queen-size bed unappealing. No one else was around to complain: I'd broken up with my sometime beau Rick that winter, or he'd broken up with me, perhaps, because he was the one who had taken the staff job as a music critic at a paper in Phoenix and left town, even if I'd been the one to decline his half-hearted invitation to tag along. I'd thought of him briefly as I finished off the bridal story, of the competitive spirit that had always kept us a little apart just as our shared career and love of offbeat guitar bands drew us closer. He'd never been completely supportive of my dream of writing full-time, just as he'd never really appreciated the old New Orleans sound that for me perfectly complemented its descendent, rock. Maybe he'd been the more realistic of the two of us about our competitive field, or maybe he'd just felt threatened.

Waiting for the e-mail to kick in and my editor to confirm that all my glowing prose had arrived sans computer gibberish, I'd wondered what would've happened if we'd stayed in the same city, if we'd have drifted toward the altar the same way we'd drifted into each other's arms. Would I still have found the nerve to quit the copy desk? Would we have stayed together? The level of passion had never been so high as to make our relationship any competition for a full-time writing gig, albeit one halfway across the country, and as the e-mail confirmation told me that my story had found its way to the right file, I told myself that it was probably just as well he'd taken the position and left—and that I had stayed in the city that felt like home to me. It was the cat I missed most, snuggling against me after I'd settled into bed, not the tall, somewhat distant man who'd sometimes shared it with the two of us. It was the memory of James that still made me stretch my arm out, feeling for that soft fur and the warm bulk of his presence. Sleeping on the sofa, I didn't miss him so much.

It also meant that I was up and showered fairly early for me, since the spring sun shining in my front windows didn't allow for sleeping in. It couldn't have been much after seven when I rolled out of the house, rotating my couch-sore shoulder to limber it up. Too early, I realized to drop by on a complete stranger. A quick stop at the neighhborhood coffeehouse, a funky independent upholstered with cast-off sofas and local art, beckoned. My circulation needed the jump-start caffeine could provide, and I could easily waste a half hour looking at the paper. Pulling up a stool to the Mug Shot's long wooden counter, I grabbed the morning's *Mail* to see who had written what. Reading all the bylines before even getting into any of the stories brought the morning up to a more sociable hour, while the barrista on duty, a petite purple-haired punkette with multiple piercings, refilled my French roast without having to be asked.

I was jazzed and happy as I strode up to the cat lady's house, singing to myself and beating out a carnival rhythm on the courier bag that held my notes. So caffeinated that at first I passed right by it. That was the house, back there, I reminded myself. The one with the sinking porch and the white paint half peeled off. But where were the cats? Without them, the building looked generic—and even more decrepit.

I walked back to the old building, hastening by the neighbor's pristine lawn. Was that a movement in the window? I waved and the curtain was pulled shut. As long as the neighbor didn't come out and start yelling, I didn't care. The building next door was definitely the right one: there was the cracked window, sealed with tape, the gutter hanging low like the brim of a slouch hat. But still, no cats. Remembering the side door, I walked up the cracked drive and knocked. Nobody answered, but I saw a movement. A cat, one of the big calicos, darting back and forth in the space where a torn blind exposed the lower part of a window, the bottom of what had once been an elegant French door. It should have been reassuring to see him moving like that, back and forth and back again. It was the kind of movement I would have thought meant a moth was loose inside, but there was something off about it. That cat was jumpy, his movements were too quick, his body and tail too low.

I crept up the drive, following the crumbling tarmac, and realized I too was bent low, walking in a semi-crouch like the cat. I told myself I just didn't want to be seen nosing around, as I followed a once-paved path around back, to where an enclosed porch seemed to have been turned into an informal storeroom. The sides were screened in, and storm windows had been added at some point, but cardboard boxes were piled high enough to obscure my vision. Looked like some wicker lawn furniture had found its way up there, too, although through the dirty, fly-specked glass I couldn't be sure.

There, finally, were cats. Two of them: a big gray darted
out of a door and ran up to me. I reached to pet him and he
ran back. Into the door and out again. Then I felt a pressure
against my shin. The tiny kitten from the other day butted her
head against me, but when I reached for her she too started
toward the door, but slowly. The gray tom easily outpaced her,
his ears nearly flat sideways, his tail down. The kitten was
limping, her left hind leg giving way as she walked. I reached
to pick her up, to see what was wrong, but with a burst of
speed she, too, darted inside.

I pulled the door farther open.

"Hello! It's Theda. Your neighbor?" I stretched the truth a bit
to explain my trespass. "I came about the kitten the other day?"

I looked about the dim porch and realized that I wasn't
alone. At least thirteen cats were there, all moving about in
jittery silence. An open doorway led into the house proper, and
there stood the kitten, left hind foot slightly raised.

"Come here, kitty." I passed the pacing cats. How odd, I
thought. None of them was resting, none of them washing or
staring out the window.

The kitten darted forward once again, and suddenly I
understood. The open doorway led into a kitchen, the kind I
dimly remembered from childhood, with a Formica table that
had once been yellow and mugs hanging on hooks above the
sink. The floor, it seemed, had long ago had a design on it, a
jolly daisy pattern that had faded over the decades to a barely
distinguishable gray. And lying face down on it, circled by her
worried brood, was the cat lady. Even before I touched her
outstretched hand, so still and so cold, the mass of blood that
darkened her gray curls told me she was dead.

THREE

"In through your mouth. Out through your nose. Breathe."

I felt a warm hand on the back of my neck and did as the voice commanded. The voice, I recalled as the blood returned to my brain, belonged to one of the two plainclothes detectives who had shown up soon after the uniform car, the first cops to arrive in response to my call. The uniforms were inside taking photos, I could tell by the intermittent flashes. I was out on the steps to the porch, my cell phone lying on the ground beside me, where I guess I'd dropped it when the world had started to rush far away and get swirly.

"I'm okay," I said, lifting my head from between my knees. The hand came off and I looked up into a pair of clear gray eyes, brightened by a hint of green. Just then, a uniformed EMT emerged from the door behind me, carrying one end of a sheet-covered stretcher. The detective took my shoulder and turned me away.

"Can you tell me who you are?"

"Theda, Theda Krakow." Dark brows raised in disbelief. "No, really, my mother was very theatrical. And my family came from Poland. It's an Ellis Island name." I was blabbering, but talking was better than thinking right now. "Theda Bara was actually a nice Jewish girl from Cincinnati. Theodosia was her name. Theodosia Goodman. I'm from New York, actually. I mean, I live a few blocks away now."

The detective kept me talking until the body and its ambulance were out of sight and he had the few scarce bits of information I could provide, like my number and my oh-so-recent connection with the deceased, as he called her. He told me little in return, except that her name was Lillian Helmhold, but I'd swear there was sadness in those gray eyes and that his salt-and-pepper hair had won its gray from such sights. There'd been no sign of a purse at the scene, as he called it, but some utility bills on the table listed her as the sole occupant of the grand old house. There were no signs of foul play either, he said.

"She probably tripped and fell."

"Over one of these animals!" His partner, whose suit pulled like it was sorely stressed, interrupted him. "They're everywhere."

It was true. The cats' worried darting had been replaced by a mix of frantic activity, as some hid, some ran about, and one yellow-eyed senior who'd wedged herself between the counter and the refrigerator hissed at everyone who walked by.

"But the wound was on the back of her head," I pointed out, recalling the grisly sight. My stomach had returned to where it should be. I could now recall what I'd seen without feeling dizzy.

The gray-eyed cop smiled at me. "Are you a mystery fan?" His voice was warm, but there was a hint of laughter in it. "Think we should be looking for suspicious threatening letters or a scrawled message in the dirt?" In truth, the kitchen in question had looked like it had enough grime on it to show multiple paw prints as well as human marks, I recalled, and smiled back at him. My fancy was getting the better of me.

"Actually, we see this kind of thing fairly often, especially with elderly folks who live alone." He was trying to be comforting, his voice as soft as his tweed jacket. "My partner's right—she could have been tripped up by one of her kitties.

A slip, a fall, and a bang on the head, maybe against that counter or one of these boxes." He gestured to the adjoining room, where a sunken sofa and shredded chair were surrounded by trunks and cardboard boxes, piled nearly as high as the ones on the porch. "A blow like that doesn't necessarily kill you right away, and often the victim tries to get to a phone or out the door."

But she was facing into the kitchen, not out the door, I thought. And I didn't see a phone in there, just mugs and appliances and dishes for the cats. I stood and turned in toward the house again. This didn't seem right. He must have seen the questions rising, and put a hand on my arm. "She was probably disoriented." I looked up at him. He stood a few inches taller than I did in my sneakers, and I saw that his nose had probably been broken at some point. "One of the neighbors, a Ms. Wright, has told us she was kind of out of it much of the time. But we will be looking over the evidence, including all the photos and such, and the coroner will have a look at her, too. Don't worry."

I opened my mouth to speak. The old lady hadn't seemed that far gone when I'd talked to her, and if he was talking to the same neighbor I'd met the day before, I wasn't sure I trusted her intentions.

"I'm calling animal control to bring the van!" His partner interrupted, his voice rising with what sounded like the first hint of panic. "There must be twenty cats here."

"Animal control?" I asked, not what I'd meant to say. "Animal control?" The cop's hand was still on my upper arm, the grip of his long fingers pressing gently, but his face had turned serious.

"What else can we do? I'm sure they'll do what they can. Theresa—Officer D'Amato—loves animals. She'll only euthanize the ones that are in bad shape."

"Bill, want to give me a hand?" the pudgy partner called from inside the stuffed sitting room. "Bill?" The panic note was higher now. "I'd like to locate a next-of-kin and get out of here!" I heard a hiss and a muttered expletive, and the cop standing next to me excused himself to help. Just then I felt a warm pressure against my ankle. Two round green eyes looked up at me. My little friend, the kitten with a limp, I thought. An injured cat.

"Talk about timing, kitty. You've got it." I scooped her up and into my courier bag and she didn't even mew.

"I'm going to head out," I yelled into the room, where various scuffling sounds and a particularly annoyed howl marked the interlopers' presence. "You know how to reach me."

"That's fine, Ms. Krakow. We'll call if we need anything," my detective, Bill, called back. Just then a box went thud, someone yowled, and I slipped out the door.

THE PHONE WAS RINGING as I unlocked my apartment door, and I grabbed it as I lifted my bag's heavy top, liberating the kitten.

"Worcester? At one?" One of the assistant editors who toiled under Tim had fielded a call from a radio station hack and been casting about, a little frantic, to find a free writer. Thrilled that I had answered, she took a deep breath and quickly filled me in.

Supposedly a fading rocker, a local boy who'd made good for a while back in the early '90s, was planning an "unannounced" surprise appearance at the station this afternoon. Unannounced, that is, except for the series of phone calls to press outlets like ours that had probably started early this morning, but the assistant editor didn't realize she was being played. Marc Starr had a new album out, so she should have expected something like this. I could have warned her. Still, it was a gig. The breathless assistant said she'd pay me for a full review if I could just get her thirty lines on the event by deadline. What about mileage? I'd asked, looking for an excuse to say no. But she was on the spot. Ralph was taking a personal day, so I was it, mileage and all. I could've requested meal vouchers, but why push my luck?

Putting down a small dish of water for the kitten, who was sniffing around the edge of my radiator, I thought about other essentials. I found an old jug of scoopable litter in the back of the larder and after improvising a tray out of a typing-paper box—and making sure she knew where it was—I grabbed my car keys and took off. I felt like I'd been up for a week already, and it wasn't even noon.

There was no reason to rush. Despite the fifty-mile drive out to the station's studios, I had more than enough time and let myself enjoy a set of vintage Irma Thomas soul after checking out a collection of Starr's so-called hits for reference. As Thomas had sung—months before the Stones—time was indeed on my side. The supposedly spontaneous event, a rooftop concert by Starr and his band, wasn't even going to start till after five, as I found out soon after I arrived. Till after the station hack had done all he could to work up the local media, that is, and till six o'clock television deadlines threatened to remove the few cameras he had gathered.

Grateful for the company, I spent the afternoon chatting with the other reporters, an intern from the Worcester weekly and a local stringer for Boston's other daily, writers for the city glossy and some fanzine contributors as well as the crew from a small cable station, all of us sitting around the station's windowless waiting room, drinking their bad coffee. Under the posters and the signed gold records—mass produced for distribution to program directors around the country—we writers traded war stories: in-depth pieces slashed to the bone to make way for celebrity photos, magazines gone bankrupt, owing us fees.

The TV folk stayed on their side of the room as we grew increasingly raucous, one-upping each other with the ways editors tended to "lose" expense sheets or forget stories that had been assigned. Of course, there were the usual copy desk horror stories as well. Meat Loaf becoming "Mr. Loaf," for example. Or the first name of local guitarist Dick Tate translated to the more formal, and meaningless, Richard while his assumed last name stayed in.

"I'd written that the piece was in 6/8 time," Larry, an older writer from the other daily, was telling us. "The next morning, I picked up the paper to see the term 'simplified' to 3/4!" We all groaned in sympathy, even though the story was an old one. If it had really happened to Larry it was the thirtieth or fortieth time, and I suspected that all of us (with the possible exception of the intern) knew it. But it was a good story anyway, an "evergreen" as our editors would say.

"Hey, I can top that," a newcomer, whom someone had introduced as Ethan, chimed in. "One of our editors was on a campaign to improve our diction, cut down on slang and contractions." The dark-haired writer with thick glasses had our attention now; all of us had experienced similar reform attempts.

"And he was as smart as the job requires. So, I guess I can see what happened. After all, it was right in my lead: 'the local authorities can't be blamed.' Some editor wanted to open that up." He paused for effect, in command of the crowd. "Except of course, that once he typed out 'can' he forgot to add the 'not.'"

"Ouch!" someone cried out loud, and at that—as well as the new guy's look of righteous indignation—we all laughed. Even as a former copy editor, one of what this crew would consider the enemy, I chuckled and moaned along. It was the camaraderie, more than the veracity I valued. After my morning, I wanted nothing more than to trade tall tales and battle stories in the company of colleagues, and if we had to make some up to pass the time, I was okay with that.

The new guy's story had trumped the lot, however, and we broke into individual conversations after the laughter died down. "Who is that guy?" I asked Larry, whom I've known for years. He raised his bushy eyebrows and fixed me with a comical look. "Why, Miss Theda, could you be interested?"

I shook my head, smiling. Ethan, with his close-cropped curly hair and those Coke-bottle glasses, had a kind of Buddy Holly thing going on, and he was certainly sharp. I pitied the editor who had to face his stern disapproval. But for better or worse I like my guys a little more happy-go-lucky. "Not my type," was all I said.

"Ah, checking out the competition, then?" Larry didn't wait for an answer. "He's a news stringer, a crime reporter with one of the Western Mass. papers," he explained. "But he's been stuck too long on GA"—general assignment reporting—"and he wants to get more into the features and arts side of things. A little sick of his editors, I gather. I wouldn't be surprised if he wants to move into the Boston market, too."

"Huh," I murmured in response. That was a lot of information, and not all of it good. But even if this guy was an ace crime reporter, that didn't mean I had to worry about losing my gigs to him, did I? I wanted to believe in that camaraderie I'd been basking in only moments before.

"He was asking about you, you know." Larry's dark eyes were watching me closely, those shaggy eyebrows slightly raised. Personal or professional interest? "Said he's seen you somewhere, and wanted to know who you wrote for." Professional then.

"Well, I assume you told him that I wasn't the great Theda K., and if I was, I had a tendency to bite."

"Of course," said my friend, looking over at the small

crowd that the new guy had gathered around him. "But I don't see him as a threat to you, Theda. He's not really a music guy. I told him he could learn a lot from you though. And that once upon a time, I'd been your mentor, too."

With a grin that made me feel even more guilty about my territorial instincts, he walked over to join the group and, after a moment, I followed. Larry was right, of course. Without his aid, I'd have had a much harder time getting established, and he'd been a freelancer then, too. This was our way: we all competed, but we all helped each other as well. It was time to make nice. I walked over to the new guy and introduced myself.

By the time Starr finally made his appearance, I'd gotten the basic Ethan outline. He was, as Larry had reported, primarily a news guy. But after years of chasing cop cars and fire trucks, he was more than ready for a change.

"The first time I reported from a fire scene, it was thrilling," he'd told me. The coffee had grown truly foul by then, despite generous scoops of pasty nondairy creamer. "I remember thinking, 'This is important, it affects real people's lives. This is what I want to do.'" I nodded, remembering my own early infatuation with the printed word. "I taught myself how to report by doing it. How to find things out by digging where you can and then getting close to anyone involved, asking questions but mostly just listening, you know?" I did. This was common ground, and I felt better about breaking the ice. Ethan, however, seemed troubled. "But after a while, all the crime stories start to read the same. It changed me, changed what I wanted. It's like everything I wrote fed the blood lust, and as a freelancer I just had to keep pushing for more to get paid. The editors always want more; they never see the big story. And the writing? They just screw it up."

He paused as if he was going to continue, but only pushed

his glasses back up on his nose. "It's like I've shed too much of my own blood for editors who don't know any different," he said finally. "They're all either tone-deaf or jerks."

I couldn't understand all of what he was saying. I'd never reported on anything more dire than a city council meeting. But I could relate to his exasperation with editors. Spurred by my memories of Larry's generosity, I gave him Tim's name—with a word of warning about *his* shortcomings—and promised to put a word in. Ethan shrugged.

"Thanks," he said. "I don't expect anything from editors anymore. What I really want is to be able simply to write. Write without worrying about the rent and only about things I really care about. Something important—and without some imbecile hanging over my shoulder asking if there were signs of arterial spray at the scene. I'm sick of these dimwits—and I've seen too many dead bodies."

I'd seen too many dead bodies, too, I wanted to explain, ready to share and maybe exorcise the horror of my morning. I started to tell him about my earlier misadventure, but just then the cry went out—Starr was in sight and we were all up against deadline. As a group, we raced up the stairs to the tarred, flat roof to find a professional sound system waiting. And even though a breeze had picked up and the setting sun didn't give off much warmth, we all stayed up there as Starr made a desultory swing through a few of the old hits, pop metal as dated as his thinning teased hair. When he announced that the next song would be the upcoming single from his new album, though, a happy murmur rustled along the rooftop. The small crowd gathered at street level might feel otherwise, but we reporters were all glad that the show was coming to an end. Not only was I shivering, I had an hour's drive ahead of me. Still, I wanted an edge, some local color, before I headed out for the *Mail*'s newsroom. Generosity only goes so far, and I managed to race down the stairs before Starr's crew blocked it with equipment. Out on the street, I cornered one of the sparse crowd before it dispersed.

"It was cool, huh? Seeing him here. Like the old days," said the fan, whose moussed coif paid tribute to her idol. "New song kind of sucked, though, huh?" Not the most articulate, but at least she looked of an age to remember Starr's fleeting fame. I had my story, and all I had to do was write it.

BETWEEN EDITING and traffic, it was after nine by the time I got home from the *Mail,* where I'd gone directly to file. It felt like midnight. The kitten greeted me at the door with a purr that belied her petite size, and when I checked I was pleased to see that she'd understood the concept of the litterbox, as makeshift as it was.

"You're a good little house kitty, aren't you?" I asked, as I scooped her tiny turds. "You're going to make somebody very happy."

Cute as she was, what pleased me most were these signs of socialization, her willingness to come into contact with me as much as her house training. Cats will always look for a way to bury their waste, but they won't always greet you with a purr. This was no feral kitten, although she seemed awfully young to be on her own. As soon as I could get her leg tended to, I was sure she'd be adopted. Kittens, after all, have a much better chance of finding a home than perfectly sound adult cats. "You'll be a wonderful pet."

"Wow," she replied, in a voice so high it barely registered. "Wow!" Litter, water—clearly there were other needs to be taken care of.

"I'm sorry, honey. Musetta, isn't it?" She followed me as I stepped into my tiny kitchenette, twining figure-eights around my ankles. "Wow!" No cans showed themselves in my cabinets, even when I reached all the way in past an ageless pack of popcorn. No dry food could be found under the sink, either, where once I had kept James' big bag of crunchies and, later, the prescription food that he had never really liked.

"Wow?" For a little cat she was growing insistent. And then, success! In the back of the fridge a roast chicken quarter from the local deli offered its juicy self to me. I'd thought of that as my dinner, but I'd be willing to share it. I pulled the flesh from the drumstick bone, shredding it with my fingers into a saucer, and placed it on the floor.

"We can share, right?" I asked. But in the moment when I hesitated, the meatier thigh in hand, the kitten cleared the plate. Sighing, I picked up the saucer and shredded the rest of my dinner for the greedy little beast, those big round eyes watching every move I made.

She made quick work of the remaining chicken, and at last seemed satisfied. Rubbing against my leg as a feline thank-you, she strode into the living room and began a meticulous, if noisy, tongue bath, beginning with her white mittens and proceeding to her face with its off-center star, and then her ears and, finally, her body. While watching her lick her rounded side was amusing—she hadn't quite mastered the art of balancing while reaching for those hard-to-get-to back spots and kept tumbling over—my own belly had started rumbling. Nothing for it but to head out again into the increasingly chill night.

When I pushed open the glass door to the Casbah, a bar and restaurant a few blocks away, the idea of a steaming casserole topped with some peppery harissa was making my stomach growl louder than a tiger.

The place was packed despite it being a Tuesday, the temperature a good thirty degrees warmer than the street outside. I looked through the sea of students and locals, a young crowd that tended toward denim and leather, searching for a seat. A pale-faced brunette squeezed by, and the black plastic of her too-tight PVC dress felt hot and sticky where it rubbed against my hand. The music was loud and almost everyone was yelling to be heard over it. Some rockabilly band, I thought, from the twang of guitar that broke through. Not my favorite style of music, but the hubbub felt like home to me. This was the sound of life, of people. I shed my jacket and worked my way sideways through to the bar.

"Krakow, come here!" An arm waved up in front of me, and I headed crablike toward it and the beckoning voice, ending up at the restaurant's high wooden bar. "Take a load off!"

Ralph was nursing a Rolling Rock, and something about the way he gestured and then fell back against the tall, polished bar made me think it wasn't his first. *"Garçon!"* he called out to Risa, the bartender, as I slid into the empty seat he'd grabbed for me, neatly ducking his slightly-too-wet kiss of greeting. "Get the lady a drink!"

"*'Garçon'* means 'boy,' Ralph," I said, thanking Risa as she set an open bottle of Blue Moon in front of me without having to ask.

"Humph," he replied, a moment of dissatisfaction crossing his round, ruddy face. For a moment he looked like an infant about to squall. "Well, you got your beer, didn't you?" I smiled and nodded, not wanting a scene, and ordered without looking at the plastic-covered menu. Shikel mishi with extra harissa, anticipating the warmth of the eggplant and lamb casserole, the bite of the pepper-garlic sauce on my tired taste buds. Warm pitas soon followed, a stack of triangular slices in a plastic basket, and I tore into the soft bread before turning to Ralph again.

"Have you been here all day?" I might be exhausted, but it was early by most standards for Ralph to look so bleary.

"Late night," he explained. "Called in sick today. Blame Connor, my new best friend. 'Scuse me." As he slid off his stool, he motioned to his left, just as the stranger on the adjoining barstool turned. Black hair hung over the bluest eyes I'd ever seen, and the smile that unfolded had just a touch of little-boy guilt, made even more endearing by one chipped tooth.

"Honest, officer, it wasn't my fault," said the stranger.

"And that was in another country, and besides the wench is dead?" I asked, on automatic, as my mind took in the unbleary vision before me.

"What?" The smile faded, the sapphire eyes seemed to dim. I was being a fool.

"Sorry. Once a lit major, always a lit major. It's from an Elizabethan—an old—play," I stuttered out my explanation. Not the time to be a nerdy English major again. "I was just asking because I got a gig today, with Ralph out. Got to cover Marc Starr out in Worcester."

"Isn't he a little past it?" No way this stranger was as drunk as Ralph; those eyes were sharp and focused. Maybe a little smug, but oh so blue.

"Definitely." I laughed in response. "But a story is a story."

"Uh, Theda, this is my buddy Connor, Connor Davis." Ralph reinserted himself between us, patting my back a little more than necessary as he clambered back onto his stool. "He's pretty new in town, but we keep running into each other at the same shows so when he called last night…" I raised my glass in understanding. "Connor, this is Theda."

"From the silent screen to the club scene, huh?" He saluted back and I felt some energy returning to tired bones. Although the two weren't eating—"Why ruin a good buzz?" asked Ralph—they sat and made me laugh as I finished my meal, though I barely tasted that good pepper sauce at all. I even relaxed enough to tell them about my morning. As I did, I saw

Ralph's face screwing up, like he was about to pop. I talked about the scene at the house, the woman lying there, but when I started to move away, to the nice cop who'd helped me out, his frustration broke through.

"Did the cats, did they…you know?"

"No, Ralph." I saw what he'd been trying to suppress. "The cats did not eat her face." Despite my answer, he smothered a chuckle at my words and beamed with glee, which I ignored. "I'm not saying they wouldn't have if they'd been locked in with her body for a few days, but they weren't and they didn't. Those cats knew something was wrong, though. It's because of them that I went in there."

All thoughts of the friendly detective disrupted, I thought, then, of the animal control officer. Those lush, gorgeous beasts had probably been rounded up for the pound by now. Or maybe they wouldn't have gotten over there so fast: despite the detective's assertion that there had been no foul play, one of his uniformed colleagues had been unrolling crime scene tape all over the porch when I left.

"I should go check on them tomorrow." I was thinking aloud.

"Is that safe? I could go with you," said Connor, and I couldn't help smiling.

"Oh, they won't hurt me." I tried to match the jokey tone he and Ralph had been sharing. "Not if I stay on my feet and keep moving."

They were making a night of it, the second in a row I gathered, but once my dinner was done I felt the weight of the day crashing down.

"If you need any help with the cats, you let me know," said Connor as I rose to leave. We'd exchanged numbers during one of Ralph's frequent bathroom breaks. Was my luck with men changing? "Happy to come by."

Despite my fatigue, I nearly skipped home. As I crawled

into bed—my proper bed tonight—I anticipated some nice dreams. A small thud nearly roused me as I drifted off, and the last thing I remembered was the brush of warm fur settling in beneath my chin and the quiet rumble of a purr.

FOUR

THE NEXT MORNING I awoke with fur in my mouth and a more rested feeling than I'd had in a long while. Both of which reminded me that this was a day to take care of cat business before more human needs.

After I checked the *Mail* to make sure my Starr story had run, it was time to start my day. A call to my regular vet was a bit of a downer. No, I had to tell her answering service, a sweet-natured older woman named Annie. I hadn't gotten another cat. I was just fostering one and I needed a sore leg checked out. I heard the sinking in Annie's voice and knew I'd disappointed her. She wanted me to be happy, just like she wanted everyone to be, ideally with the warm companionship of a spayed or neutered pet. But I had to pay attention to my own internal clock. There would be a right time, and that time was not yet.

Our chat did provide some interesting information, however. Rachel, my vet, was working at the shelter this morning, Annie said. The animal control officer had called her to help out because they'd brought in eighteen cats of various ages found in a house in Cambridge. The cats would be put in isolation for a few days, Annie told me, until the cops found out if there was a will or a next of kin determining their fate. In the meantime, Rachel and any other vets on call would be busy giving them blood tests and routine care, just in case they ended up in the adoption center when their quarantine was up.

I left a message to let me know when I could bring the kitten in and looked around for the little beast. She was the picture of relaxation, stretched out in the sun on the back of the sofa like a starlet at St. Tropez. Her injured leg hadn't seemed to deter her from climbing up to one of James' favorite spots.

"Don't get too used to this, kitty. It's all temporary," I called out to her. She didn't respond, except to extend her pink and white toes in a yawning stretch.

I grabbed my keys and headed out. I'd swing by the shelter later, but clearly all the other cats were in the system already and I'd have to trust that they'd be looked after as well as they could be for now. Reasoning that I'd want my car later, I drove the few blocks to what I'd begun thinking of as Lillian's house. The crime-scene tape wasn't visible from up front, but I parked on the street anyway and made my way quietly around the back. Just one day had passed and the aging gingerbread looked saggier by years, the peeling paint sadder somehow and the windows, without their watchful cats, dead and cold. Belying the trend toward gentrification that seemed to perk up a different block each week, this house had become a husk overnight, slipping from a picturesque bit of local color to a decrepit old building without its owner and shorn of its feline inhabitants. I trod gently up the walk. Respect, if not outright nerves, was making me careful.

Crash! Someone else didn't share my concerns, and the muffled expletive that soon followed let me know that no remaining cat had made that noise. Thud! What sounded like a box full of papers hit the floor and shook some paint flakes off the porch's sagging overhang. The house was not as deserted as it had first appeared.

"Anybody there?" I called in. Asking the obvious seemed like a good chance to alert any looters or neighborhood kids that it was time to hightail it home. "Hello?"

"Come on in," a female voice called back from deep inside, and then started coughing from the dust. "You're not with the cops, are you?"

"No, I'm a neighbor. Were the cops here again today?" I slowly crossed the porch and turned left into the sitting room. That's where the noise was coming from, and besides, I didn't necessarily want to linger in the kitchen.

"Oh yeah, they took the tape off," said a voice from behind a high-backed chair and what looked to be a solid column of newspapers. "Not that that would have stopped me from coming in." The voice stood and revealed itself to be emanating from a twenty-something woman in a Clash tee shirt and matronly kerchief. The few strands that poked above the bandana were of light magenta, appropriately clashing with both the orange shirt and the red kerchief. A welcome bright spot in the too-still house, she held a dustpan and brush in one hand and started to reach out the other. The slight shock on my face must have made her think better of the move and she paused, wiping her hand on her denim-clad thigh instead.

"You're from the coffeehouse!" Beneath the grime, I recognized that smile, not to mention the hair.

"French roast, keep it coming in the morning. Skim latte if you come by after noon."

"I don't think we've ever been properly introduced." I reached out my hand, not caring about her griminess. "Theda Krakow."

She took it, with a grip amazingly strong for her size. "Like the film star? Cool. I'm Violet. Violet Hayes."

I couldn't resist the smile that came over me. "You play the guitar?"

"Just like Jimi." A wide grin split her face as well. "How'd you guess?"

"Reporter's intuition. What brings you here?"

"I could ask you the same thing. I'm a fixture at Lillian's," she started and told me how she'd been helping the old woman out for the last eighteen months. She'd been coming by after her shift at least twice a week ever since Lillian had posted that notice in the coffeehouse, the one asking for volunteers for her "feline haven."

"She spelled it Feline Heaven on her flyer, but I think that was, what do you call it? A bit of wishful thinking on her part," Violet remembered. "She was getting on in years, but she was still incredibly independent. Sharp as a tack. Just slow and stiff going up and down the stairs. Between the number of litter boxes and her visits to her son, she just needed a hand keeping it all together."

"She had a son?" I thought of this grand old house—and all those incarcerated cats—and started dreaming.

"He's not well." Violet was shaking her head. "Emotional problems. He had some kind of breakdown when he went away to college and has been living out near Amherst ever since. I don't know the details, but Lillian went to visit him pretty regularly, and recently things had gotten worse with him. Another breakdown and he ran away or something."

"Do the cops know about this?" I was thinking of the detective, Bill, and his partner, rummaging through the mess of papers in search of a next of kin. Legally, this son sounded like it. But Violet heard my question differently.

"Oh, he's never really been violent. I mean, not really. And I don't think he'd do anything to hurt his mom. I mean, he's just a little out of it, most of the time, you know?"

I told her about Bill and the other detective looking for a contact, and she relaxed a bit. "That neighbor, the woman, she doesn't like him," she explained. "Lillian brought Dougie—that's the son—up for a weekend a month or two ago. There was some problem with his group home. And that Wright bitch was close to calling the cops on him. All he was doing was singing. Sitting on a lawn chair and singing."

Having had my own run-in with that particular neighbor, I didn't ask the obvious, like, how loud, what time of night, and which particular lyrics. I'm a live-and-let-live type at heart, and I figure it takes all kinds.

"Who lives on the other side?" I asked her. We'd been acting like this Ms. Wright owned the neighborhood.

"That's a rental building, about a dozen units. Everyone there minds their own business. And the building behind hers is owned by the university. It's offices, mainly, so nobody is there after five. This would be a great neighborhood, really, if it weren't for some people." Who those some were was clear. "Lillian used to let kids come in and play with the kittens, when she had them. She taught them all how to pick them up and how to be gentle with them so they'd purr and the momma cats wouldn't get upset. She was a total asset to the neighborhood. To me, as well."

She paused, her round, pink face beginning to wrinkle up beneath its colorful topping. "I'm going to miss her. Who'd do this to her?" Her voice was growing louder. Anger was preferable to tears. "Who, and why?"

"So you don't think it was an accident?" I didn't tell her of my own instinct that foul play was involved. I wanted to hear what she said. "The cops seemed to think that she tripped and fell."

"The cops. Tweedle-dumb and tweedle-dumber? They think she'd tripped over her own cats. They did *not* know Lillian." She grabbed a box off the floor and threw it on the chair. A few paint chips fell from a ceiling that sagged ominously. "Lillian was slow, but she was steady." She ripped the top flaps open and a puff of dust went flying with the dry, old tape. "Lillian shoveled her walk all through the winter. The sidewalk, too, until I took over." She reached in and pulled out a pile of ledgers. The thump they made on the end table as she dropped them only accented her determination. "Lillian was a dancer when she was younger. Did she tell you that?" She whipped the top book open with a thud and leafed through its pages. "She taught yoga until the arthritis got her." My mind wanted to remind Violet that people age, that even formerly lithe legs can become unsteady. I didn't have the heart. She slammed the book shut and grabbed the next one.

"And Lillian wore one of those one-touch medic-alert panic buttons around her neck." My mind went blank. "Her son saw the ad and wouldn't shut up until she bought one. You know, the 'I've fallen and I can't get up' ad?"

She leaned on the books and her voice grew slow and low, as if she was swearing an oath of blood on them. "Lillian would not have tripped. Lillian would not have fallen over her cats. But if, a big if—" she looked up at me, her eyes blazing. "If she had, she would've finally used that damned necklace. She'd have pressed the damned button and waited for the damned ambulance to get here.

"Someone killed my friend Lillian." I had no breath to respond to the fury in her eyes. "Something here is going to tell me why. And I'm going to find out who."

FIVE

"ARE YOU CRAZY?" I couldn't keep my voice from rising. "Have you lost it?" I started listing reasons why this was a very bad idea. One, we weren't detectives. Two, it could be dangerous. And three, despite what she said—and despite my own piqued instincts—we didn't even know if there was a murderer to be caught. By the time I'd finished enumerating all these reasons, with significant elaboration and the occasional colorful expletive, I'd paced the crowded room twice and raised a new cloud of dust by hitting at boxes and piles of paper. Violet just kept working, opening boxes, leafing through letters and scrap books, then refiling years of accumulated papers.

"You can't investigate what you think is a murder all by yourself." I'd almost forgotten my own suspicions. "You cannot. You *will* not do this." Although I probably only had ten years on her, that decade and our serious difference in height— I was a good six inches taller than Violet—made me feel vaguely protective of her. Someone had to be, I thought. "I've got it. Together, we'll go to the police. You'll tell them about the panic-button necklace thingy. You'll tell…" Any other thoughts I had were broken off by a coughing fit, which threatened to choke me as I inhaled the dust and dander of years.

"No cops. Absolutely not. Hey, c'mon." She took my arm to lead me out of the dust-filled room. "Now, blow your nose." She handed me a large, lace-edged hankie, not the style I'd have pegged her with. "Wipe your eyes. Good. Now, it's no use lecturing me about the police," she started, when a hideous shriek pierced the air. Half howl, half hiss, it brought us both out the back door in a rush, just in time to see a white and gray blaze zip by low to the ground. A flash of fuchsia and cream, this time human-sized, followed close behind.

"That animal!" The human said it like it was an insult. I recognized the impeccably turned-out neighbor, but now the front of her silk suit heaved with emotion. "That animal was on my roof, stalking my birdfeeder!"

"It's Sibley!" Violet's glee would have provoked her further had the purple-haired punk not immediately turned to seek the cat in the confines of the dust cloud behind us.

"I thought those beasts were all taken care of." The neighbor turned to me instead. "You were here the other day, right? You're not with animal control, are you?" She looked me up and down, taking in my mussy hair and jeans, and answered her own question. "No, you're another cat person."

"I'm Theda, Theda Krakow, and I'm a journalist." I struck a pose that I imagined did my namesake proud, and extended my hand.

"Patricia Wright. Patti. I'm a realtor," she explained, straightening her jacket. Her voice had dropped half an octave to sound almost smooth, a professional voice. "And I'm a concerned neighbor, as well, but you know that. A journalist? You don't mean there's going to be a story about that, about…all this." She waved one beringed hand in a vague gesture, taking in the decrepit house and overgrown yard. Her tone rising again to a tight squeak. "Or about her—the lady who, who…" Her face was growing white.

"Who died? Your neighbor Lillian, you mean?" I didn't really want to help her out, but the look of panic coming over her intrigued me. "No, I was going to write about her cats," I continued. In front of this woman, I didn't want to talk about hoarding. She obviously had enough anti-cat feeling as it was.

"Oh good, then it's over." She breathed again. "We don't want some unnecessary fuss. The accident, whatever, it's bad for business." She leaned toward me, speaking now in a con-spiratorial hush. "Nobody wants a property where the last owner, well, *expired,* even in this market. And I'm dying to get this listing."

Poor choice of words, I thought, since someone had done just that. But before I could say anything about her neighborly concern, Violet emerged, her arms around a large white cat marked with big gray spots, one placed just so like a cap between his ears. "Here's Sibley. He's had a good scare, hasn't he?" The cat, calm now, had his front paws wrapped around her neck. In a moment he'd be suckling her earlobe.

"Disgusting." Wright stepped back. "And dangerous."

"Oh, he just likes to watch. Don't you, Sibley?" Violet stroked the smooth gray saddle that covered most of his back, and sure enough, the cat reached up to mouth her ear, the one without the rings. He closed his eyes and a rumbling purr quickly became audible.

"Well, he's not going to stay here. I'm calling those animal control people right now," said Wright, turning on her heel. Clearly, she'd been upset to leave the house without a cell phone.

"I better take this big guy to my place," said Violet, hefting the placid cat a little higher on one shoulder and reaching behind her to close the door. "You won't tell, will you?"

I wasn't sure if she meant about the cat who'd escaped the round-up or the cops, who'd missed whatever evidence she'd hoped to find. The first had my complete sympathy, but I still hadn't heard her reasons for the second.

"Don't do anything, at least not without letting me know first." That was a non-answer, I knew, but it seemed to work.

Smiling once more, she accepted one of my cards before she took off down the driveway, top heavy with a happy cat who no longer had a care in the world.

THINKING ABOUT SIBLEY and wondering about the fate of his former housemates, I too took my leave, driving to the shelter across the river where the bulk of Lillian's cats had been taken. Clean, if somewhat sterile, the low brick building housed a well-lit public area with cages of animals up for adoption. Index cards posted on the front of each unit listed the animals' names and special needs, if any. Several were decorated with smiley faces and stars, as well as notes reminding potential pet parents that older animals make great pets, too.

"Hi, Sandra, is Rachel in?" I'd been on a first-name basis with most of the shelter staff since last month, when I spent a weekend reporting a Sunday piece. The glossy story, accompanied by heartbreaking photos, had brought in a flood of donations and helped a few animals, the featured ones at least, find new homes.

Sandra buzzed me in, and I opened the glass-windowed door to the shelter's working rooms. Reaching automatically for the disinfecting hand cleanser, I wiped my hands together to spread the alcohol gel as I peered into the separate isolation rooms seeking the vet.

"I got your call," the tall brunette greeted me as she came out of a room of cages and reached for yet another plastic dispenser of cleanser. "I'm glad you've gotten another kitten!"

"It's not an adoption," I stopped her cold. "It's a foster situation. This is one from that house that I hear got dumped on you."

"Do you think she's sick?" The vet looked concerned. Young kittens too small for vaccines can quickly sicken and die from such common illnesses as distemper, but not so quickly that they don't bring an entire neighborhood—or shelter's worth—of litters down with them. "Vomiting? Diarrhea?"

"No, it's her leg," I answered, describing the kitten's limp and following Rachel into another isolation room. I kept talking as she opened a cage where a mother and her kittens were waiting out their days before they could be moved to the adoption center out front. "Plus, she probably needs worming, ear mite drops, and treatment for whatever else you're finding on the cats from that house."

"Bring her by tomorrow. I'll see her on my lunch break, around one," said Rachel, examining one mewling little guy. She looked first in his eyes, which had a bit of gunk on them, then turned the complaining kit upside down to examine his healing navel and then his bottom, which his mother had cleaned well. "But you'd be surprised. Those cats seem in great shape. I'd been warned—Officer D'Amato in Animal Control had called me—that it was possibly a hoarding situation and there were a lot of cats. But they're all well fed and none of them seems dehydrated. Most of them have been neutered, too. We've got some fleas." She replaced the kitten and picked up his sister. "It's finally warm enough for the outdoor cats to be getting them. But unless the blood tests come back with something unexpected, I think that entire lot is all moving on to adoption."

On that happy note, I took myself home, picking up food for Musetta and myself along the way. Parking in Cambridge, a city of tow zones and regular street cleaning, can be a challenge, with temporary No Parking signs sprouting like mushrooms after a rain. Despite one such notice warning of a mover's van and another for repaving, I found a spot less than a block from my building. As I balanced the bags to unlock the door, I heard the impatient mew of welcome. Raising one foot to do the kitty-blocking maneuver I'd perfected with James, I felt that life, finally, might be going my way.

THE FIRST MESSAGE on my answering machine burst that bubble.

"Krakow! What happened? Photo says they're not going

to shoot a stiff for you. Call me." Damn, I'd forgotten to cancel the photo assignment. I'd forgotten to tell Tim about the new development on the story, too. I'd have some back-tracking to do.

"Hey hon, how's it going? Did you get those clips I sent you?" Bunny's friendly voice warmed me. "We're hoping you'll come by this weekend, test drive the new sofa. It has been way too long." She and Cal had been nesting, but in an inviting and not-too-obnoxious way. I'd been the one to let time slide by.

"Theda?" The deep, soft voice of the third message wasn't familiar, and then I remembered with a little thrill of pleasure. "It's Connor, Ralph's friend. I was hoping to catch you in." He paused and I could hear my heart beat. "But I guess I'll see you around."

That was it, no suggestion to get together. No request for me to call him back. Which was probably just as well, I told myself, stifling the sigh of disappointment. I'd had enough ex-perience with the guys in clubland to know that a cool start could heat up if I gave it time. Let it play out, let him make the moves. Following Bunny's call, I could hear her voice in my head giving me the time-honored advice that neither of us had followed too well in the ten years we'd been friends. Still, despite a tendency to gripe, she'd ended up with Cal, who loved her, mishegas and all. And I knew that despite her complaints the two were a great match. I should be so lucky. Since I didn't have a choice, I might as well tell myself I'd have done the smart thing. After feeding Musetta and making a turkey and salami sandwich for myself, I settled in with a pad and prepared to do damage control on my career.

"But it's a great story," I found myself protesting minutes later. One of the few times I could get my editor on the phone and he wasn't having any of it.

"No, it's a crime story. And you're a feature writer. What

am I saying? It's not even a crime story." Tim's voice faded as he stood up and paced away from the speaker phone. Not a good sign. "It's a dead old lady story. And I'm not interested in a dead old lady story."

"What about all her cats? They'll go up for adoption in seventy-two hours and then they have something like a week to find a home or they'll be destroyed, maybe less. I mean, unless the police find an heir who wants to take them or a will that provides for their care. Writing about them would help."

"You did a shelter story already for the magazine. Real nice work, Theda." The compliment didn't follow through to his tone of voice, and I remembered how jealous editors could be. I guess it meant he valued me.

"Why don't you get out to the clubs and get me something on nightlife. What's going on with drugs out there?" I could almost see him drawing broad gestures in the air. "Is anyone doing anything new anywhere? Has anyone famous been busted somewhere?"

"I think a lot more people are interested in animals than you think." I tried to talk him down, but he must have heard something else in my voice.

"You're not still all upset because of your cat, are you?" My continued silence gave him his answer. "Christ, Theda. It's been a month. You've got to get out more." I didn't need his hamfisted sort of sympathy. What I needed was work; I'd been counting on the cat-lady piece. So murmuring what I hoped could be taken for assent, I suggested a profile on a new Wednesday night series, a local singer who was booking acoustic blues and jazz at a restaurant in nearby Jamaica Plain. She'd had a name that Tim had recognized and I hinted, with absolutely no basis, that local celebrities were considering it the latest cool hang.

"Midweeks are the new weekends now," I heard myself saying.

"I thought those were Mondays," he replied in all seriousness, and the deal was sealed. A quick call to Bunny secured me a brunch date for Sunday. I told her that the cat story was on hold, at least for now, and that I'd explain later. We agreed that I'd pick up fresh bagels on my way over, and then it was time to work.

I'D BEEN INVOLVED WITH newspapers since I was a kid. My junior high school hadn't had a paper, so I started one that we copied and stapled by hand and gave out once a month. It was only eight pages, but it was good enough to outlast me, and provided a solid training ground for the young writers I then edited on my high school paper. In college, I'd mixed my English major literature courses with writing workshops, trotting out my singsong attempts at verse and some highly autobiographical short stories for an endless series of meetings and discussions. It wasn't an entirely useless exercise: I'd learned to hide my feelings when the criticisms grew really cutting, and I also probably mastered some craft through, if nothing else, the repetition of rewriting. But whether it was all the more confident students in my writing classes, the ones who wore black all day and smoked clove cigarettes, or the fact that I kept one foot in the more pedantic literature camp, I never really believed I could make it as a writer. Newspapers, yeah, sure, I loved them. But as an editor, a grammarian and fact checker and maybe, if I were very good, an assigner and shaper of stories. Not as a writer, never that.

A few years out in the real world taught me that my caution wasn't completely misplaced. Good editors, particularly good copy editors, were always in demand. I'd snagged a job right out of school as an editorial assistant at my alumni magazine.

The post called for a glorified secretary really, but I was proud as hell of the "editorial" in the title. Plus as soon as I started catching typos and, much to my boss' dismay, inaccuracies in the regular columns handed to me to input into the computer, my duties expanded. It was rudimentary editing, more fact-checking than anything, but it beat simply typing. I started writing professionally that year, too, freelancing stories about the local rock scene for a free weekly. But I told myself that this side of my life was just for fun. If I covered a band, I'd get on the guest list next time they played. If I wrote something that made my friends laugh, it made me happy. That wasn't work. And because the alumni magazine already had a copy editor, after a year I started looking around for another job.

In some ways, I was lucky. The weekly that had been publishing me—adding the princely sum of twenty-five bucks a story to my meager salary—was hiring a fact checker, so I applied. That job soon lead to full-fledged copy editing, which meant learning grammar on the job, reading newspaper copy with *Strunk and White* on my lap and a cubicle full of sticky notes reminding me "if 'to' then 'from'!" and "farther along, but further in." When a position opened up at the *Mail*, I'd taken the test and held my breath, waiting for the call telling me I was invited to join the major league.

I got it, and with it a raise and my first non-roommate apartment. But despite my increasing prosperity—the *Mail* paid wages that could and did support some of my colleagues' families—I had grown increasingly dissatisfied. For one thing, the higher up I went in the publishing world, the further—or was it farther?—apart the editing and writing worlds went. At the weekly, everyone did everything. I'd never had the stomach for crime reporting, but I'd done my time at City Hall licensing hearings. Hell, our drama critic

doubled as the typesetter. But by the time I had some senior-
ity at the *Mail,* I was lucky to sell so much as a book review
once a month. Every other editor I approached looked at me
funny when I tried to pitch stories, as if a fish were asking
them for wings. A copy editor writing? Didn't I get paid
enough? They didn't understand that I missed it. I missed
writing. Missed the thrill of researching a story, the joy of con-
ceiving it—of twisting it this way and that to find the angle
that would give me the best access to the parts that mattered.
I even missed filing on deadline, the adrenaline rush of turning
in the pages or sending the electronic file with the knowledge
that my words, with my byline, would next see light in lovely
black type. Which was why, even though I had money in the
bank and only had to work occasional holidays and Sundays,
I had quit and tumbled myself back into relative penury.

If I didn't make a go of it, I had only myself to blame.
Which on this particular afternoon meant buckling down to a
round of phone calls, first to the club I'd be reporting on later
to make sure that the folks in charge would be around and
available to chat. Then to one of my most reliable, if dull em-
ployers: a home section editor who could usually be counted
on to throw an assignment my way.

"Bookshelves? I can do bookshelves." Fifteen minutes
later we were agreeing on a story. "Built-ins and custom work,
sure. I've got three contractors at my fingertips." Those fingertips were reaching for the Yellow Pages as I spoke, so my
assurance wasn't totally false. Besides, the basic rule of freelancing, our source of pride, is that we can reach anyone with
three phone calls. I'd find sources for a home renovation piece
easier than that.

It was still the workday, so I left messages on five answering machines, figuring that the first three to call me back
would make it into the story. Just to see what else I could find,

I switched my computer on and tooled around the Internet,
pulling stories on local bookshelf manufacturers and a couple
of interior designers who might be relevant. To really make
it as a journalist—especially if you wanted to survive as a freelancer—you had to get more than just what your story
required. You needed to have background, to understand what
was going on, even if only a fraction of your research
appeared in print. While those articles printed, I let myself
play, slipping a White Stripes CD into the computer and
cranking it as a new-mod soundtrack to some basic computer-
age snooping. Bopping in my seat, I called up a search engine
and plugged in Connor's name. No matches came back, and
I wondered about the spelling of his last name. Davys? Daves?
Three songs slipped by in pure guitar-pop fury, but the
computer didn't respond, though one close miss—"Connor
Davitz"—did turn up a local Irish-Jewish caterer who might
make an interesting story at some point. Finally, I gave up.
So many of my friends were writers or musicians, I was used
to finding some kind of paper trail on them. Reviews, publicity, or whatever. But if this guy wasn't so bohemian, maybe
that was for the better. Now Lillian, that might prove more
interesting. Maybe I'd turn up an ancient enemy, an old rival
in love—or in cat collecting—who had proved deadly. I typed
in "Lillian Helmhold" and sang along to the music while my
iMac did its business.

No tales of geriatric feuds surfaced. Instead, I found a
death notice for a Lillian Rosbach Helmhold, which had just
run in that morning's paper, reminding me that my fun and
games involved a real woman and a real life. I sobered up a
bit and turned the music down, but my curiosity was piqued.
A legal ad listing her full name again and asking any heirs to
come forward made me wonder about Dougie—obviously
Doug or Douglas—and whether he even knew about his

mother's death. I typed his name in, wondering if it would help me find him. What I got were a slew of stories from the Berkshires area newspapers, out in the western part of the state, starting from about two months before. "Grief at Green-leaf House," read the first headline. One Douglas Helmhold, age thirty-eight, was listed among the residents who had had to be evacuated when a private Northurst residential facility was damaged by fire. The fire, said the report, was probably caused by the residents' propensity for smoking.

"They light up all the time," one of the home's live-in counselors was quoted as saying. "We try to keep them from smoking in the house, especially in their rooms, but they don't want to go outdoors in the winter, and who can blame them? Plus, the nicotine is calming to many of them and it's hard to get them to quit." An accompanying editorial on the crusade to ban smoking at all mental health care facilities had me rolling my eyes halfway through, but at least it was better than the usual "not in my backyard" screeds. Northurst sounded like the kind of liberal college town that would kill these people with kindness before kicking them out, and for that I was glad. I'd read enough about mental illness to know that finding a quiet, low stress, and safe environment can go a long way toward making life—and treatment—bearable. People like Dougie might never actually recover, but if he could settle into a regular routine, he'd be more likely to stay on his medications and out of trouble.

THAT BUBBLE WAS BURST by the next round of stories. The fire, according to a piece in the *Northurst Eagle,* had not been caused by an errant butt. A cigarette had served as a fuse, but the couch it had been dropped on had been doused with lighter fluid, too. Plus, someone had jiggered with the gas in the kitchen, loosening the pipe that ran into the stove and turning the kitchen into a potential bomb once the fire spread. Only luck and the sharp nose of one of the eight residents had kept the fire from reaching beyond the common room—and kept the hundred-year-old clapboard from exploding. The next day's front page explained why someone had gone to all that trouble: Social Security checks, the disability monies that supported most of the residents, had been disappearing into an unauthorized bank account, as well as monies that were supposedly paying for the residents' many prescriptions, and that account had been emptied.

Some of the drugs seemed to be unaccounted for, as well, according to a follow-up written by one Ethan Reinhardt, *Eagle* contributor. Could he be the freelancer I'd met at the Marc Starr press party? Whoever he was, he was good: he'd interviewed the overnight staffer who had been quoted in the first news story, but obviously had spent more time digging up background material, too. I remembered him talking about the importance of listening and observing, and I could tell he practiced what he preached. By the time Ethan had filed his second article, he'd found more news to report. The overnight counselor who'd first spoken to the press—the one who'd pointed a finger at the residents' smoking—had gone missing. Police wouldn't say if he was suspected of involvement, but they did let out that he was wanted for questioning.

There was a third story, too: the counselor's unexplained departure on the heels of the fire—and the subsequent investigation into both—had seriously upset several of the residents, and their temporary displacement while Greenleaf House was repaired disturbed their fragile equilibrium still further. The writer had done his homework on the treatment of mental illness. If this was the same Ethan, it was a pity that he was leaving news. But if it was, I really would have to share my contacts with him. Despite the residents' conditions—and despite Ethan's griping about how his editors mangled his prose—he'd managed to draw coherent portraits of them, and had clearly spent time with them. Incorporating additional input from medical sources, he'd explained how two had withdrawn into themselves and were hospitalized in near catatonic states. One, Douglas Helmhold, had become severely agitated and then gone AWOL, walking away from the unlocked ward without a word to his doctors or any of the other patients, at least to any who could talk. He'd been missing for close to a week, long enough for the drugs to wear off and his psychosis to come back full force, when he was finally picked up by the cops, rambling and unresponsive, on the Cambridge Common. It took nearly two weeks in Cambridge General's psychiatric ward before he was balanced enough to be released, first to a family member and then to the temporary shelter that had taken in the Greenleaf House's other residents.

So this was the "problem" that Dougie had had a little while ago, the reason Lillian had brought her son back home for a few days. Between the fire and the hospitalization, she'd probably seen her home—the old house they'd once shared— as the safest place for him. It was certainly better for his agitated mind than some unfamiliar temporary housing, and I could see why she wanted him there while Greenleaf House was being restored. But given the shape Dougie had probably been in when Lillian had brought him home, it was no wonder the neighbor, prim as she was, had been unhappy. My instinct was to dismiss her concerns. Any woman who disliked cats deserved to be shaken up a bit, but I had to be fair. She might have been truly afraid, made nervous by Dougie's strangeness. She wouldn't have been the first neighbor to complain when a mentally ill child came home.

Maybe the conflict had been unavoidable. Ethan had cer-

tainly understood it, the visceral reaction that supported the
"not in my backyard" stance, and had used his illustrations
well to demonstrate what had become a truism of mental
health: that people with diseases like schizophrenia are much
more likely to be the victims of violence, theft, and fraud than
they are to perpetrate them, no matter how many Hollywood
"psychos" hack up starlets on the silver screen. The missing
monies at Greenleaf House—still unaccounted for two
months later—proved his point.

But I'd done enough reporting for the *Mail*'s health section
to know the darker side of the story as well, and that gave me
a grudging sympathy for prim Patti. Although advocates for
the mentally ill didn't like to admit it, not everyone who had
a mental illness cooperated in their own treatment. There
were many reasons for people to stop taking their drugs. De-
lusions, which were often part of the illness, convinced people
that they were "all better," a sure sign that their last dose of
halperidol or fluphenazine was wearing off. Paranoia, another
symptom, often made the best intentions of doctors or family
members suspect. Sometimes it was a simple dislike for the
powerful psychotropic drugs' many side effects, which could
range from dry mouth, stiffness, and dizziness to the weight
gain and nervous tics that marked the longtime antipsychotic
user. And as good as the new treatments were—so-called
"miracle drugs" like clozapine and risperidone—when the
patients stopped the daily pills or medicated syrup, when they
ducked the monthly injection, the story changed. Those who
didn't comply with their treatment could be dangerous.
Although advocacy groups tried to stress the positive, statistics showed that unmedicated people with mental illnesses did
get violent. They did shove people under subways and go on
shooting sprees. Part of the tragedy was that, often, no
meanness was involved. Maybe a loving, but ill adult son had

battered his mom because he thought she'd been taken over by demons. Maybe he saw flames shooting out of her and wanted to put them out. Whatever, it happened. And the victims, most often, were family members.

Could Dougie have killed his own mother? It was possible. Even if he'd not meant to harm her, if it had been some kind of horrible accident, the violence—the sight of his mother lying there—might have scared him into hiding. If he'd walked away from a hospital once, there was no reason he couldn't again, and clearly even when he wasn't at his best he knew his way back to his mother's place. Here, he could easily blend in among Boston's many homeless, sleeping by the river now that the weather had warmed up and huddling by the library's heating grates if the frost came back. I made a mental note to locate him and to get some kind of sense of whether or not such wanderings were common; perhaps a call to the Greenleaf House would suffice. But the hour was getting late, and I had paying work to take care of first. I had time only to heat some soup before the Wednesday night showcase opened. Musetta joined me at the table, purring on my lap as I stroked her with one hand and tried not to drop hot mushroom-barley on her. She was so trusting, I found I wanted to protect her from everything. Especially after all she'd been through.

With an effort, I placed her on the sofa, and she grunted softly, as if she disapproved.

"Sorry, kitty, time to earn the kibble," I told her and watched her curl into a neat circle before I stepped out into the night.

SIX

I ALWAYS GET lost in Jamaica Plain. The maze of one-way streets and missing signs means I have to allow twice as much time to find anything in this funky urban neighborhood as I do at home. I know JP residents who feel the same way about Cambridge. Situated on opposite sides of Boston, we each had retained a bit of countercultural spirit, in part because of our tiny and inaccessible maze of winding streets. But this kinship didn't help much as I found myself for the third time driving over the trolley tracks to find myself facing the vegetarian restaurant that Rick had loved. My mood wasn't helped by memory, either of him or the tasteless tofu stir fries I'd endured, and I was settling into an angry funk when suddenly an SUV pulled out right in front of me. I slammed on the brakes, honked, and saw it. The SUV had vacated that rarity, a legal parking space. And right beyond it was the Central Café, my destination for the evening.

I zipped my Toyota into the vacancy, double-checking that I'd locked it—this wasn't my neighborhood, after all—and walked up to the café. Like so many of the more fun, funky businesses in these outlying neighborhoods, the café seemed to have grown through accretion, to have evolved as the neighborhood had changed. Undoubtedly a pub in its first incarnation, its small windows had been knocked out for a friendlier glass front that had probably boasted lots of ferns ten years ago. These days, it boasted a menu, taped to the glass above the brass railing, with a bill of fare that recalled the Caribbean rather than Dublin. Inside, however, the pub layout dominated: a long wooden bar ran down the left side of the room, with tattered vinyl booths on the right. A barkeep of an age to remember how to pull a pint with just enough head was doing his job beautifully, delivering what looked like a very honest drink to the single diner at the bar, a man in a blue cableknit sweater whose unfolded newspaper almost concealed what smelled like a bowl of Jamaican pepper-pot stew before him. I regretted my meager dinner as a whiff of spice and fish broth reached me, and continued on to the back room, where the music would be starting soon.

The back room, which actually ran parallel to the long bar, had been set up as a restaurant, and a few couples and one group of friends were already seated at the little tables, made up nice with white cloths. Carole, the organizer, had dragged one of the tables over to the doorway. She'd be taking the low cover—three dollars, her sign said—in a few minutes. Me she waved right in, and I hung around as she counted her singles into the cash box, waiting to ask for more details about the music nights.

The acoustic café, as she had dubbed it, had long been a dream of hers. As a denizen of the club scene, she knew there were a lot of musicians out there who longed for a quieter outlet, someplace on the side where they could try out songs with just a guitar or pay tribute to a blues or folk influence from their past. Nothing too high profile would be necessary; this would be for the musicians and their friends as much as the fans. And nothing could be planned on the weekends: those nights were reserved for the bands—and the paying gigs. And so she'd started this Wednesday night series three weeks before, promising the restaurant owner that it would bring in more diners and offering the musicians whatever the door came to. Thus far, it seemed promising. Word of mouth among the musicians and neighborhood was bringing in more people each week. More important to my purposes, nobody had written about it yet. If I could get Tim to run my piece by next Wednesday, I'd be credited with discovering the outlet, and it couldn't hurt Carole's promise to build up business either.

Carole gave me the rundown on who would be playing that night: among them a rockabilly guitarist who wanted to try out some country blues and a singer who had a fondness for torch songs. I took a place close beside her, intending to observe the audience as well as the performers, and watched as people, first singly and soon in a small queue, lined up for the tables and mismatched chairs in front.

That was my plan, anyway, and I made a few notes that would later help me describe the scene. But as I was writing a piano started playing, skating over the keys in an almost random pattern. A low, soft voice started singing soon after, settling the piano into its chords, and I found myself transfixed.

"If I could read your mind," sang the voice, sweet and slightly flat, bringing a blues touch to the jazzy sound of her song. "I'd know better where the danger lies…" On she sang, a song of disillusionment and love. I craned my head to catch a glimpse of who was making this magic and saw the raven-tressed singer of a local goth band. Her lips were outlined in their customary black, matching the kohl-rimmed eyes she had trained on a space beyond her listeners; she was singing one of her band's hits, a staple of Boston college radio. In this setting, though, the angry volume of the rock version had been replaced by a contemplative resignation. Her fingers played over the keyboards, filling the space usually occupied by a guitar solo with intricate variations. I leaned in to listen.

"Theda, Theda Krakow, is that you?" I looked up at a blue

sweater, the solitary diner from the bar, and recognized the detective from the day before.

"Bill, uh, Detective Sherwin?" Out of what must have been his regulation on-duty jacket and tie, he looked younger and more relaxed.

"It's Sherman. But call me Bill," he smiled into a big wide grin and then ducked his head, as if to hide it. Maybe it was that broken nose. "What brings you across the river to darkest JP? Had you heard about Carole's acoustic experiment?"

"I'm writing about it, actually." Coming back to my senses from the music-induced high, I realized that here was a patron I could interview. "Could I ask you a few questions?"

"Turning the tables, huh? Sure. Can I buy you a drink, or are you on duty?" I assured him that the journalistic discipline wasn't that strict and let him get me one of those perfectly poured pints before the interrogation began.

"So what brings you here?" I asked him, once we'd both settled in at my table. "Do you come here often?" The heat rose up my neck and we both laughed at the line, but he took it straight.

"Matter of fact, I do. I live around the corner and up the hill and I've been coming here for dinner ever since they got Charles in the kitchen. He does a pepper pot that will warm you even in February. Do you like spicy food?"

I love it, and told him so, but I wanted to keep the conversation on him. Between pauses to listen to the music, I learned that he was one of the regulars Carole had confided in. Although he was basically a jazz fan—"Monk, Miles, and Mingus!"—he'd been coming to the Wednesday showcases since the start, at first in support of Carole's plans and now, he admitted with that shy smile again, because he'd been won over by the quality of the music. His one regret—he leaned

toward me with a conspiratorial air and lowered his voice—
was that my story would bring too many tourists in.

"I want the series to be successful. But I want it to stay a
neighborhood secret, too."

"That's a great kicker," I told him. "Look for that quote at
the end of the story." I reached for my bag to stow my pad
and move along to the next interview. But he must not have
noticed because he started asking me questions. How was I
doing? What, besides this story, was I up to?

I found it hard to believe a cop would be so concerned
with a witness. But then I'd never been the one to find a
body before.

"I'm okay," I told him. "You know, I checked on those cats,
the ones at Lillian's house, and they're doing well, too. None
of them have had to be euthanized, at least not right away.
They'll all get a chance to be adopted."

"That's a relief." The room had quieted down to a soft
buzz between performers. "There were some fine looking
animals in that bunch."

"Are you a cat man?" I found the idea amusing.

"Yes, I guess I am." He seemed to consider my question
seriously. "I wasn't originally, you know. I grew up thinking
that a dog was the proper pet to have. But then, a few years
ago, I had a girlfriend who had four cats. It was kind of a 'love
me, love my cats' situation. Truth is, when that ended I missed
the cats more than I missed her."

"And now?"

"I'm not seeing anyone now."

That flush returned. "I meant the cats. Do you have a cat
now?" I didn't want to imagine what he must think of me.

"Oh no, no cats." He was chuckling. "I never got around
to getting a cat of my own."

"When the timing is right, the kitty appears." I paraphrased my favorite Zen koan at him and he seemed to appreciate it, not hiding his smile this time.

"You could even adopt one of Lillian's in a few days," I suggested, seeing a way to save at least one of those lovely felines.

"Well, first we have to see if there's an heir who wants them," said Bill, and I remembered.

"There is an heir! Dougie. Do you know about him?"

"The mentally ill son? Yeah, we found some paperwork and the department has contacted him, or been trying to, anyway. I wouldn't count on him saving the day, however. Legally, he may be the heir, but I don't think he'll be able to take the cats. I don't even think he'll be able to take over the house, and it will probably end up sold for taxes. The last records we have show him at some kind of permanent halfway house for people with schizophrenia, and there's a question of competence, in a legal sense. I haven't followed up on that end personally, but we have people looking into it. And the residence may take one of the cats as a mouser." He looked pleased at this last bit. "So how do you know about Doug? As I recall, you'd just barely met Lillian."

"Violet told me about him," I said, and as I did, everything she'd told me flooded back. Her declarations about Lillian's competence, the medic-alert necklace, and her conviction that the woman had been murdered.

"I went over there this morning and she was going through boxes," I started to explain. "She's convinced…"

"Whoa. Back up." Bill was sitting up in his seat now, beer forgotten. "Who is this Violet person and how did she come by permission to 'go through' the deceased's possessions?"

"She's another neighbor and a friend of Lillian's," I explained. "She works in the local coffeehouse, but she used to come by and help Lillian with the cats. She'd cover when Lillian took the bus to go visit Dougie."

"And was she gathering food or materials for the cats, when you dropped by?" His tone was inquisitorial now. The music, which had started up again, forgotten.

"Well, no. She was going through boxes of papers and books." What exactly was she hoping to find, I wondered? I'd not thought to ask. "But what's important is what she told me. She's convinced that Lillian was murdered."

Bill paused. He looked at me for a long moment and not with the shock or surprise that I'd have expected after I dropped that particular bombshell. It felt instead like he was appraising me, and I sat up straighter as a result.

"She says that Lillian wore one of those medic-alert necklaces. You know, the ones that let you call an ambulance if you fall?" I figured it would be best to get to the hard evidence first.

"Theda, slow down a moment." He raised a hand, as if to stop traffic, and I shut up. "Now, how do you know this Violet?"

"I just met her at the house. But I've seen her before. She serves me my coffee almost every day."

"And do you always trust everyone you've just met?" He couldn't be more than a few years older than me, but his tone was definitely that of a teacher or older brother now. "This Violet may be a perfectly nice young woman, but she shouldn't have been there. Animal Control is responsible for those cats now, and it sounds like you know that they're perfectly good at their job. And the house, legally, is in the care of the city until the probate is decided. That's a legal distinction, but it is practical too. We can't allow looters, even looters who may have—I repeat, *may* have—known the victims. Especially in a case like this, where there's an elderly person who collected lots of junk, if not cats, there are always rumors of hidden riches, stories that all the junk was covering up buried treasure, and what not. They're never true, but it doesn't matter. Violet should not have been there."

"Maybe she was looking for evidence or a lead." I might not have known Violet for long, but I did trust her. There was something open and honest about her face, even with the nose stud. "She really does believe Lillian was murdered."

Bill paused again, but this time when he started speaking his voice was back to its less formal mode. Officer Friendly. "Theda, Lillian Helmhold wasn't murdered. I shouldn't be telling you this because the finding hasn't been officially released yet, but I will. We had an autopsy. Lillian Helmhold died as I'd thought, of a subdural hematoma, a slowly bleeding wound under her skull. Her time of death was sometime between eight and midnight, and she probably injured herself as much as an hour before that. A lot of elderly people meet with accidents right around dusk, Theda. There's even a word for it: sundowning. With no evidence of foul play, it is most likely that she fell, as we'd originally thought. Her death is going to be ruled accidental."

"And the medic-alert necklace?"

"I'll look into that." He had the grace to look mildly chagrined. "But I wouldn't count on it leading anywhere. A lot of older people sign up for these personal alarm services and then forget to keep up with the monitoring fees, or they find the necklace annoying and stop wearing it. Or they take it off at night or in the tub, just when they're most likely to fall. They're like burglar alarms: homeowners put a lot of money in them up front. They go off once or twice by accident in the next six months, and they become a bother. Within a year or two, they stop setting them and soon the codes are forgotten. That's why selling them is such a great business: the companies know they're not going to have to spend that much on follow through services."

I didn't have anything to say to that. For all I knew, he was right. He was a cop, after all. And although I knew that Violet hadn't wanted me to say anything to the police, this had just kind of come out. It was better this way. I was done with it.

"Yeah, well, thanks for the beer." I pointedly pushed away the remaining half pint that now tasted sour and flat. The peevishness in my voice was obvious, even to me, but I couldn't help it.

"Theda, I'm sorry." He reached out and took my forearm. "I will look into it. I promise."

"Thanks. I do appreciate it." I tried to muster a smile. "And think about adopting one of those cats, will you? The older ones probably only have till next week to find a home."

He smiled back. "The crusading journalist returns! I'll think about it, Ms. Krakow. And you remember what I said about trusting people you've just met."

"Excellent advice, seeing as how I just met you!" I replied as I stood to leave. His mouth was slightly open, but no words came out as I swung my bag over my shoulder and walked away. I'd have to call Carole tomorrow to fill in some of the facts for my story, but the opportunity to make a dramatic exit was just too much fun to resist.

SEVEN

I PAID FOR MY dubious wit the next morning, rolling out of bed a little before eight to the realization that I'd played too much and done too little work the night before. As I made my coffee, extra strong French roast, and booted up the computer, I mulled over all the people I could call for follow-up. Musicians, scene regulars…nobody who'd be up at this hour. Penance makes for discipline, however, and in lieu of the club story I tried the contractors again, this time catching two of them who were—in their words—running late. They both agreed to chat with me that evening, and one even came up with the name and number of a recent client who had offered herself as a reference.

A full pot of my best dark brew, heavily sweetened, accompanied by Raisin Bran and the morning papers, carried me up till nine. I checked my e-mail—mostly spam—and figured it would be okay to call the contractor's client. The warmth of her greeting nearly knocked me off my seat.

"Scott told me you'd be calling!" She sounded as if I'd made her day. "I'd love for you to come by and see what we've had done. The work is just beautiful! How's eleven?"

Musetta's vet appointment was set for one, so I suggested ten, half hoping that she'd refuse. Nothing would make her happier, though, and with a lilt in her voice she gave me directions to the ritzy side of town.

I sighed and lumbered into the shower. Time to make

myself presentable. Truth was, of course, that I didn't need to be. As a freelancer, unaffiliated with any real professional organization, all I really had to be was clean and decently attired, and I knew other freelancers who severely stretched the definition of both those terms. But I still had to summon up an extra dollop of energy when I went out to do interviews like this morning's. Maybe it was the subject matter; no matter how many "action verbs" I chose, this was fundamentally a dull story. Useful, maybe, but dull, the kind of assignment that I hoped to be able to phase out eventually. Maybe it was that months of self-employment had made me unfit for human society, better company for a cat or a computer than another living, breathing person. Or maybe it was that I knew that because this woman's life—and bookshelves—were important to her, I'd end up spending several hours with her, a complete stranger, for the two or three salient quotes that I'd have gotten from a fifteen-minute phone interview, if only I'd had pictures to draw from.

But I didn't, and so after showering and dressing, feeding the cat and scooping the litter, I slumped out the door. The day that greeted me shone like a jewel, completely shattering my burgeoning self-pity. Overnight it must have rained, because more of the new leaves were opening, their brown-gold casings lining the gutter, and the buds still waiting glistened. One stately old beech, right by the corner where I'd parked, shone black and silver, still wet and bright, and the air had that freshness that reminds me how close we are to the sea. Knowing full well I'd not have been up and out this early were it not for Mrs. Bookshelves—I fumbled for my pad to make sure I had her actual name—I made a mental note of gratitude and vowed to be patient. Karma might not work that directly, but it didn't hurt to be sure.

Fresh air, warm enough to merit open windows as I drove,

banished the last of my morning fog, and I was singing along with the radio by the time I pulled up to Mrs. Bookshelves, a lovely Georgian mini-mansion, set back behind a severely pruned hedge.

"You must be the reporter!" A woman was standing at the top of the porch stairs to greet me, her impeccable hair and makeup making me think that she'd risen long before me to get dressed. "Did you bring a photographer?"

That could have explained the makeup, as well as the perfect pale lemon twin set, the pearls, and elegantly pleated pants. But she looked like the kind of woman who dressed like this anyway, just as her mother had. Close up, I would have said it all was a bit old for her; she seemed to be within a few years of my own age. But I was being nice.

"Uh, no, uh, I'll be passing your contact info onto my editor though, Mrs. Book, I mean Mrs. Hudson."

"Please, call me Sally." I wouldn't dare. Why did posh always make me uncomfortable? Already my morning lift was wearing off. It tumbled further as she led me into her house, more a showcase than what I'd call a home. Not that it wasn't lovely. Fresh flowers nearly overwhelmed a receiving table and, to the left, I could see the kind of cream and yellow furniture that wouldn't have lasted a night with my friends.

"This is the living room," she said, although I'd have been afraid to do much living in it. "And here," she led me back across the wide, well-lit entrance hallway, "is the office." Sally smiled as she said it, as if the word were a private joke. I peeked in at a rolltop desk that looked antique, a love seat that I'd seen in magazines, and a framed diploma that made her only two years older than me.

"This is your office?" The decorations were clearly feminine, but I had to ask. "And what do you do?"

"A little research, a little reading." She lowered her voice. "I'm thinking of starting an interior design firm. That's why I was so excited that you wanted to feature my house!"

"Yeah, well, okay." I took a deep breath. "And your bookshelves? Which ones did Scott do for you?"

"All of them," she said brightly. "These built-ins and the window seats and the cherry shelves in the living room that you just saw! We consulted together on the design. I conceptualized the project."

Looking around, I saw very traditional cases built into both rooms, her office shelves painted white with a seat upholstered in a sunny floral fabric filling in the space beneath the big bay window. Then she led me into a third room, much more masculine, and announced it as "the library." These were the real deal, and I made notes on the floor to ceiling shelves that lined the interior walls. Except where they gave way for a huge, marble-topped fireplace, they dominated the room with a dark red sheen that glowed from regular polishing. No small porcelain figurines here, although a few silver-framed photos of the senior Hudsons and two tow-headed kids took pride of place in front of some handsome leather-backed volumes. A lot of bookshelf for a decent collection of books, nothing milk crates wouldn't have taken care of. I pegged Mr. Hudson as a lawyer, corporate, and very well paid. In this room alone I was looking at a good thirty thousand dollars' worth of custom cabinetry, easily, but who was I to question the expense? Contractors have to eat, too.

"My husband is with Hudson, Hudson, and Brandt." She looked proud, as if I'd recognize the name. I smiled back. "And you, you work for the *Mail?*" Clearly I'd been silent too long, taking notes and a few measurements.

"I'm a freelance writer, actually. I'm not on the paper's

staff, but I contribute stories to the *Mail* and for a couple of magazines."

"A freelance writer." Sally sighed audibly. "That must be *fun!*"

I did my best to smile. "Are these real cherry or veneer?" By the time I got out of there, ninety minutes later, I felt both drained and broke. So much for how the other half lives.

CAN CATS SENSE when we need loving? I returned home to find myself the object of affection in an almost aggressive sense. Musetta was growing stout as a linebacker. Her weight, which she threw against my shins as I entered holding my bag and that morning's mail, was warm and solid.

"Good morning to you too, little kitty." I bent down to scratch her spine right at the base of the tail, getting a growling, guttural purr in response. "Isn't this nice? I hope you don't hate me after your vet visit today."

There would be time for more coffee, I noticed. Life was perking up. But first, two messages that were blinking at me from the machine. I grabbed a pad.

"Hi Theda. This is Bill, Detective Sherman, again. I wanted to let you know that we followed up with the emergency-alert necklace. We didn't find the actual device, but we were able to find the service that she'd registered with. As I'd thought, she'd never used it, which makes it more likely that she never wore it either. But they did confirm the contact information we have for her son. They had the information about a prepaid cremation service, too. Mrs. Helmhold must have taken care of herself at one time, anyway. So, thank you for the tip." The voice paused though the tape kept rolling. I figured he was worried that he'd said too much. "And, well, anyway, it was nice to see you last night. Feel free to call me back with any other questions."

The message ended with him repeating the number he'd given me before.

That was gentlemanly of him. I suspected that he wasn't supposed to tell me, a reporter, all that information, and I appreciated it. I guessed he could tell how emotionally invested I'd become in Lillian's death.

"Hey, Theda." The next voice on the machine was worth saving. "Connor here. Are you an early riser, or did you just never come home?" The suggestive chuckle with—was it just a hint of frustration?—made me give silent thanks to the Hudsons' extravagance. "Anyway, Ralph was telling me about some band from Brooklyn that's going to be playing at the Casbah tonight. Don't know who's opening. Maybe I'll see you there." It was a statement, rather than a question, but I knew an invitation when I heard one. Who needed more coffee? I cranked the stereo and danced around the apartment, sending Musetta skittering for cover. "Ooma-wallah-wallah," I called out to her, echoing the nonsense refrain of Professor Longhair's classic, "Tipitina." She glared at me from under the sofa and I turned the volume down. Going to the vet would be traumatic enough, I remembered, and went to search for James' old carrier.

"GOOD TO SEE YOU, Theda! I'll be right with you." Dr. Rachel was backing out of one of the isolation rooms when Sandra buzzed me in, her shoulder holding the door open as she rubbed her hands together with the ever-present Purel. Motioning for me to follow her into an empty examining room, she headed right to the room's sink, taking advantage of the real soap and water.

"It's good to do this. That alcohol cleanser really irritates my skin after a while," she said, drying her hands. "Okay, who do we have here?"

I'd placed the green plastic carrying case on the stainless steel examining table and Rachel opened the top. Lifting the uncomplaining kitten, she deposited her first on the scale and then on the table, taking notes and chirping to her patient as she went along.

"Teeth coming in, very nice. Aren't we sweet? Let's see that troublesome leg of yours. Not still limping? No, not that I see. And now the ears, little bitty ears. Belly feels good, yes it does! Now let's see your bottom!" Rachel wielded a mean-looking thermometer. At this indignity, Musetta started to scramble away, her white boots not getting much grip on the smooth metal surface.

"Come on now, baby. We're almost done." A few more pokes and prods and she was.

"You'll want her shots today, right?"

"Might as well, whatever she's due for."

"We'll do the usual new kitten inoculations. Watch her?" She turned to the table behind her and its well-stocked cabinet. "I'd put her at between six and eight weeks. A little young to be out on her own." She reached again for her patient, calm now despite the needle that was coming up behind her. "What a good little girl you are! Good thing you've got a good mama right here to take care of you."

Musetta didn't flinch, the little trouper. I did. "I'm not her new mama, Rachel. I just want to take care of her till I can find her a good home. A kitten this cute, shouldn't be hard."

"Wouldn't be if it weren't already kitten season, Theda." Rachel prepped another injection and looked at me a little harder. "Spring is when intact cats breed most. We're already full up, and that means no more stays of execution for all the animals we already have. Six days, that's it. And that's just not much of a chance, especially for the older cats." She saw the look on my face and sighed. "I don't like it any more than you do." She gave the last shot and stroked the little girl into a purr. "But we don't have the space and we don't have the resources, even with all the volunteers."

"But a kitten, surely?"

"Yeah, a little beauty like this will probably get snatched right up. But that means some other kitten won't find a home."

I looked down at the examining table and away, out the window where a still-bare tree had begun to toss in the wind.

"I'll think about it," I said, meaning, "I'm not ready." Musetta made her way over to my edge of the table, still purring, and butted her head against me.

"Do, Theda. This little girl looks to be in fine shape. Her leg must have gotten bruised somehow, but it seems to be healing. I don't see any need for X-rays. And I think she's already made her choice."

MUSETTA MEWED A LITTLE on the drive home, then curled up and slept, exhausted by her adventure. I kept the radio off so as not to disturb her and instead let my own thoughts wander. I didn't want to be pressured into another cat. James was my cat, and always would be. I didn't even want to think about it and instead mused about more pleasing developments. Connor in particular. I was looking forward to meeting up with Connor tonight. But first, it was time, once I got home and liberated the kitten from her temporary imprisonment, to do a little research. Not the three-call rule on something this sensitive, but some in-person questioning. Time to head back to the Mail and corner Ralph.

Boston traffic is miserable. The city streets, legend has it, were laid out by a snake and paved by a cow, and neither the years nor the ongoing construction known as the Big Dig have been kind to the result. That traffic, a day-long mess of snarls and honking, along with my growing aversion to talking with real humans, makes me very fond of filing everything electronically. But on occasion eye contact is still useful. And editors do like to see that their reporters leave the house every now and then. That was my excuse, anyway, as I pulled into one of the guest parking spaces in front of the *Mail* and bounded up the stairs to the features department.

"Theda!" Tim's booming voice headed me off on my way to Ralph's cubicle. "Do you have a moment?"

It was a command, not a request. But then, he paid much of my rent. "What's up, boss?" I tried for jovial as I weaved between desks toward his office, where he stood in the doorway looking flustered and annoyed.

"Who is Sally Hudson and why is she calling me?"

"Sally Hudson?" It hit me: Mrs. Hudson, Mrs. Bookshelf. She must have called the paper looking for me and gotten directed to my former section and, thus, to Tim as my editor. "She's someone I'm writing about for Home. She called you, I gather? I'm sorry."

"Crazy lady," he muttered as he retreated back to his desk. I think he was referring to Mrs. Hudson.

"I'll call her in a minute," I promised him, following him into the small office out of habit, and he looked up, vague hope in his eyes.

"Do you have something for me?"

I almost stumbled into his desk. Of course! He thought I was here on business.

"Went to that acoustic café last night," I said, settling into his one guest chair. "It is becoming quite a scene. Great music, great food. Real atmosphere. The neighborhood is catching on fast. And," I leaned forward in a conspiratorial way, hoping to hype my one bit of news. "Nobody else has written about it yet. *Nobody*."

"Excellent. Get it in by Monday, we'll run it on Wednesday." He pushed back from his desk and swiveled to face the computer. I was dismissed.

But I have a conscience. "One more thing, Tim." He looked up, surprised to still see me there.

"Hmm?"

"Do you know a writer named Ethan, Ethan Reinhardt?"

"Never heard of him." He started to turn away. Either Ethan hadn't started pitching stories yet, or he was having second thoughts about leaving news. Still, I'd said I'd put a word in. Freelancer solidarity and all that.

"Well, I've read some of his stuff. He's looking to get into features, and I was wondering if I could give him your name."

"Suit yourself, Krakow. If you want to make your own competition…." He turned away and I swallowed, hard. There had to be some karmic payback in this life for good deeds, right?

"So, RALPH! RALPH?" He had his earphones on. I swung his chair around with him in it, causing him to scramble as the Discman slid off the pile of press releases and cardboard mailers that obscured his desktop.

"Hold on. Wait a minute." He took the headset off. "What's up, Theda?"

"Who's playing the Casbah tonight? Your friend Connor called to tell me it was going to be a good show." I was hoping I sounded casual.

Ralph didn't buy it. "Connor called, huh?" He looked at me in a way I couldn't read at all. I thought about clearing a space on his desk to sit on and pulled over another chair instead, putting my feet up on his opened top drawer.

"Yeah. Why?"

"Nothing. Nothing at all." He reached for headphones again, and I reached to stop him.

"Come on, Ralph. Give it up."

"Well, I'm just surprised, that's all." He sulked, momentarily, lower lip out. Could that be jealousy, or just hangover-fueled grumpiness? "I'd have thought maybe you were too bookish for him. Must be the red hair. But don't look to him for anything like domestication. He's out almost every night. And sometimes I don't hear him come back."

"He's staying with you?" He'd given me a number, but I hadn't used it. And although I've known Ralph for years, I've never had reason to call him at home.

"Yeah, didn't I tell you? He's new in town and he needed a place to stay." This was food for thought. "He's a nice enough guy, though, Theda. I mean, we just know each other through the clubs, but he's fun and, thus far, he's done his share of the grocery shopping." I envisioned Ralph's fridge and shuddered. "I just thought you should know, I don't think he's exactly boyfriend material."

Great. Well, he'd been pursuing me, right? "Is he a musician or something?" Maybe he just wanted some press coverage. "I did a Google search, but nothing came up."

Ralph glowered again and I knew I'd crossed a line. In club circles, it was incredibly uncool to ask what someone did for work. So many of us were in the "slash" category: poet-slash-waitress, painter-slash-cabbie. But I was looking for a rationale. And besides, despite Ralph's warning, I was curious.

"He's some kind of artist, I think. At least that's what he tells you ladies." From the way he rolled his eyes, Ralph was unimpressed. "He's definitely done a lot of things. And, yes, he did ask me about you, more than once."

Had I been that obvious? No matter. I could feel the smile splitting my face and grabbed a lock of my own hair to chew on as cover. Ralph wasn't buying that either. "Ah, spring," he said. "Romance is in the air." He started to push the headphones back over his ears, then paused. "And the band tonight is the Brought Low from Brooklyn. They're really worth hearing. Get there early."

"YOU DON'T NEED a new man, you need a new cat." I'd pulled Bunny away from her cubicle for a confab in the *Mail* cafeteria. She was firm. "Get settled in your home life first. The rest will follow."

I'd made her take her break with me, dragging her away from a huge pile of barely legible library search request forms, and then filled most of it with descriptions of Connor between bites of a tuna salad roll-up. I was starting to get silly, to read too much into too little information, and she wasn't having any of it.

"He calls you, but not to take you out on a proper date? He doesn't offer to pick you up? And his best friend warns you that he's not the domestic type? I don't like it." Whatever version of an afterlife my parents had settled in, they didn't have to worry that I was being looked after.

"Let's just see what happens with this one," I tried to reassure her as I finished my sandwich and pushed the chips aside. For myself, I had no doubts. "I don't even know how close Connor and Ralph are." That raised Bunny's eyebrows. "Hey, I'm a big girl, remember."

"You're tall, Theda. That's not the same thing. Be careful."

She had to go back to work. Shouldn't have taken the break at all, she grumbled. Shouldn't have eaten so many of my chips. So I walked her back down to the library and drove home singing. I didn't know what I sounded like to those contractors I'd promised to call when I reached them about an hour later. But, hey, they'd get publicity out of the story. Three quotes from each and I made my farewells, typed up my notes without reading them and turned the computer off. Another bowl of Raisin Bran for dinner, and it was time to get ready for my night out.

EIGHT

I'M NOT ONE for dressing up, and club lighting—furthered by the atmospherics of alcohol—isn't too particular. Still, I wanted to look nice and made sure my black jeans were clean and flatteringly snug from a recent spin in the dryer in my building's basement. I mulled a bit over what top to pair with them: silk was way too fancy, but except for one or two good blouses the rest of my wardrobe consisted of band tee shirts and those durable polyester work clothes I hoped never to have to don again. A run through my closet yielded up a man-tailored blouse, dyed a brilliant turquoise by one of my favorite second-hand stores. By some miracle, it appeared freshly pressed, and the color set off the gold in my red hair without making my winter-pale face any more sallow than usual. Musetta sat on the bed as I buttoned the blouse, turning to and fro to check how it looked from the back once I tucked it in. She was an adorable kitten, with those wide eyes appraising me. She looked so pensive I was tempted to think that something was wrong.

"Don't you like it, kitty?" I swooped around, startling her for a moment as I gathered her up for a cuddle and a kiss. "Not everyone can be as perfectly groomed as you are, or as stylish! Or are you thinking about your cousins?" The thought of all those cats stuck in the shelter made me hesitate about my own happiness, and I hugged the little kitten harder. She squirmed, and I set her back on the bed. "I'll see what I can do, Musetta.

I promise," I said, but she scampered away. I'd have to do without her best wishes on this sort-of date, but she was too young to know better anyway.

THE CLUB WAS HOPPING when I got there, a little after ten. Already it was steamy, the windows fogged up and the noisy room too hot for the black leather jacket I'd grabbed on my way out of the apartment. Not that I regretted it: outside, the May warmth had faded with the dusk, and besides, I liked bowing just this much to rock and roll convention. A quick glance around the room yielded a few greetings and a couple of familiar faces, but not the one I was looking for.

"Hey, stranger!" I looked behind me and saw Violet in full regalia: hair spiked and newly colored and wearing a cut-off tee shirt that showed the bracelet-like tattoos encircling her upper arm. "You here to see me?"

"You're playing tonight? Cool, I didn't know!" To be honest, I wasn't sure she'd told me the name of her band, but as I followed her toward the bar, she tapped on the set list that was tacked to the adjacent wall: 10:30, The Violet Haze Experience, I read, to be followed by some band I'd never heard of and then "From NYC!" The Brought Low, closing the night with a 12:30 start time.

"First time for everything," she smiled. The bartender brought her a bottle of Bud and waved away her offer to pay. "I'll put you on the list." She slapped a dollar on the bar and turned to head back to the music room, the big downstairs area where the bands played. "Oh, I almost forgot." I caught a glimpse of a particularly intricate Celtic knot design on her shoulder as she turned back to me. "There's going to be a memorial service on Saturday. Behind the house, if the weather's good. If not, maybe the coffeehouse. I'll post something there anyway."

Her words sparked a memory. "Violet, before you go." Not good timing, I could tell. She was due onstage in a few. "You've really got to stop going into Lillian's house. You know it's illegal."

"I'm not breaking and entering, Theda. I've got a key. Well, I know where Lillian always left her spare key, right under the last slate on the path."

"But the cop, the detective who I spoke with that day. He says that it's off-limits until they figure out who inherits and what will happen to the house. He says you could be arrested for trespassing."

"You talked to the cops?"

"It came out." I rushed to intercept her anger. "It was an accident, sort of."

"You spoke to the cops. By accident." I had her full attention now.

"I ran into that detective, Bill Sherman, at the Central Café. Over in JP?" She nodded, willing to accept that cops went to hear music sometimes. "He started telling me that Lillian's death had been ruled accidental. So I had to tell him what you'd told me, about the medic-alert necklace and everything." He'd seemed really reasonable and accepting of everything I'd told him, I remembered. Quite nice, really. But I wasn't going to try to convince Violet of that.

"I getcha. It's okay. I mean, I haven't found anything that could have caused anyone to want to hurt her, not yet. It's just that, well, cops and I don't get along. I have my reasons. And I can't stop looking through Lillian's stuff. Not yet."

"But if you're busted…."

"Look, I can't explain now. That's my drummer and if she's waving to me then you know I'm late."

"Go! Break a string!" I waved her off. I wanted to talk to her about the cats, maybe get some more information, but she was clearly too busy. I'd catch my breath and have one more look around before following her.

"I'll be looking for you down there! And we'll talk. Later." She disappeared into the crowd.

I made one more slow sweep around the room and ducked into the ladies'. As suspected, the hot damp had already taken the starch out of my shirt collar and caused the natural curl in my shoulder-length hair to burst forth in abundance. Ah well, Connor had first seen me after a day of death and Worcester and he'd still called. Twice.

With that happy thought I made my way through the crowd, weaving slowly and almost sideways, to the back door that led into the music room.

Downstairs, the air was a good ten degrees cooler and, except for the ashy smell of old cigarettes, a lot more comfortable. Only about twenty people mulled around the large dark room, gathered mainly at the bar rather than in front of the still-dark stage. I felt a twinge of guilt at letting Violet guest-list me; her band could have used the five bucks. But then the soundman wandered over to his station, the lights over the raised stage switched on, and Violet took the stage with a bang.

With a crash, actually, as she tore into her guitar and her drummer jumped on a kit that had been pared down to hard-beat essentials. Fast repeated chords—part Eddie Cochran, part Billy Zoom—filled the almost empty room, almost loud enough to obscure the solid bottom of bass notes that supported the whole structure. It was brilliant noise, and I felt my body begin to move. Already the drinkers were turning toward the stage. And then Violet began to sing, or more accurately to caterwaul, high and urgent but somehow or other exactly right.

"Yeah!" I yelled, and the short girl in front of me turned around and smiled. Girl! Despite her moon face and innocent smile, she was probably a few years past the legal limit of twenty-one. I was thinking my age. But the music was as exciting as it had been when I'd first started sneaking into clubs as a teen. And age be damned: we were all dancing, moving as a unit now, the few faces in attendance bobbing and weaving as Violet's trio stopped on a dime and broke into another number without any appreciable loss of energy. I turned around and saw the crowd had nearly doubled, another couple of people pushing through the door as I looked. None of them was Connor, and I thought he'd be sorry to be missing this. I started dancing again, knowing full well what my hair would look like. Ah well, Medusa herself would have appreciated this band. Bam—another song ended and the three launched into a slow number, an intricate bass pattern taking over, and I could almost hear Violet's words.

Something about love and anger, I made out, and then she soloed, sharp and fast as befitted her punk origins. Her drummer was soaked, her neck and arms glistening with sweat, the front of her pink baby-T already stained dark. But her bassist was smiling, tall and proud, with only her hands revealing the effort of keeping each three-minute whiplash on key and in rhythm.

"Great, huh?" The short young fan I'd noticed before was shouting up at me, round face all aglow. Somehow I'd pushed up beside her and now I nodded back, smiling. "I've loved Violet for years!" she yelled. She was either older than I'd thought, or shared the habits of my younger days and a good fake ID.

"I'd never heard her before!" I yelled back when the music next went into a lull. She looked at me, pierced eyebrows raised in astonishment. Clearly, I *was* old. I danced on, anyway, facing the stage as the three instruments started into a syncopated assault, a reggae-filigreed structure that allowed Violet's shrill-sweet voice to soar. Then the bassist joined in, a strong alto counterpart to the near hysteria on top. Instrumental breaks let them breathe, and then back again and just that fast, another song was done.

"I know her through the cats!" I yelled over to the short dancer. Even in the moments between songs, the noise level had grown.

Nodding, the young fan responded, "Yeah, Violet the Vet. If she ever can afford it. I want her to keep on playing though."

Another song began, a slow one again, with the two voices intertwining over a simple repeated riff. A tall, skinny young woman—easily three inches above me, and probably a few pounds lighter—squeezed in and wrapped her arms around my conversation partner. The tempo picked up and we all danced again, breathing as one for as long as the music lasted.

AFTER THE SET, I surfaced for air. I couldn't believe Ralph and Connor had missed it, but there they were when I went back into the front room, sitting by the bar.

"Ah, there's our rosy-cheeked lass!" Connor immediately dismounted from the high wooden bar chair and swung it around to welcome me.

"You look all hot and bothered," added Ralph, with his usual tact.

"You wouldn't believe what you just missed." I started to tell them, taking the seat and swigging down the full water glass the waitress placed before me. The hair I pushed back from my face felt damp and springy with curl. "The Violet Haze Experience. They were incredible."

Connor looked interested. Ralph, however, rolled his eyes. "Oh yeah, they send me fliers all the time. Nuevo-riot grrl, with a touch of speed metal, right? Sleater-Kinney wannabes."

"C'mon, Ralph, that's not fair. I mean, yeah, you can hear

their influences, but they've got an energy and they've also got some great songs."

"I forget you were such a pop fan, Theda." He said it as if a sense of melody and song structure was a bad thing. "A good hook and you can dance to it, right?"

"Ralph…." I started in, but he had already turned to look for the bartender. "Risa? Risa! We need a refill here." He turned back to look at me. "Too much estrogen. I need the antidote."

Before I could respond, Connor had his hand on my seat back, his arm almost around my shoulder. "Don't mind him, Theda. He's never comfortable with women who can kick his ass." He leaned in close, as if to let me in on a secret, and I couldn't help breathing in the warm, slightly spicy scent of him. "I, however, admire feisty women."

Whoa, girl, I told myself as I smiled up into those deep-blue eyes. "Thanks." That was all I could say without losing any dignity I had left. I didn't really know this man. And besides, we were in a public place. Much to my surprise, Ralph saved me by shoving me with his elbow.

"Whatcha having?"

"Don't bother, Ralph, Blue Moon coming up," Risa answered for me, by which point I'd recovered enough to respond like an adult human.

"Thanks, Connor. I just get so mad. That attitude is why I'm no longer focusing on music criticism," I told him. That, and I couldn't get enough assignments to make the pitching worthwhile, but that was more information than he needed. "We're supposed to be out there, listening. In print, we all say we're dying to hear something new, and we all would love to discover the next big thing. But god forbid anyone should appear uncool by liking something that doesn't pan out in the great artistic race. And the result is new bands don't get heard."

"Especially new bands led by women, right?" If he was

trying to win me over, he was doing a great job. I nodded my assent, but didn't trust myself to speak.

"So, you ready to hear a real rock band?" Ralph grimaced and bit his lower lip as he mimed a guitar solo. "Get ready to rock!" He knew he'd gotten to me and was trying to make nice. The result was charming as a lovestruck eleven-year-old. Next thing, he'd put a frog down my shirt.

"I'll give an honest listen to your boy-rock," I teased right back. Two could play at that game. Or three. I smiled up at Connor to invite him in on my side, and we all began to talk at once, praising bands we'd heard—or heard about—and generally showing off our fandom and our expertise. The mood restored, I couldn't bear not knowing what my hair looked like after the sweat and frenzy of Violet's set, and after a few verbal parries excused myself to hit the head, which was back by the music room. Although I lacked either a brush or a pick, a quick finger comb separated out some of the worst tendrils, giving me what I liked to think was a pre-Raphaelite crown of curls. My face was glowing, though whether still from the heat of dancing or from Connor's attention, I couldn't tell. Not bad for thirty-three, I told the reflection in the dim, chipped mirror. Not bad at all, I cheered myself on, and turned to return to the men.

Stepping out of the bathroom, I nearly ran into Violet. Wet with sweat still, but triumphant, she was oblivious to the room around her.

"Violet! Great set!" I would have clapped my arms around her, had she not been so clearly sticky.

"You really liked it?"

"I loved it. I was dancing up by the stage like I haven't in years."

She looked honestly pleased. "Wow, thanks for checking us out. Hey, I've got some more loading out to do, but then

I'll come talk. Where are you?" I pointed over to the bar. Her eyes followed the line of my hand.

"Yeah. Well, work to do." She was gone.

She was distracted, I knew, with the post-performance buzz and the more pressing need to move all her band's equipment off the stage so the next band could come on. I walked back to the bar, and this time both men dismounted from their bar seats, ready to offer me theirs.

"Thanks anyway, I'll stand awhile." They looked at me quizzically. "Hey, if I'm making the point that women can rock, then I better prove I can stand my ground, too."

"Fair enough," said Connor. "But watch mine, will you? I'm going to try to head off this bartender for another round."

Risa did look swamped, but I don't think it helped that Connor went to join what was rapidly becoming a pack. Thirsty drinkers had swarmed the service area, hindering the club's one waitress. I slid into his seat—just for the duration—and found Ralph leaning toward me on the bar.

"So, you and Rick aren't still an item, huh?" While his query wasn't the most articulate, I read his meaning. The spirit of competition, it seemed, had awakened a spark in Ralph.

"No. I don't know that we ever really were." I didn't want to encourage him, but his question hit on something I guess I hadn't made my peace with.

"You seemed so down for a while this winter."

"That was because of James, my cat." I really didn't want to talk about this. I certainly didn't want to hear his response, and so I spun around to stare into the crowd. There was Violet, coming back from loading out.

"Hey, Violet!" She turned for a split second and just as fast looked away. I was sure she'd heard me, but she spun on her heels, heading toward the music room, and didn't look back.

"What's up with her?" I didn't know what had happened.

"Oh, she recognizes me," said Ralph, who had swung around soon after I did. "She probably read my manifesto in Sunday's paper on the new rock chicks and how bogus they are." I was tempted to tell him what I thought of his misogynistic little rant, but he wasn't done. "Plus, clearly I'm in the front room and I didn't go back to see her. She keeps sending me those fliers. Poor girl, she probably had her hopes up."

I couldn't imagine Violet would have any illusions about old Ralph here, but maybe she did have some about me. Did it bother her that I was sitting with Ralph? Had it finally sunk in that I had talked to the cops? When I'd run into her just now, she'd been fresh from the stage, and I'd been full of praise. Maybe as she was carrying amps and guitars out the door she recalled what we'd started to talk about earlier. She said she had her reasons about not wanting the police involved. But maybe she didn't, or not any good ones. I didn't know her well enough to tell. Whatever she'd planned to tell me before, clearly she had changed her mind.

Connor came back with our drinks just then, and I tried to put my new friend's strange behavior from my mind. We told some more stories and then made our way back to the music room, just in time to catch the last of the middle band. That gave us enough time to secure a good place for the headliners. The space that had held a cool ashy chill before was packed with people, and I allowed myself to be sandwiched between the two men as they bullied their way over to the side of the stage. There, with the bar behind us, we could almost see. We could certainly hear, as the main attraction kicked in with a big, bass-heavy sound that had the crowd around us moving in no time. The band had something, almost a retro Southern rock style, with blues powered by the metal attack of well wielded guitars. But their music didn't move me like Violet's band had. Maybe I was more self-conscious now, standing here with Connor. Maybe I was just feeling the beer and the hours and the week that had passed. Connor was still charming, cracking me up with impersonations of various rock types, but I was pooped. In a lull between songs, I reached for his arm.

"I've got to crash," I yelled into his ear. He looked disappointed. "I'm sorry," I continued. "I'm just wiped out and I'm not going to be any fun soon."

"I doubt that," he said, and brought his hand up to cradle my face. I forgot my fatigue for a moment but then it, with the band, came crashing back.

"See you around." I attempted a light-hearted smile.

"I'll call you," he promised. And with a slight spring in my step, I made my way out of the crowd and toward the comfort of my own sweet home.

NINE

THE PHONE WAS ringing before I knew what it was.

"Argh," I complained, pushing the kitten off my pillow as I responded blindly to the sound.

"Argh?" Somehow I'd found the receiver and grabbed my bedside pad and pen.

"Theda? This is Mrs. Hudson. Sally. I tried to reach you yesterday." Damn, I hadn't called her back when I'd told Tim I would. I looked at the clock: eight a.m. Felt like five. "When you were here, looking at my shelves, I forgot to tell you the most important thing." Something like a hangover was settling in, pounding right above my left ear. I cursed that last round I'd let Connor buy. Keeping up with him and Ralph was foolish for a woman my size. At least I'd worn earplugs once the headliner had started. If I hadn't, maybe I wouldn't be able to hear the bookshelf lady right now. Then again, maybe that wouldn't have been so bad.

"It's the window seat. The one in my office? I wanted to point out how they were constructed." She seemed on automatic pilot and soon I stopped taking notes. I don't think I dozed much, but suddenly she was talking resale values. "By building around the original casement, they highlight the original design," Sally was saying. "Which really ups your value. Especially with everyone rediscovering the architectural gems we have right here in town."

I woke up a bit, trying to think of realtors I could call for confirmation or, at least, a quote. Adding value to your property wasn't a bad angle. "That's fascinating," I interrupted her monologue. "Do you know a Patti Wright? She's a realtor near me."

"Oh, Patti. Yes, of course," came the burbling response. "Going into real estate was the smartest thing she did after getting free of that husband of hers. Did you know George, too?" Her voice had sunk to a hungry whisper, but I had to disappoint her. Too early for gossip, and definitely not my crowd. "Ah well," she sighed at my negative response. "He was one of her less-than-stellar moves. The other was accepting that white elephant she lives in as her entire settlement."

"The house?"

"Of course, the house. That was her big project and I personally know that she's sunk a load into it. A load! Can't sell it now, of course. That neighborhood isn't quite ready for redevelopment." I swore I could hear a smirk.

"How do you know she wants to sell it?" I was waking up now, my community pride—and my curiosity—pricked.

"My dear, it's been on the market several times over the last year. Thomas has seen the signs. He cuts through that area on his way to the turnpike. And we all know how, well, how *difficult* things have been for her, you know, in terms of finances, what with the property taxes and all."

Hmmm…. I murmured my assent and let her ramble on for a bit. So perhaps Patti Wright's dislike of her neighbor, with her rundown house and multiple cats, wasn't just prissiness. Could Lillian's stodginess—or her poverty—have had that big an impact on Patti's real estate dreams?

"I should call her, of course." Sally Hudson hadn't missed a beat. "But, well, she hasn't really been around lately, has she?"

"She hasn't?" I felt slimy, priming her for gossip in this manner. But if she knew something that might have bearing on Lillian—or my neighborhood—I wanted to know. Sally was more than willing to share.

"It's not just that she's working all the time, you know." She said it like it was a scandal. "But I heard Patti also had to leave the club. Something about a check not clearing for the dues…."

Her voice had dropped to a whisper, but I heard what she was insinuating. And if Patti Wright was falling out of her accustomed social set, her desperation could be personal as well as professional, particularly if she was trapped in a white elephant of a house by a seemingly disreputable neighbor. Real estate was a high stakes game in our rapidly changing city, but how much had she gambled? Enough to give her motive to kill an old lady simply because she was set in her ways? Hudson rattled on a bit before ringing off. I hoped that I was polite, but when I looked at my notes they read simply, "cabinet, upholstery. Wright???" Clearly, Sally had left me with more questions than she'd answered. I balled up the paper and tossed it. Out of nowhere, Musetta pounced.

"Okay, kitty. Talk about a rude awakening." Musetta hadn't been too happy to be expelled from her pillow, but now she reared up on her hind legs, looking for all the world like a little gopher as she batted the wad of paper. It disappeared under the radiator, but even when I sent it scurrying across the floor once more she seemed satisfied with having made her goal.

"Meh-eh?" she said, instead, looking up at me.

"Breakfast? Coming right up, your highness." Being a freelancer didn't mean you were free. It just meant that you served a whole slew of different bosses.

AFTER I'D SPENT a good five minutes watching the kitten eat, empty can and plastic spoon still in hand, I realized that I'd not fully come to life yet. Time to do something about that.

And even though bed beckoned, I could see from my window that yet another glorious spring day had begun. A head-clearer stronger than caffeine was called for.

"Ow! Stop that! Ow!" I moved to clap my hands and hit my head instead. Finding the first sneaker had been easy. But although I'd finally located the second, back in the corner under my bed, rescuing it in the presence of a rambunctious kitten took a little effort. I wasn't feeling too limber as I crawled under the bed, and she saw my outstretched fingers as her natural prey.

Instinctively, I'd reared up when she pounced, forgetting where I was. I'd trained James not to do that kind of thing by clapping whenever he pounced inappropriately. But the loud thud my head made as it hit the metal frame seemed to serve the same purpose, and I emerged just in time to see her scampering out of the bedroom. Lacing the second shoe on, I thought I could already feel my head clearing, but that was probably because of the counter-irritant from the bruising. Nothing fresh air and sweat wouldn't cure, I told myself, feigning an optimism I didn't really feel.

The air outside did feel glorious, slightly damp and just cool enough. I stood on the stone steps of my building looking around, trying to remember how I used to stretch before running, and generally stalling the inevitable. On the trees that lined my street, buds had finally been outnumbered by small, light-green leaves; in the shallow beds alongside my building the daffodils' sprouting green hurried to make up for lost time. Time to follow suit. Although I felt leaden, each step a drag, for the first two blocks, life began to return. My stride lengthened and I started to move with some grace. Soon I was flying. I'd be sore tomorrow, but I couldn't resist a real run, like I'd used to do last fall, when life had been simpler. I decided to make a circuit of the entire neighborhood, really give myself a workout.

Down to the river? No, I needn't have fooled myself. I knew I was heading for Lillian's even before I reached the corner. If I kept this up, I promised myself, I'd run along the Charles tomorrow. For today, however, I'd just jog by the old house, see what was happening. My encounter with Violet the night before had shaken me up. The way she had just walked off must have meant she was really pissed. I knew she thought her old friend had been murdered, and my instincts had agreed. But if she was right, it was best left for the cops to handle, no matter what she thought. Besides, in the light of day, I couldn't back Violet's conviction with anything other than a gut hunch. Bill Sherman seemed like a decent cop, a smart one as well, and he'd had answers for everything. More likely, I thought as the old house's lilac hedge came into view, Violet's belief came from a natural aversion to sudden death. She's so young, I thought. She's probably never lost anybody before. I passed the Wright house and slowed to a walk for a breather. Still, I didn't want Violet to get herself in trouble with the cops. I'd talk to her again, if she'd let me. See if I could make her see reason.

Standing on the sidewalk, hands on my hips, I realized I wasn't moving forward any more and might as well stretch. A nicely solid oak stood on the edge of the lawn, and I leaned into it, feeling the tightness at the back of my calves give way ever so slightly. Then, it wasn't a noise exactly, but some combination of rustle and movement. I looked up at the side of the house just as it disappeared. Some flicker in an upstairs window made me think that the grand old house wasn't empty.

Was it Violet? I feared that she was rummaging through boxes again, and wondered what to say to her. Having access to a key wasn't the same as permission, and whatever she was looking for wasn't worth getting busted over. Or could it be another cat? The one she'd called Sibley had escaped the round-up, and it was quite possible others had as well. Maybe I'd seen some stray who nested in the attic making his move toward an unsuspecting rodent. I stood for a moment longer, watching the window, the only one up on the third floor. Nothing else moved. Maybe it had been a trick of the light. Maybe all I had seen was a hallucination of my oxygen-deprived, endorphin-pumping brain. Maybe I was stalling before starting to run again, but there was something creepy about the old house, now that the cats were gone. Those windows felt too much like eyes. Enough! One final stretch and I was off.

A half hour later, I was singing in the shower. Sex could be great and chocolate was reliable, but nothing consistently lifted my mood like exercise. How could I have forgotten this wonderful feeling? I toweled off, trying to gauge the extent of my buzz. No, I would still need coffee. I laced my sneakers back on and positively trotted over to the Mug Shot.

I was lucky to get a stool at the counter, the little coffee-house was that busy.

"Skim latte coming up!" Violet yelled over the whir of the espresso machine. She was fixing a row of chai teas, all to go, but brought my tall, foam-topped glass over with a smile not long after.

"Hey, Theda. How's it going?"

"Great," I could honestly respond. "But...last night." I wasn't sure how to broach the subject. "Did I piss you off? Was it because I told that cop?"

She looked at me blankly. I wasn't making sense.

"I thought you were going to come over and chat after, but you sort of took off." In the light of day, I sounded like a hypersensitive fan. Maybe she'd just been tired or had some other perfectly sound reason not to want to socialize. We didn't know each other that well after all.

"Oh, at the bar? Hold on, one mocha latte coming up! That was nothing." She grabbed two empty mugs off the counter, wiped the pale brown rings beneath them and headed back toward the machines. "I saw a creepy guy I sort of know. Real bastard," she said as she walked away. "I just didn't want to have to talk to him."

Relief tasted as good as that warm, thick drink, and curiosity followed. Could it be Ralph she was avoiding, as he had suggested? Ralph's dismissal of her music had been more than cavalier, it had bordered on cruel. Maybe he'd said something. Worse, even if he didn't want to admit it to me, maybe he'd written something that had knocked her band. To me the pudgy, aging critic was a bit of a buffoon, but for a fledgling musician trying to get gigs in this town, press was important—and a slam in a major paper like the *Mail* could set you back months. I'd have to work on Ralph, I decided. Get him to actually listen to a song, if not a set, next time the band played out. Right now, I had more pressing concerns.

"Violet, have you been working all morning?" She'd taken a damp rag and was wiping down the counter as she nodded, stopping to work on one particularly sticky spot.

"Yup. I did set-up today, and we're ready for customers by seven, why?" She looked up, curious.

"I thought I saw something—or someone—in Lillian's earlier. Just a movement in the window. You've got Sibley, right?" She nodded. "Could there be other cats still in there?"

"Could be." She bunched the rag in her hands as she thought. "I think all the house cats were taken. Maybe a feral, but you're not likely to ever see one of them. They're hiders."

She moved along to help another customer. I must have been fooled by a trick of the light. All along the street, the budding trees had just begun to cast fuller reflections.

"You coming tomorrow?" Violet had swung back to my

end of the counter to hand over a bag of ground coffee. She took the customer's money and pointed at the bulletin board. "It's been moved to the church. One of her friends works there." I read the notice: "Lillian Helmhold, a life remembered." Friends and neighbors of the late Lillian Helmhold, a.k.a. "The Cat Lady of Cambridgeport, "were invited to share memories and pay their respects at an informal gathering to be held Saturday morning at eleven at First Baptist, in the church's downstairs common room.

That was tomorrow. I felt like I'd begun to know her. "Yeah, I will," I called back to Violet as I drained my glass. "Maybe we can talk after?" That might not have been her in the house this morning. Still, I had the feeling she didn't take my admonition to leave the place alone any more seriously than a cat would. I didn't like losing Lillian just as I'd found her, and I didn't want to lose Violet too.

"Sure. I'm going to try to get some people over to the shelter afterward, too. You know that Lillian's cats are up for adoption today?" I nodded. How could I have forgotten? The clock had started running on those beautiful beasts, and if we could place some of them with sympathetic friends, it would be an afternoon well spent.

On this day, however, work took first priority. With the energy from my run and the latte's healthy shot of espresso, I cranked out a draft of the bookshelf story. There were only a few "TKs"—"to comes" in newspaper parlance—to fill in. I left a message for one contractor, reminding him that he'd promised to give me his price range for the story, and logged onto the Home You Go supply store web site to get their prices for do-it-yourself materials that would provide the budget option in my story. Then, because the sun was now over the yardarm, I made the calls I needed for the Jamaica Plain café story. Musetta was sleeping on the old corduroy easy chair beside my desk, and I could have kept going, cranked that one out too, had my stomach not started rumbling loud enough to almost wake her. I'd forgotten how hungry exercise made me, but I'd earned a break and a little more fresh air. There was a greasy spoon three blocks away that served breakfast all day, a survivor from when much of the neighborhood worked all shifts at the candy factory. Somewhere in there a cook had a plate of eggs with my name on them. Careful not to wake the sleeping kitten, I slipped out the door.

Wiping up the last of the runny egg yolk and Tabasco mixture with the end of my well-buttered whole wheat toast, I surveyed the damage. I'd had the eggs poached instead of fried, and congratulated myself on that. But the stiffness that kicked in as I was walking down my front stairs reminded me that my exercise regimen was going to have to become a lot more regular. At least I'd gotten a good chunk of work done already. The bookshelf piece I'd hold till Monday, then read through again to catch the glaring errors and silly phrases that become clear after a few nights' sleep. I'd still be sending it in ahead of deadline. The café piece left me more room to play, and I let my mind wander, wondering which quote to make my lead or if I should start with a description of the layout or the music.

Thinking about the night led me to thoughts of Bill, Detective Sherman. He'd been a surprise, stepping down from his kindly Officer Friendly role to show up just like a neighborhood guy. If I hadn't met him in his cop guise, I'd be wondering about him as a man. I laughed, startling the cook, who looked up from his grill, then quickly looked away. I left a couple of bills on the check and hit the street, limping only slightly. Who was I fooling? Bill Sherman was a cute guy, smart and nice, too. At least from what I'd seen. Up close he was probably morbid, always poring over photos of his unsolved homicides. Or a neat freak, picking up hairs and stray fibers to store in little plastic bags like evidence. He'd said he wasn't coupled; he'd been eating alone at least on Wednesday. And that reference to a former girlfriend made me pretty sure he wasn't gay. But I'd been wrong before. I did a few stretches before attempting the stairs to my apartment and was greeted by a wide-awake kitten who scooted out the door to sniff my neighbor's door mat.

"Enough of that now." I scooped her back up. Lord, she was getting plump! I set her on the sofa. "Now, who called us?" Musetta sat up and batted at my hand. She didn't care; she wanted to play. "Business first." I reached for a piece of paper, something to crumple up into a toy, and hit the button.

"Damn, woman! You are hard to reach." My hand froze. It was Connor, sounding deliciously sleepy. I could easily imagine those blue eyes half-lidded and that black hair mussed. "Well, we're just waking up here at Casa de Ralph, so maybe you're sleeping in, too." Musetta batted at me again, aware that she'd lost my attention. "What say we meet at the Casbah tomorrow? Let's make it early-ish, say eight. We can have dinner. Make a night out of it. I'll be looking for you." He didn't ask me to call him back, but that was fine with me. I knew that he was staying with Ralph, and I didn't want any third party tagging along either.

"Musetta, we've got a date!" Something about the tone of my voice put her ears back, or maybe it was the volume. No matter. I ran into the bedroom and pulled the belt off my terrycloth robe. Trailing it behind me, I limped and skipped up and down the hallway, letting the crazed kitten leap and pounce on my trailing tail until both of us were exhausted.

I TOLD MYSELF I was getting back to work, but it was really still play when I logged back onto the Internet and began to poke around. In all fairness, I did a few cursory searches for references to the Wednesday night happening, but I trusted Carole when she said nobody else had written about it yet. Instead, I went back to those clippings I had bookmarked, the ones covering the fire and embezzlement at Greenleaf House. Many of the best stories—the follow-up ones exposing the money stolen and the employee who'd gone missing—were written by the same *Northurst Eagle* staffer, though I spotted a few more by Ethan, too, including a long interview with Dougie and the halfway house staff. This must have been the biggest story to hit the town in years. No wonder Ethan had felt like he needed a break. I'd have to nudge him to send some clippings to Tim. But now it was time to put the freelancer's most powerful weapon to work. I reached for the phone.

"Northurst. Massachusetts. I'd like the number for the *Northurst Eagle,* please. Editorial, news department if you have it."

The paper was small enough so that one number sufficed for everyone who didn't handle advertising. Small enough, too, that a real human answered the phone and I could ask for Jim Brett, the staffer who'd authored those first Greenleaf House stories. If my instincts were correct, he covered the local mental health beat, or at least had some understanding of the issues.

Rather to my surprise, a real person answered his extension.

"Brett here."

"Hi, I'm Theda Krakow." I introduced myself as a freelancer, although I left out that I wrote features, and explained that I was doing some follow up on the Greenleaf House crimes.

"That was bad." He remembered it immediately. "The state subsidizes the home, and everyone there is on disability. There's not a lot of spare cash floating around at the best of times. A lot of people volunteer their time—including the lawyer who was supposed to be overseeing the handling of money, the conservatorships, and such—but everyone is kind of stretched. This really set them back."

Brett, it turned out, was a general assignment reporter on the staff of the small daily. He'd originally picked up the story on the police scanners in the newsroom, when the first reports of the fire came in. But he also had a particular interest in mental illness. "I have a cousin with schizophrenia," he explained, and quickly outlined how such group houses work. Eight residents lived together along with two full-time counselors. All the residents were seriously, chronically mentally ill; all were on some form of medication, but the house wasn't a locked ward. It was, in fact, a nice suburban home, with a yard that the residents kept mowed and neat and a simple sign-in system that allowed the residents to visit friends or relatives, even spend weekends away. The counselors, Brett explained, weren't medical professionals, though usually they had some interest in the field. They were there to make sure everyone stayed on their meds, basically, and to keep track of everyone's progress. Illnesses like schizophrenia were often cyclical. If someone wasn't getting out of bed in the morning, the counselors were there to ask why and, if necessary, call the doctors. Beyond that, they handled administration of the house, from posting rosters of chores to be done to making sure prescriptions were refilled. They also did a lot of the routine paperwork, both for the Social Security disability insurance and for the household upkeep. That's where the trouble had hit.

"It's really a pity. They'd had no problems for years," Brett was saying. "A couple of the residents worked, but most just went to day programs, group therapy and the like. They're mostly back to normal now." He paused. "As normal as they can be, I guess. But it caused a stir. Alarmed a couple of the neighbors who hadn't realized there was a group home nearby. And it really threw some of the residents for a loop. A few had to go back into the hospital to be restabilized."

He'd led me right up to the question I'd wanted to ask.

"Was one of those folks Doug Helmhold?" I heard a pause on the line. Of course, confidentiality was an issue. But I was a fellow journalist, and if it was a matter of public record….

"Dougie. He's a good kid." Brett laughed. "Kid! He's my age, but so shy and trusting you'd think he was much younger. Yeah, he was pretty shaken up by it all, by the fire and everything. Dougie was very attached to one of the counselors, too, the guy who took off. The cops were looking at him for the embezzlement, but I haven't heard any developments on that front. It's possible that the work just got to be too much for him. Much of what the counselors do is baby-sitting. The pay's lousy and there's an extremely high burn-out rate."

I heard the rustle of papers over the phone line and knew he'd anticipated my next question.

"You know who you should really talk to? Anna Nussbein. She's one of the counselors with a real interest in the work. She's been there pretty much since the house was established and has been working toward her doctorate at the university out here for probably as long. If anyone can give you the lowdown on any of the residents, she can."

He gave me the number and we rang off. My luck wasn't completely on: I had to leave a message for Ms. Nussbein, but I was encouraged. Heading back to my computer, I figured out the lead for the café story and was just reading through my notes when the phone rang again.

"Ms. Krakow? This is Anna Nussbein here." A faint German accent clipped her tones, and for a moment I had a horrible vision of a bad World War II movie. "How can I help you?"

I identified myself as a stringer for the *Boston Morning Mail,* as I had on my message. It was the literal truth, even if

I wasn't on assignment. "I'm calling because I'm doing a story on Lillian Helmhold. She lived in Cambridge."

"Oh, I know all about her. Dougie used to talk about his mom all the time." The warmth in her voice melted my image of a Nazi nurse and replaced it with a warm, grandmotherly type. "Such a pity, it is. But I guess she was as old as my nana, my grandmother." So much for stereotypes.

"So, they were close?" It seemed a silly question, but I had to ask it.

"Close? Well, you have to understand." She paused, not sure how much to explain. "With Dougie's sickness, he can't—he doesn't like being too close. Especially to family. It's too much stress for him. She would visit him and every now and then he'd go visit her, just take off and catch the bus. Not too often, but he loved her, yes he did. He loved knowing she was there, a hundred miles away."

"You're speaking about him in the past tense. Is he still living at Greenleaf House?"

"Oh yes. He had an incident, but he's back now." I wondered about the severity of the "incident." I also wondered if he'd made one of his impromptu visits to Cambridge that last Monday, but her tone made it clear that no details would be forthcoming. From her, anyway. I took a chance.

"Is it possible for me to speak to Dougie?"

"Sure. If he wants to, that is. He'll be in your neck of the woods tomorrow."

The memorial, of course! Anna answered a few more questions I had, and we rang off. I checked the clock. It wasn't quite four. If I hurried I could make it.

Much to my amazement, I found a meter right in front of the hulking brick courthouse that holds most of Cambridge's important records. Feeding in quarters, I gave silent thanks to Eric, the actor-slash-lawyer who had initiated me into the mysteries of probate and public records. A good friend of Bunny's, we'd bonded over community theater, which I occasionally wrote about, and he, in turn, helped me get my feature-writer brain around some legal terms that had come up when my parents had passed away eight years earlier. Without his know-how, I would probably have been too intimidated to ever return to the huge building, which loomed like a red-brick monument to paperwork and bureaucracy over the eastern edge of the city, and I would have lost access to a valuable resource. Inside, as I dashed across the worn linoleum and up the huge, curving staircase, I still felt cowed by the weight of centuries of jurisprudence. What was it about a courthouse that could make me feel eight years old? No matter, I knew what I was looking for, even if I felt like a child. Four-ten: I noted the second hand on the plain hallway clock ticking by. I pushed open the heavy wood and glass door marked *Probate* and dived into the records.

One of my last questions to Anna Nussbein had been about the legal status of Dougie Helmhold. Was he competent, in a legal sense? And if not, who handled property matters for him? The answer, as I'd begun to suspect, was complicated by time and loss. Officially, his mother had been his guardian until her death. Now the lawyers who handled affairs for Greenleaf House would probably take charge, to some extent, untangling the initial legal knots. Anna wasn't sure, but she thought they'd been appointed to limited conservatorships, which would enable them to kick-start the transfer of Lillian's property. Still, the Greenleaf House lawyers wouldn't be out here, handling the day-to-day of settling taxes and selling assets. For that, they'd probably have to hire someone to administer the estate. Someone local. I rifled through files that smelled faintly of mildew. Behind me a door slammed: the employee's exit. The large clock over the file cabinets clicked a minute closer to four-thirty: closing time. I was being silly. Probate moves with a snail's pace, as Eric had taught me. Probably nothing would be decided or even filed for weeks yet. Then I saw it. Name of decedent: Lillian Helmhold. Application for Administration. I skimmed the legalese. "The petitioner(s) hereby certify…." And there it was: Patricia Wright, realtor and notary public, had requested the court's permission to be named the administrator of Lillian's estate.

TEN

THIS DIDN'T LOOK good. I sat on the hood of my Toyota reading over the copy of the paper I had made. Trying not to jump to conclusions, especially not to Violet's conclusion of murder for some kind of profit, I began to list the possibilities. Why would Patti Wright want to control Lillian's estate? The air was beginning to cool and the damp wind smelled of rain, but I was thinking too hard to drive just yet.

I knew she didn't like Lillian's cats. She probably didn't like Lillian, either, if she'd ever bothered to talk to her. And her few comments about Dougie hadn't made it sound like she would be concerned with his interests particularly, so it wasn't neighborly concern that was at work here.

What was she after? If what Sally Hudson had said could be trusted, she wanted to sell her place. Needed to, in order to regain the life that she'd once had, and I gathered that the rundown property abutting hers, especially with all those cats, was scaring away buyers. Patti had told me herself that she wanted the listing for the Helmhold property, and I'd read—and written—enough about the local real estate scene to know that two lots side by side in the middle of Cambridge could mean a fortune to the right developer. I saw that old house as a shabby queen. She probably had images of luxury condos dancing in her head, if that neat, tight coif had room for them.

But if she administered the property, what was the advantage to her? I wasn't sure of the details, but from what the clerk in the probate office had been able to tell me, it did limit her options. It probably meant she wouldn't be able to act as the realtor for it. Of course, that didn't mean she couldn't covertly control it, maybe pass it along to a colleague—a confederate who'd split the fees and profits with her down the line. She'd certainly get to exercise some say over who ended up with the grand old house and its considerable yard. Direct profit aside, she'd be able to shape the neighborhood in her image, I realized. She'd be able to unload her own house, and maybe change the character of the neighborhood. I thought of how taxes and rents would rise, of families priced out of the homes they'd inhabited for generations. They would matter little to the realtors who'd start flocking, looking for a share in the millions that were already changing hands in my lovely little city. And Cambridgeport—right by the river, closet to the university—was the city's heart, a diamond in the rough.

Or maybe it was all innocent, a concerned neighbor doing what she could to help out, and Sally Hudson's gossip just that. I knew I was working up a head of steam, that I was creating fiendish scenarios out of only the tiniest shred of information. Violet must be rubbing off on me, or else conspiracy theories were as contagious as spring fever. I smiled at the thought of my upcoming date, and folded the form to slide into my pocket. I needed to think about this, to see what else I could find out. I heard the five o'clock bell of a nearby church and pondered knocking off for the day. Just one more stop, I promised myself, and ducked back through the gathering traffic toward my own neighborhood.

Patti Wright wasn't in when I rang her bell. Or wasn't answering anyway. Up on tiptoe, I tried to peek through the tiny windows inset into her door. This was becoming ridiculous. Still, one brief chat with her might clear everything up. Dismounting her mosaic-inlaid steps, I followed a slate path around back, stepping gingerly and trying to look casual.

"Patti? Patti Wright, are you working back there?" I knew I was talking too loudly and that my fake friendliness wouldn't fool anyone, but I kept it up anyway. "Yoo-hoo, Patti?" The back of her house was as neat as the front and just as deserted, its two flowerbeds bare and hemmed in by white stone borders. Even her side of the lilac hedge appeared to have been tamed, trimmed back to make a flat wall that nearly concealed Lillian's house up to the second floor. I looked over the hedge, my eyes traveling up the peeling clapboard wall. Could this house really be a motive for murder?

As I sat staring, my reverie was suddenly broken by a movement. There it was again. Or was it? The third floor on this side, facing Patti's, had two windows, and just for a moment I could have sworn something had flickered inside one of them. I stepped back to get a better view. The window toward the front was mostly obscured by two lace curtains. The other window, further back, seemed to have boxes piled against it, and those boxes had served to push the curtain out of the way. That's the one I thought had shown some sign of life, some small shift of light, as if something or someone had moved among those boxes and they, in turn, had jarred the curtain.

Or had it been an encroaching shadow? Although it was early for dusk on a spring afternoon, the day certainly seemed to be fading fast. Clouds were moving in, and I could see how a flash of late sunlight, angled just so, could have mimicked movement.

"Violet?" If she was in there, I was going to warn her off. This was getting ridiculous. "Violet?" I ducked around the front of the hedge and into Lillian's yard. The back door was closed and locked tight.

"Violet!" I rapped on the metal frame and waited for her

to appear, shame-faced and dusty. Silence. If it wasn't the purple-haired punk, I wanted to know who was in there.

Where was the spare key? Under the last slate? I could see where the chipped blue stone had been moved recently, its imprint in the new grass showing where it had lain. But when I lifted the slate, I found nothing but an earthworm. "Violet?" I knocked again and called her name, yelling up at the third floor where I'd seen that movement. Nothing answered, not Violet, not a cat. I looked for a loose window, but everything was battened tight. Could I make it up to the second floor, maybe climbing one of the overgrown yews? Even as I grabbed at the spiny branch, I knew this was ridiculous. If I kept this up, one of the renters who lived in the brick building opposite would see me and start wondering. Or Patti Wright would come home and call the cops on me for attempted breaking and entering. Besides, it was starting to rain. Thick, fat drops were already darkening the slate path. I knocked once more, rattling the door's thin metal handle for good measure, and gave up, running to my car just as the thunder broke.

THEY CALL CAMBRIDGE the City of Churches, at least in the older guidebooks, because there seems to be one of every possible denomination on almost every corner. Of course, despite the preponderance of scenic white steeples, our citizens aren't as observant as they were in the city's Puritan youth. Plus, these days synagogues and mosques offer further alternatives, so these churches tend to function as all-around civic buildings. One was known for its political involvement, with speakers heating up an audience every evening. Another hosted yoga for seniors on weekdays, and a third shared its space with pagan worship circles once a month. So I wasn't too surprised that First Baptist right nearby would be hosting

Lillian's memorial service, even though I hadn't heard any evidence of any religious affiliation in the old woman's life.

Not that I'd know. I was just lying in bed, having awakened early, and found myself wondering what it would be like, religious or casual, and depending on that, what I should wear. The sun sneaking around my curtains promised a bright, clear day, the night's storm as much a memory as the pizza I'd devoured by the TV the night before. Black might be a bit much, especially since I'd only barely met the deceased. Maybe dark blue: my nice jeans and a formal top. I wanted to be respectful. I also wanted to blend in, just in case there was anything to find out.

But first, a run. I was determined not to let my exercise habit slip away again, and felt the need of exorcising some of that pizza as well.

The first step out of bed stopped me cold. "Ow!" Musetta, who'd stretched out at the foot of the bed to almost its full width, looked up. "Ow!" I'd gotten both feet on the floor, but that was it. Every muscle cried out for relief. None of them wanted to work.

"Ow. Ow. Ow." I hobbled to the bathroom to brush my teeth and tried leaning on the sink, my left leg stretched out behind me. I could feel the tension from heel up to butt. Switching hands on the toothbrush for symmetry, I stretched the other leg and waited. No popping sound. This might be okay.

"Musetta, what did I do to myself?" I asked the kitten who had come to stand in the hallway and look quizzically at me. I spit and rinsed. "What did I do?" In answer, she flopped to the floor and stretched luxuriantly, arms and legs extended with her paws grabbing at the air.

"You're right, more stretching." Out in the living room, where I could follow her example, I treated myself to a good twenty minutes of every warmup I could remember. Sweating, even in the shorts and tee shirt I'd put on, I could feel my body forgiving me. The exercises seemed to amuse Musetta, too, especially when I bent low enough for her to bat at my hanging hair.

"Free weights!" I announced, and hefted her up in one hand. Man, she was becoming a little butterball. "Left side!" I switched her to my other hand and hoisted her up toward the ceiling. "Meh!" She sounded a little panicked. That was enough, obviously. I put her down, where she proceeded to ferociously attack my untied sneaker lace.

"You win, little kitty. You've chased the enemy off." Giving her a kiss on the top of her smooth black head, I tied my laces, grabbed my keys, and set out.

Forty-five minutes later, I was glad I had. Sure I had limped more than I'd flown, but it was coming back. I wasn't the most graceful on the corners; stepping off one curb I'd swear I scared a driver into slowing down to keep from hitting me; at any rate, he crawled along at a snail's pace for a while. But within minutes after I'd passed Lillian's block, I could feel the warm buzz in my muscles, from my legs through my butt, and by the time my own building was in view I was cruising. This morning, I made sure to cool down for ten minutes and repeat all my early stretches. Feeling all right with the world, I fed a homemade Neville Brothers compilation into the CD player and went dancing into the shower. Aaron Neville's ethereal falsetto wafted in with the steam, reminding me, "Everybody plays the fool…" and I sang right along.

I GOT TO THE CHURCH about fifteen minutes early, thinking maybe I could grab Violet and finally get some answers to my questions. Maybe I'd even find other people to query. A paper sign posted on the dark wooden door of the squat stone structure directed me to a community room, down the stairs to the right, where the cement walls were warmed by appliqued hangings depicting life in Cambridge. Tall windows, cut thin and high in the basement wall, let spring sunshine in to illuminate the colorful hangings, the felt-and-fabric version of medieval tapestries, and the overall effect was cheery, rather than dreary, an impression furthered by the lively hubbub that had begun filling the room. Already a group of about a dozen people were gathered, mainly around the portable podium placed by the room's far end. I saw Violet talking to some women who seemed to be of Lillian's vintage, and as I approached was nearly run over by three dark-haired little boys, all in Sunday suits, whose mother followed close behind, hushing them with reminders that they were in a church.

"Hi, Theda." Violet looked up from discussion. "Glad you could make it."

I walked over, and Violet made the introductions. "Sylvia and Rosie were friends of Lillian's, and Gerta took yoga classes with her. That's Mrs. Rodriguez over there; I don't know her first name. But her boys—Eddie, Richie, and Marco—were over at Lillian's all the time, especially when a new litter of kittens had been dropped off."

I said my hellos and explained that I'd only just met Lillian, not that I'd been thinking of her as a potential cat hoarder. Mrs. Rodriguez—who came over and introduced herself as Oona—apologized for the boys, explaining that she wanted them to tire themselves out before the service began.

"We weren't thinking of a service, actually," one of the tinier older women interrupted. She introduced herself as Betsy, the community organizer for the church. "Lillian never really cottoned to religion or any kind of organization," Betsy explained. "Instead, we thought that we could all share some memories of her. I'll talk first, and then anyone can take the podium who wishes."

Everyone murmured assent and, since the crowd was starting to grow, moved to settle into the metal folding chairs that had been lined up in neat rows. This could be useful, I realized, following the crowd. By listening to these people talk about Lillian, maybe I could get some idea if—or why—anyone might have wanted to harm her. In the meantime, I sidled up to Violet, who still stood by the podium.

"Violet, can I ask you a few questions? This is getting serious."

"What? Sorry, I was looking for someone."

"Yesterday afternoon, late in the day, was that you at Lillian's house?"

She looked at me strangely. "What are you talking about?"

"The key was missing and I thought, I could've sworn, I saw some movement up on the third floor."

"Squirrels, probably." She waved at another young woman with bright red Pippi Longstocking braids who'd just come in. "And I never take the key. Maybe you looked under the wrong stone."

"Maybe, but Violet?" She had started walking away. "What's with you and the cops? Why didn't you want them involved?"

"Because they're incompetent." Her friend gave her a hug and they clasped hands. "Look, we can talk afterward. You're coming to the shelter, right?"

I hadn't planned on it, but maybe that would help me get some answers.

"I guess so. One more thing," I stopped them as they started to walk away. "Is Dougie here? Could you point him out to me?"

She craned her head around. Most of the crowd was taller than her. "I don't see him. Maybe his bus was late." I looked around too, not sure what I was seeking. There were definitely faces from the neighborhood I'd seen before, even someone who looked like Ethan. I started to call out to the stranger, to see if it was the reporter, but just then someone shushed us, and I saw that Betsy had taken the podium. Everyone else was already seated, so Violet hustled off to join her friend and I looked for an empty seat, finding one about midway back.

"We're here this morning to remember Lillian Helmhold," began Betsy, peering at the crowd from just over the podium. I could see her eyes resting on the three boys and several of their young friends who'd been shepherded in by parents. Her wrinkled face was kind, but something in her stare made the children grow still before she continued. "Lillian was not a member of this church, but she was a member of our community."

For such a small woman, Betsy's voice was deep and low. Clearly, she was an accomplished public speaker. But the talk she was giving—I doubted if she'd let it be called a eulogy—was personal, rather than practiced. Rather than describing an oddity, a strange old lady who might have made enemies, it painted a clear portrait of a woman who had been active and involved in the world around her. Lillian had come to Cambridge as a young woman, Betsy told us, a young wife who was giving up a life as a dancer to settle down and raise a family. She'd built a career despite the ravages of World War II, but was willing to turn her back on what sounded like considerable fame in order to forge ties and build a home, a new people-centered life to replace all those she had lost during the war years. Her husband, Piers, had been an academic here in Cambridge and also, like Lillian, a refugee from a war-torn Europe when they met at a reception after a performance. He was tall and dashing, in Betsy's memories, and he clearly loved the woman who had given up fame to be with him and to bear and raise their son.

About that son, Betsy spoke gently. "He loved his mother dearly," she recalled, and her gaze settled on a stout man toward the back whom I hadn't noticed before. Balding and somberly dressed, in a dark sweater that looked too warm for the day, he seemed to be rocking back and forth in his seat, and I wondered if he was listening. "Lillian in turn worked hard to help him find his way in life, because Lillian loved Dougie, too." The man in the sweater looked up furtively and quickly lowered his eyes again. Clearly Betsy was connecting with him, and just as clearly, from the dampness visible on his scalp, she made him nervous. "Lillian loved her son," Betsy repeated, her voice low and calming, but the man just kept rocking, and she let her oratory continue. The two of them, Dougie and Lillian, had been on their own for more than a decade, Betsy explained, once again addressing the assembled crowd, and they'd found ways to make things work. But Lillian was always quick to remind her son that his father had loved him as well, loved him above all else, and that he was with them always in spirit.

"Now," she said, looking over what had become a congregation, "we have to believe the same about Lillian. She was a survivor, a woman who thrived and rebuilt after destruction and despair. And what she built will live on, in our hearts and our minds, as well as in our community."

Pausing for a moment of reflection, Betsy looked honestly moved. Rather than wanting to question her about her relationship with Lillian, I found myself envying her, wishing I had made the effort to meet the old cat lady long before. As I mulled over my regrets, Betsy began talking again, inviting those who wished to share their thoughts or memories to come up to the podium.

Several people stood up, most of whom looked to be of Lillian's vintage, skewing the average age way past sixty. None looked likely as a potential suspect, but by then I wanted to listen anyway. The first of this crew who stood to speak was as wide as she was tall, and as weathered as a stone. More likely to injure herself than anyone else, she slowly waddled up to the podium and stood there for a moment, catching her breath.

"Lillian loved her kitties. She did what she could for them," she began, and the small congregation murmured its assent. "She said she loved them because they were so warm and so caring. They responded when so many didn't in this world. She also loved them because they were graceful, like dancers, just like Lillian used to be. They moved in such lovely ways, she always said she could watch them for hours. And, like her, they always landed on their feet."

Not that last time, I thought, as the eulogies continued. More's the pity.

Another woman stood. As tall and lean as her predecessor had been round and squat, she recalled stories of Lillian's youth in a clipped, Eastern European accent. The woman she remembered had been a dancer, lithe and gay.

"She would have been a star, but for the war," she said, the echo of her own youth turning "war" to "var." "But after—even with all the years of training she missed out on, with all the years of chaos—she had her followers, her admirers. She performed all over the world before she came to marry Piers." This was news to me. Could something from her past have come back to haunt her?

"Lillian had known hardship. She'd gone hungry," the speaker continued, her long hands clasping the sides of the podium. "That's why she liked to have her belongings around her. Why she liked to have enough." Her dark eyes scanned the crowd looking for an argument. Others must have noted her tendency to collect cats, and perhaps other things as well. That could heat some passions. But no, the speaker continued. "She had her quirks, our Lillian. She never could quite trust 'the state' again. But her friends and neighbors? Always!

When Ruby, her neighbor, was ill? Lillian was there every day, helping out. And you didn't have to be sick. Our Lillian always shared. Nobody went hungry, if Lillian knew about it. Nobody was evicted. No animal was mistreated. Lillian Helmhold was my friend."

That sentiment echoed in every voice that morning, even when the three young brothers rose and, under their mother's encouraging eye, read a brief letter thanking "Mrs. H." for teaching them about animals. My cheeks burned as I recalled how I'd counted cats and jumped to conclusions, and I gave up my intentions of questioning the mourners here. I finally understood Violet's vehemence. If anyone had caused Lillian Helmhold harm, it wasn't one of the friends gathered here today. Whoever it was, though, that person deserved to pay.

I wanted to say this to Violet, or at least make some ac-knowledgement that I understood her loss. And as pushy as it felt, I wanted answers to my questions, too, if for no other reason than to clear away any suspicions lingering about her interest in the old house. But first, I needed to talk to Dougie.

"Doug—Mr. Helmhold," I called over to the stout man in the cardigan. From the back, hunched over, he looked strangely like his mother, with fewer and darker curls. He was standing by the door with Betsy. She was reaching up to say something to him, but at the sound of his name he turned. The face that looked up to me was all eyes, dark and wide, the rest sagged damply, useless with pain and loss.

"I just wanted to say…to say I'm sorry." How could I question this man now? If he'd done anything, it had to have been an accident, right? Behind him, I could see Betsy nodding at me. She put her small hand on his shoulder, just gently touching him, and he started forward, lurching out of the room and away from her.

"Betsy?" She'd been watching after him and turned back

toward me. I wasn't sure how to ask, but I had to. "I'm trying to figure out…. Could Dougie have…? I mean, how is he doing?"

She shook her head, but as soon as she started to speak, I realized she'd misunderstood my question. "As well as he can be, I guess. Poor boy." She paused, lost in thought. "Lillian always said she'd take care of him. I know she wanted to. I always thought she'd put something by for him. She'd talked about leaving him something. Wishful thinking, I guess." She reached forward and patted my hand with her featherlight, cool palm, then turned to follow Dougie out the door.

Following her to the sidewalk, I saw Violet surrounded by children. The petite, purple-haired rocker seemed to have inherited the mantle of neighborhood "cat lady." Standing on her toes in what looked like black high-top sneakers, she was busy counting heads and checking with mothers. A convoy was going over to the shelter and the kids were excited.

"We're going to have to say goodbye to Mrs. H's kitties, now. Remember that," she said, her hands on the shoulder of one shy-looking girl. She glanced up at me with a look of pain on her face. "Five days," she mouthed, silently, over the children's heads. How could I have forgotten? On Wednesday, any of the cats that had not been adopted would be destroyed. I knew Violet was hoping to place some of Lillian's cats today, counting on the presence of their children to make some of the parents relent. But there were more cats than parents here, and I suspected that a good number of these mourners were renters, working people who probably had the standard "no pets" lease and couldn't afford to move. Dougie was already gone; I'd have to find another time to talk to him. Violet, meanwhile, clearly had her hands full.

"Who's coming with me?" I asked, trying to keep my voice bright, as I nodded toward Violet. She smiled in relief. "Let's go visit some kitties!"

ELEVEN

I ENDED UP WITH a full carload in my little Toyota: the shy girl, whose name was Luisa, her mother, Eva, and Luisa's buddy Kristen were all getting comfortable when Violet came over to where I was parked.

"Room for one more?" I nodded and she slid into the back, next to the girls.

"You don't have a car?" I was a little surprised.

"My drummer has a van," she explained. "But she's using it for work today. Floral deliveries."

I'd forgotten that not everybody's economic situation was better than mine, but Violet seemed happy enough squeezing into the tiny back seat. She made sure the girls were buckled up, and we were off.

"Make sure Rosie sees you," Violet reminded me. I was leading a convoy of three cars to the shelter, which boded well for the cats, but it took a few minutes of stopping traffic on Mass Ave before we were off and across the river.

"Will they let us pet them?" Kristen suffered from none of Luisa's shyness.

"I don't know, honey. I think so." Violet had slipped fully into the role of den mother, or pride mother if we were talking cats.

"I want to see Blackie. I want my mother to let me take her home," said Kristen. I didn't risk turning around, not with a carload of kids, but I was dying to read Violet's expression.

Surely some of the parents in our group would permit the adoption of a cat today, wouldn't they?

"Let's talk to her later, okay?" Violet seemed to have the same agenda I did.

"Okay." We rode in quiet for a while, with Luisa occasionally whispering to her mom.

"I don't know, sweetie. Maybe you should ask Violet."

I could hear Violet turn in her seat to face the shy girl, and when she spoke there was an extra gentleness in her voice. "Is there something you want to know about, hon?"

"What will happen with Mrs. H's house?" The tiny voice was clear, if soft.

"Well…." Violet paused and I realized she might not have the answer.

I stepped in. "Do you know Dougie, Mrs. H's son?"

"Uh-huh!" Both girls nodded eagerly.

"Well, because he's her son, everything Mrs. H had now belongs to him. But because he lives so far away, a judge will probably ask someone else to help him take care of everything." I wasn't about to explain probate to nine-year-olds, partly because I didn't fully get the intricacies myself. "So someone else, maybe Mrs. H's neighbor, will clean out the house and figure out what to do with things. She might have to sell the house." I figured I should begin to prepare them for what seemed inevitable. "But if she does, then the money will go to Dougie."

The administrator would be paid handsomely for his or her efforts, of course. I wondered if the cut would be enough to keep Patti Wright afloat, even before she manicured the neighborhood into her own image.

"She's gonna sell the house?" Kristen had understood me, even as I'd tried to soft-pedal my suspicions. "But what about the cats? Where will people take their cats?"

"What about the treasure?" Luisa's softer voice chimed in. I'd forgotten about the imagination of children. "If we found it, we could buy the house for the cats."

I looked at Violet, but she just shook her head. Another child chimed in. "Yeah, the jewels!" She pronounced it "jools."

"You were her treasures, kiddos," said Violet, her voice unusually soft. "You and your families and her kitty-cats." Her eyes met mine, but I already understood. These children wanted a happy ending. "Too much TV," she murmured for my ears only. "Every time there's a special on the Discovery Channel that comes up and I tell them...."

"But the kitties?" Luisa, interrupting us, wasn't going to be deterred.

"We'll do what we can for them, honey." Violet's voice sounded as sad as I felt. "We'll see what we can do."

I feared an outbreak of tears, and knew that I'd be joining in. But Eva had been a mother too long to allow that. "Why don't we all sing a song," she suggested, with a lightness in her tone that none of us felt. "What's that new one you really like, Luisa?" She started a round of something I vaguely remembered from summer camp. Her voice was truly lovely, effortless and clear, and the two girls quickly joined in. Counting games and Britney Spears took over, and by the time we pulled into the shelter's parking lot trailing the other cars, everyone was in a much more chipper mood, ready to go visit the kitties.

"Don't run! Look both ways!" It was no use, kids were bursting out of cars and racing to the front door, led by Violet, who sprinted as fast as any of them. I stayed to lock up and found myself walking with Rosie, one of the elderly women who had spoken at the memorial.

"They're so happy, going to see the animals." I pointed out the obvious as an ice-breaker.

"The children gave Lillian a lot of joy," her friend responded. "I always suspected that was one of the reasons she took the cats in. Cats—especially kittens—are like catnip for children."

"It sounds like she was really good for these kids."

"They were good for her." Rosie nodded at the memory as we followed the group across the lot. "She needed them. She always felt so guilty about Dougie, you know."

"Because she couldn't take care of him at home?" I held the shelter door open for her and she stepped in and turned to me, eager to explain.

"Because she thought she caused it. That's what they told her, that's what they told all the mothers in the bad old days." She chuckled, but it was a grim laugh. "Your child's problems are all your fault. Piers was a scholar. He kept up with the research, especially after Dougie was hospitalized the first time. Piers knew that it wasn't Lillian's fault, that it wasn't anything either of them had done. He brought all the studies home and told Lillian all about the genetics, all about how one percent of the people always have schizophrenia, everywhere in the world. But she was a mother, and she felt bad. If she didn't give it to him, she thought at least she should have been able to save him. She kept him at home as long as she could. You know, after all she lived through, she never could quite work through her distrust of institutions, the law and all. But it didn't work. Eventually she had to move him out, and so she found the nicest, homiest place she could." Rosie sighed. I wondered about why, but wasn't sure how to ask.

"Were there ever big problems?" I was trying to be delicate. "Safety issues?"

"You mean, was he ever violent?" She cut straight to the point, and I nodded, but she paused before answering. "He was…he could be…scary." She finally decided on the word. "He got loud, and he heard things, had fights with voices in his head. He was never mean, but it got to be too much, especially as he got bigger and Lillian grew older."

"He seemed in control this morning." I was wondering if he were always that composed, or if his "scary" moods ever crossed the line into action.

"He's good now. He has been for a while." Rosie was nodding to herself. "The last hospital he was in tried him on one of the new drugs and it seemed to help a lot. He and Lillian actually got a lot closer in the last few years. As long as he stays with his program, I think he'll do fine." She turned and walked through the inner door, where our group and two other families were raising the volume level to ruckus proportions. Somewhere an excited puppy had started barking.

The last thing Rosie had said stuck in my mind as I entered the din. Schizophrenia was becoming treatable, but it still wasn't curable. Quitting the drugs and the therapy could easily make the voices, the scariness, come back. Dougie's program—as Rosie had called it—had already been disrupted once recently, by the fire at Greenleaf House. Had Dougie really settled in again after that, or had he gone off his meds again, gone missing, and maybe—just maybe—headed back toward Cambridge? This is what I needed to find out. But then Luisa and Kristen came running, each of them grabbing a hand and demanding my presence so they could go into one of the other animal rooms. I didn't feel much like an adult in charge, but I allowed myself to be half led and half dragged through a glass door and into one of the shelter's quieter cats-only rooms where the girls had found some of their feline friends.

"TOMMY, TABBY, TIGGER…." Violet was counting cats. She'd been in the other cat room first and now she looked worried.

"Where's Domingo? Where's Butterfly? Click and

Clack?" I didn't know how to answer her, but just then a vet tech walked in.

"Excuse me." Violet cornered the young woman, who was struggling with a large bottle of water. "There were other cats with this group. Can you tell me where they are?"

"The gray longhair and the Siamese? They were adopted out this morning," said the tech, reaching into a cage for a dish. "We moved that litter up as soon as the cage was cleaned." She pointed to a large metal crate where four adorable tabbies wrestled with each other and with two fuzzy toys. "Space is so tight here, we're trying to give everyone a chance."

"And the others? A kitten and some tabbies?"

"That's all we got in. I'm sorry."

Violet looked relieved. "They must have gotten away." She turned to me. "I was afraid they'd jumped the gun on euthanasia. Some of them were older cats."

I nodded. I knew what the odds of an adult cat being adopted were, especially when they were competing for attention with a frisky litter like the one that had taken their shared, if temporary, bunk.

"Can you take any of them?" I asked and remembered the birdwatcher who had happily nursed on her ear. "You have Sibley, right?"

"Yeah, and I shouldn't even have him. My apartment, well... it's not even an apartment, really. It's our practice space. Just a loft. I'm living there illegally." She straightened up, a look of determination coming over her. "But I'm not giving that cat up, even if I have to move to keep him. What about you?"

I didn't want to explain. James, my mourning, all seemed beside the point here. "I've got that black and white kitten, the one she called Musetta." Violet eyes widened in surprise. "She was limping," I explained. "Animal Control was on its way, so I just scooped her up." She smiled.

"Good for you, Krakow. You've got the right instincts."

Just then I felt a tug on my shirt and turned to see Luisa holding one of the huge tabbies I had first seen on Lillian's porch. Draped over the little girl's bony shoulder, with much of its round bulk leaking through her matchstick arms, the floppy cat didn't look comfortable, but I clearly heard a purr.

"This is Mrs. Thompson," said the girl, her face nearly obscured by the cat's tawny stripes. "She was a momma before she had her operation." Clearly she knew the animal. "I'm taking her."

I automatically looked around and saw Eva, who smiled and nodded. Although Luisa started to fumble as more of the relaxed cat began to slip through her too-small hands, Mrs. Thompson seemed to be smiling, too.

"Has your mom filled out all the forms?" I reached down to scoop up the falling feline, replacing her more solidly in the girl's outstretched arms.

"I called in advance," said Eva. "They just told me to bring written permission from the landlord." She reached to relieve her daughter of the purring tabby.

"No!" Luisa started to wail.

"I'm just going to put her in her traveling box," Eva explained and then turned to me. "We'd been planning on taking one of Lillian's cats, but I thought Luisa would rather have a kitten." She shrugged. "This one will be easier to care for." She placed the pliable beast in the cardboard carrier the young vet tech had brought over. "It's that little one I feel sorry for." She motioned to Luisa's friend, Kristen, who stood quietly in front of a cage that held a large black cat. Without a word, the girl pushed her fingers between the bars and the cat reached back. Claws sheathed, it gently batted a velvet paw at the small girl's hand.

"I'm going to work on her mother, see what we can do,"

said Eva softly, just for me to hear. "C'mon girls! Come on, Kristen! Time to take Mrs. Thompson home!"

Violet said she'd catch the bus back to Cambridge—it went right by her practice space—but I was famished by the time I dropped off Eva and the girls. Visions of yuk kai jang swam in my head, but I made myself drive past Korea Garden, abjuring my favorite spicy noodle soup, and pulled up instead in front of Carberry's café. Minestrone and a sandwich would fill me up just fine. I wasn't worried about the calories. Hell, I hadn't had breakfast and it was close on four p.m. But I didn't want the aroma of garlic, lovely at first but less attractive second hand, to be seeping from my pores later that night. Despite my hunger, I hadn't forgotten that I had a date.

By four-twelve, I was picking up crumbs with the tip of my finger and wondering what to do next. It had been a while since I had a first date, even one as casual as this, but not so long that I didn't remember how well I could work myself into a worry frenzy. Going home and trying to get some work done seemed like an invitation to fret, and now that my blood sugar level was approaching normal I realized I shouldn't have let Violet off so easily. Even if she never gave me a straight story about why she didn't trust the cops, I wanted to hear her reasons for going back to Lillian's. Was she searching for something specific, some kind of clue or giveaway that she knew existed? Did she have any solid reason to believe that the old woman's death had been murder? Had she even considered Dougie as a suspect, and that maybe he'd had an accident or breakdown that could have resulted in tragedy? I wondered if she knew that the yuppie neighbor had applied to administer the estate, and realized that I needed to find out more about the whole administration process as well. For all I knew, Patti Wright had already been given the job and was over there measuring curtains for luxury condos. Which made up my mind for me. I'd drive over to Lillian's, see if anyone was around. Maybe I'd get a chance to talk to Patti or even Violet. At worst, I'd waste a little Saturday pre-date time.

I should have guessed by the empty driveway that Patti Wright wasn't home. Nobody answered at Lillian's either, when I rapped on the back door. When I checked out the slate in the walkway, the key was there, where Violet had said it would be. Maybe I'd lifted the wrong stone the other day? Whatever, I had it now, but I didn't know if I dared to venture inside. What would I find there? Dust, cat waste, whatever bits of our spirits we leave in places after we've gone? Perhaps Patti in her role as trustee had secured the empty house with an alarm system. I started to imagine silent guard dogs, crouched and waiting to attack. I might be named for a famous vamp, but some things—like fear of bodily harm—make me into more of a shrinking violet.

A brush against my leg made me jump, but it was fur I felt, not teeth. Looking down, I found myself staring into the mis- matched eyes of one of the ugliest tabbies I had ever seen. A scar had taken the fur from over one eye, the yellow one, and the green eye didn't look too healthy. One ear was ragged, the other folded down like a bad fashion statement. And the mottled tiger fur, a strangely colorless mix of greys and browns, looked moth eaten, barely covering the animal's thin ribs.

"Were you left here?" I asked, wondering if this poor beast was one of Lillian's who'd been missed in the roundup. Perhaps he was a new cat, a stray dropped off by someone who hadn't heard the news—or a local regular who came by on his own occasionally, hoping for a handout. "Did anyone ever feed you here?"

"Ne-eh!" The tabby squeezed his mismatched eyes closed with the effort of the mew. "Neh!" he said again, butting my leg with his balding head. He expected a response.

"What can I do?" I asked him. I'd have to start carrying cans of tuna in my pockets, I thought. Or stock the car with Fancy Feast.

As if in response, the tom moved toward the door and stretched, reaching his long thin body up to grab at the metal door handle and flex his paws. He was positioned to scratch, marking the door as his property, I knew, but for all the world it looked like he was trying to open the latch. This was a cat who wanted to go in.

"Neh!" he said again, still stretched up to the door handle but now turned to stare right at me.

"I get it. Hang on." I wasn't hopeful, but it was worth a shot. As if he understood me, he came down, butting his irregularly furred head against my leg. With a sigh I tried the key in the door. It fit. What I was doing was against the law, and against my better sense. Besides, there was no guarantee that any of Lillian's stock of cat chow remained. No assurance that I could find it, if it did, or that the alarms and mute Dobermans of my imagination would not materialize.

"Ne-eh-eh!" The little tiger tom was growing impatient. I turned the key and opened the door.

"Wait a minute!" Might as well try to stop electricity, I realized, as the scrawny cat zipped by me and into the kitchen. He certainly knew where he was headed. So did I, which made me hesitate a moment as I remembered how I'd found Lillian there. Then another imperious cry summoned me. He was waiting by a cabinet, trying to pry it open with one paw. I pulled it open for him and we were both rewarded. About two dozen cans of generic cat food were stacked there, sorted into tuna and chicken flavors, right by an industrial-size bag of dry food. I looked through the upper cabinets for a dish, my progress only slightly impeded by the happy cat doing anticipatory figure-eights around my ankles.

"Here you go." I pulled the top on one of the chicken-flavored cans and emptied it into a saucer—there didn't seem to be any dishes devoted especially to the cats. But if I'd expected the half-starved animal to wolf his food, I was mistaken. He dove into it eagerly enough, lapping and biting off chunky bits to chew in that particular open-mouthed cat fashion, head held sideways so he could really get his teeth into it. But when he was a little more than halfway through, he stopped, sat, and proceeded to wash his face and paws.

"Watching your boyish figure, are you?" He eyed me for a moment and then moved on to his ears. A cat washing himself, even an ugly cat, is a beautiful sight and I was lulled. Standing there, leaning on the counter, I didn't think what I would do with this stray or whether I should bring him down to the shelter. I just observed as he moved on to forelegs, then hind legs and bottom, finally reaching around to wash the hard-to-get places in the small of his back.

"Are we done now?" I asked as he began to slow his pace. The phrase "criminal trespassing" had jumped into my head, although I doubted the cat would understand. "Shall we go back outside?" I reached for his somewhat sleeker fur. But the shaggy tiger who had been so overtly friendly before now had other ideas. Slipping between my hands, he darted out toward the porch.

"Okay, we are going out." I stood to follow him and stepped onto the enclosed area. The cat was nowhere to be seen.

"Kitty? Kitty? Come here?" I cursed my complacency and started making the whispering hiss call that works on almost any cat. "Kitty? Psst psst psst psst?" I bent to look under a woven vinyl lawn chair and behind some cardboard boxes. Nothing. "Kitty?" Then I saw a head, a head with one ear, poking up from the very edge of the porch, where more boxes and some magazines tied with twine rested on an aluminum chaise lounge. "Kitty?" He ducked back down, but I'd seen him and carefully picked my way over. He'd cornered himself between the boxes and the wall and now hung loose-limbed and pliant as I lifted him by his thin middle.

"New!" He mewed louder than he had before, perhaps because of the indignity of my grasp. He didn't struggle, however, and I found myself following his gaze. Doubled over in my hands he was staring straight at the floor. There, almost wedged between the box and the corner, right where he'd been sitting, was a thumbprint-sized white plastic oval strung on a broken metal chain. I transferred the tabby to my left hand, he was that light, and reached for the object with my right. I took both of them out to the yard and put the cat down to examine what he'd shown me in the bright afternoon light. I didn't have to, really. I knew that I was holding Lillian's safety device, the missing medic-alert alarm.

TWELVE

THERE WERE DOZENS of possible explanations for how that little plastic pendant could have ended up on the floor in the corner of the porch. I went through them, once I was home, as I picked up around the house and filled Musetta in on the events of the day. The chain might have broken months ago, when Lillian was loading those boxes or tying up that bundle of magazines, and the miniature alarm fallen unnoticed to the floor. She might have pulled it off in annoyance when it got tangled in her curls once too often. Perhaps it dangled and enticed a plumper kitty than the one I'd met—one who had hung on it until it broke, ending up as a feline trophy. Maybe she had several and liked to toss them in corners. Who knew? I gave up on my apartment and its piles of books and magazines—it was what it was—and stepped into the shower. Violet's paranoia was really getting to me. But I'd bring the white plastic bit over to the police, or at least give Detective Sherman a call, maybe on Monday. This was Saturday night, and I had other plans.

Planning was what I was doing, once I was out of the shower and beginning to get dressed. This was a first date, but who was I kidding? Connor was smart and funny, as well as cute. I pulled out the satin bikinis, the purple ones edged with lace, and the matching flimsy, but decorative bra. Bunny would have my head for moving so fast, but that was why I hadn't called her, wasn't it? By tomorrow's brunch, I'd have more to tell. For a moment, I thought about canceling that date. What if we wanted to lounge?

No, that was going too far. Nice undies were being hopeful. Clearing out all of Sunday was obsessive. Musetta, watching from the bed, seemed to agree.

I opted for the same jeans I'd worn to the service. Despite the shelter visit, they still seemed clean and were undoubtedly my nicest pair. Then I fussed with my hair until quarter to eight, when I finally accepted that it would do whatever it wanted, date or no.

I walked the couple of blocks to the Casbah and opened the door on the familiar din. Connor had already secured a table, over by the wall, and he stood and waved me over with a big welcoming grin.

"Hey, gorgeous!" He leaned in to give me a quick kiss of welcome, startling me and thus stopping my automatic bullshit detector that says guys call women "gorgeous" when they don't remember our names.

"Hey there," I replied, aiming for casual. I sat down harder than I meant to, already a little flustered. "Sorry I'm late." What was I apologizing for? I gave myself a mental kick.

"You're not late." I glanced up from the menu and he was leaning toward me. He almost took my hand, but seemed to stop himself, content to look right at me. "You're right on time. You're perfect, and I'm glad to see you." Oh god, he could tell how nervous I was. "I took the liberty of ordering some appetizers." He leaned back in his seat, the serious moment forgotten. "Hummous and baba ghanoush. Marisa's baba is the best in town. And what about beverages?"

I was daring and ordered a rye and ginger, rather than my usual Blue Moon. I needed to calm down, and fast. If Connor could tell how ill at ease I was—and how could he not?—he was doing his best to be gracious.

But Risa poured a strong drink and the sweet rye whiskey did its job. Before long we were digging pita triangles into the messy, tasty dips, laughing like children as we competed for the last olive that had studded the Middle Eastern treats. He had told me about moving to Boston, how he had heard that the scene here was happening. Ralph had been right: Connor was an artist. In Boston he was hoping to actually find professional support, maybe a gallery, and a social network to boot.

"You paint?" He hadn't specified his medium, but I could envision his tall, lean frame standing before an easel.

"Oils, mostly. And houses. That's how I did this." He tapped his chipped front tooth. "Ladder accident." He laughed and I joined in. Most of the visual artists I knew had day jobs of some sort; the writers, too, for that matter.

"Well, the painting season is starting." I thought of the peeling coat on Lillian's house. In New England almost all outside employment is crammed between April and November, though I'd seen a few hardy souls up on ladders in down parkas and wool hats in March. "Unless you're already working?"

"No, not yet. I should, but I've been caught up in one of my own pieces." I should have noticed that his hands didn't have the usual cold-weather chapping. I looked down at those hands now, at his long, strong fingers, and was momentarily mesmerized. "I was painting all afternoon, trying to get this last canvas done before earning season." He sighed. "It's hard, you know? One of these days, I won't need to work for jerks." I understood that well enough. We raised our glasses to such a future. "But enough about me. Tell me about writing. How did you end up doing that?"

"I need another drink for that." I smiled at him and he signaled our waitress. She was bringing our entrees anyway, we'd both ordered the eggplant, and she followed with another round as I explained my progress from copy editor to free-lancer. By the time we'd cleaned our plates, I'd told him about my career path, such as it was, and even a bit about Rick, about how his doubts had fostered mine.

"I think it was a question of confidence, as much as anything." I found myself saying, trying to explain why I had left writing for so long. "I don't know that I've ever really doubted my basic skill—I don't know if I feel comfortable calling it talent—or my perseverance. I mean, I know I can do a serviceable job, write a printable, articulate story and get it in by deadline. I know I can do that as well as most of the bozos I read in the paper. It's just that it's hard to rely only on yourself, you know?"

"I do, Theda. And I know, too, that until you believe in yourself it's really hard to get others to trust you." I looked up at him. He got it.

"Does that affect your work?" I was curious now. Painting—fine art—seemed solitary by nature.

"It's a different field," he said as if reading my mind. "But the confidence aspect is the same. You've got to market yourself to dealers, to gallery owners, if you want to sell. Even if you want to be seen. It gets tiring." He looked down at his plate.

"Do you have a gallery in Boston yet?" I didn't want to push, but it seemed the natural follow-up.

"No." He looked up again, smiling. "I told you I've been lazy, right? Hey, how about another drink? Then we can go hear some music."

So he wanted to change the subject, that was okay. How many men would spend an hour listening to my story? And how coherent was I at that point? Stopping the waitress before she could place her order, I switched mine to a beer, and let Connor pay the tab, promising to get the next round as we both stood and walked toward the back room.

"Hey, Theda! Good to see you!" I turned and saw Tess, an old friend from the club scene. Another friend, I realized with a stab of guilt, I'd lost touch with over the last few months.

"Tess, you're back!" The tall, lean beauty played bass well enough to get studio work, and her exotic good looks—the inheritance from her Angolan father and Irish mother—helped open other professional doors as well. Even enveloped in my winter's haze, I'd heard she'd left to try her luck in New York. "This a visit?"

"No, I'm here for good." She smiled and chuckled, shaking her head at my inquiring gaze. Her long jet curls fell in her face, and with a shy duck of her head she brushed them aside. "I'm back about a month now, girlfriend, trying to figure out what to do next. Where've you been? I'm the one who should be lying low, licking my wounds."

"Long story." Connor coughed gently. "Tess, this is Connor. Connor, Tess." They shook hands and Tess shot me a smile and a look.

"Call me, Theda. We need to catch up."

"Will do," I promised. She clearly had a story for me. Maybe I'd even have some news for her after tonight.

Leaving Tess with a quick hug, I walked Connor by the door man, who looked at me and waved us both in. A small crowd had already gathered for the first band.

"Theda!" Nick and Lucy, both fanatical garage-band fans, were already waiting. "You're here!" Lucy hugged me, and I introduced them both to Connor. "We thought about leaving a message for you," said Nick. "These guys do an entire set of Outsiders covers, it's amazing!" I looked at Lucy. "I know," she said, grinning. "I told him we'd have a better chance of getting you out to hear them if he didn't tell you that."

Connor raised his eyebrows, and I resisted the temptation to elbow him in the ribs. Boston music fans followed trends that never registered on any Billboard chart, but surely rooming with Ralph he'd become accustomed to that. Or maybe he hadn't; I thought of Ralph's taste, his little prejudices. If Connor had gotten his indoctrination into Boston rock solely from Ralph, the whole garage scene might be new to him. He may never have realized that an entire subculture existed here that dedicated its money, free time, and listening hours to the pursuit and re-creation of British Invasion-era American rock, Farfisa organs and all.

"Get ready for a truly hi-fi experience," I leaned over to whisper in his ear. "These guys would play in mono if they could." Just then, the band kicked in with a roar of distorted guitar and the wheezy wail of an electric organ. Both arms flying, the drummer threw all his weight into a simple beat and the crowd began to bob. Nick and Lucy turned from us to push their way up front, exposing another layer of the crowd. In its midst, I recognized Ethan. Signaling Connor that I'd be back in a moment, I pushed my way up to him.

"Hey, stranger! You following me around?" I trusted my grin would signal the joke.

Ethan smiled back. "Hey! Theda, right?" He caught his glasses just as they started to slide. "Warm in here, isn't it?"

"It's a good crowd. You here with friends?"

He shook his head no. "Just poking around really. Trying to find out what's up."

He was new in town, I reminded myself, and remembered my resolution. "There are a couple of folks I know here tonight. Hang on, I'll introduce you." I looked around for Nick or Lucy or Connor, but Ethan was shaking me off.

"No. Don't bother. I really don't want to deal with the whole social thing."

I smiled, trying to think of what else to say. "So, are you interested in trying to break into the *Mail?*" He leaned forward, staring at me. The volume had gone up. I tried again. "You're looking for assignments?" I was nearly yelling.

"Yeah. Maybe. If—" The music drowned out his words.

"Call me." I was mouthing the words so he could read my lips. "I'm listed. I may have some ideas." He nodded and gave me a thumbs-up. I thought he was going to say something, but then he turned and disappeared into the dancing pack.

"Thought I'd lost you," said Connor, coming up behind me. Poor Ethan, he must not have realized I had a date.

"Too much for you?" I shouted back.

"It's not the music," said Connor. I could barely hear him over the roar. The heat from the crowd was rising with the volume, as well, and I could feel his breath on my ear. "It's the crowd. Who was that?" He paused and I thought about trying to explain. It was too loud for details, and after a moment he was laughing anyway. "Do you know everyone in this club?"

"Just about!" It was an exaggeration, but I'd been captured by the music. The keyboard player had taken the lead, banging out chords to a tune I knew, and soon the bass and guitar were joining him in a simple three-chord riff that circled and filled the room like smoke. I grabbed both our empties to put them on the bar, and started to dance, pulling Connor to face me.

He was a good sport, and more graceful than most men I know. But after two songs, he pulled away with a grin. "Air! Air! I need a breather!" I could feel moisture on my brow and the sweat dripping between my breasts and followed him without complaint to the back of the room-length bar, the end farthest from the stage. The drummer had picked up a syncopated tattoo designed to mimic the guitar's vibrato effects.

"Blue Moon, right?" I nodded, still short of breath, and held my damp hair up off the back of my neck. So much for all my fussing with it.

"These guys rock!" Connor mimicked the drummer, tossing his head to the beat, but his shorter dark hair didn't quite fly around like the band members' did.

"You need more hair," I yelled back. "Like this!" I tossed my own mop of curls forward and then back, and felt tendrils sticking to my damp and no doubt rosy face.

"You've got it," said Connor smiling, as he reached forward to brush a curl off my cheek. I was feeling the alcohol, the music, and his presence and didn't trust myself to speak. We smiled at each other. The cold beers went down fast.

"Another dance?" I grabbed his hand and pulled him toward the stage, not waiting for an answer. Soon we were right up front by Nick and Lucy, all jumping around more or less to the beat as the set drew to a frenzied close.

"Let's get out of here." Connor reached for my hand as the sound man's tape mix came back on. The volume was lower, but just barely. I followed him, expecting him to lead back to the main room, where we could catch our breath and have another beer. He veered left instead, toward the door to the street.

"We're leaving?" The night, I had thought, had just begun.

"Let's try the Friar," he said as he pushed open the door to the cool night air. The Friar, back across town, was a tiny pub with no windows and a sound system that fit into one packing case. On weekends, however, the old regulars made way for an enthusiastic young rock crowd, winning the club the nickname of "fryolater" during summer months.

I hadn't had a chance to say goodbye to Nick and Lucy, and I had been enjoying the music. But Connor had already hailed a cab, so I followed him inside and up to the Friar's front door, where a booming beat promised fun inside.

"What are you drinking?" he asked as soon as we'd each forked over the five dollars cover. The Friar did not deal in specialty beers.

"Bud!" I called out, scanning the room for familiar faces.

"See anyone you know?" Connor asked as he handed me the longneck.

"Don't think so." I took a long pull from the bottle. Dancing had given me a powerful thirst.

"Good." His voice was low and close to my ear, and I felt his lips on my neck, cool from the beer. I turned and we kissed, then broke away as the band started.

"Excellent! I love these guys," I said, pointing with my bottle to the two women who'd just taken the stage, a slightly raised platform at the end of the bar. The night was filling up with happy surprises. I really did like this duo, and the kiss had been wonderful. I could still feel its warmth traveling down my body. But I wanted a moment to think, to gather my resources or maybe just to savor the moment. I took another long drink, the metallic beer taste not quite erasing the feel of his lips.

"Mmm." Connor might've been saying something, but I didn't hear him, only felt the movement of his lips against my hair. I watched the band, as conscious of his breath and his hands on my waist as I was of the musicians and the bluesy rock they played. Connor was behind me now, and I leaned back on him as we both swayed to the music. One chord, I thought, but that was all that was needed as the guitarist pushed her capo down a fret and started another long solo all moans and whispers.

"Dance with me, Theda." I heard his voice in my ear and turned. He took our empty bottles and reached over to leave them on the bar, then pulled me toward him. The slow song ended and we kept dancing, moving over to the side of the room as the drummer kicked into a rocker and the people beside us began to pick up the beat.

"So sweet," I think he said, kissing me. I couldn't reply. I opened my mouth to his and pulled him closer, both of us pressed against the wood-paneled wall. I could feel the heads of pushpins against my back and knew I was dislodging posters for weeks of upcoming gigs. The music kept going as we paused for breath and kissed again, shifting slightly to arrange arms and legs and tongues in new and interesting ways. He tasted of beer and the bourbon he'd been drinking before, and I felt drunker on the taste of him.

"Let's get out of here," he said, finally, when we both realized that the band had stopped. He stepped back and I stood up straight. Both of us were breathing heavily. I nodded and he took my hand, weaving through the crowd until we reached the street.

Out in the air we turned toward each other and he grabbed me again, pressing me against the stucco wall of the bar as if he would devour me. "That empty house is near here," he said, when we both came up for air.

"I have my own place," I replied, remembering that he still roomed with Ralph, and stepped toward the sidewalk. Luck or fate brought a cab and I gave him directions before letting Connor pull me back into a long, sloppy kiss. Condoms, I said to myself. Don't act drunker than you are. Condoms. I knew I had a pack in my night table, but I also knew how close I was to forgetting any sensible part of myself.

"Ahem," said the cabbie, making little effort to make his fake cough sound real. "We're here." Connor slapped down a five-dollar bill for a three-dollar fare, and then pulled me out of the cab. I stood up and we kissed again. I pulled away only long enough to extract a key from my pocket.

"Upstairs." He followed me and we both tried to embrace as we walked, tripping on the stairs as we did. I started to giggle and then he did too, although he also kept trying to kiss me into silence, which didn't help us climb to the second landing.

"Shhhh!" I pulled away, just a bit, as we fell against the wall. "My neighbors!"

"The hell with your neighbors," he growled and slammed me into a door, kissing me harder than before, his hands now pulling my hips to his. This was my door, though, and I managed to hold up my key between us. He nodded and I turned, fumbling with the lock.

"Come in." I opened the door and stepped in, pulling him to follow.

"Raow!" Connor had just stepped into the door when we heard an ungodly noise. "Eeeooowww…roaw!" A high-pitched whine that ended in a growling roar called my attention down and to the left. I flicked on the light. There was Musetta, my cute little kitty, puffed up and hissing like an adder. "Rrrraow!" She was twice her normal size.

"Kitty, what's the matter?" I knew better than to approach a cat who looked like that.

"Let me see." Connor reached for her. Too late I put my hand on his arm to pull him up. "Heh!" the cat spat and fell back. But not before lashing out with both claws. Connor stepped back, and I saw blood on his hand.

"Musetta!" I yelled, but the cat continued her whining growl. Her ears were pinned flat to her head and she drew back as if threatened, both front paws raised to strike again. I backed away.

"Connor, are you okay?" I turned toward my date and found him sucking the back of his hand. I took it from his mouth and saw six deep scratches. "I've never seen her like that before."

"Had her long?" He didn't sound amused. Behind me, the cat's low whine was gaining in intensity. "Eeoorrr…."

"Here, let me put some antibiotic on that." I started to step around the cat, toward the bathroom, but Connor didn't follow.

"No, no thanks." He was holding his bleeding hand like it hurt him. The mood was clearly broken. "I think I'd better take off, Theda. It's been fun."

With that he turned and walked out and all I could do was stand in the open doorway and watch him retreat down the stairs. Damn that cat. What had come over her? I turned toward my kitten, expecting to see signs of madness or rabies or rage. But the puffed-up beast who had just ruined my evening was now sitting calmly on the hallway floor, looking up at me all wide-eyed innocence once more. Her fur still looked a little rumpled, but her ears were up and her mouth was closed.

"What is it, Musetta? What was all that, Musetta? Just tell me what?" But the small cat didn't answer, except to bend over and start licking her toes.

THIRTEEN

"THAT CAT HAS more sense in its little body than you have in your college-educated brain." Bunny stood glaring down at me, her round face tight with anger. "What am I talking about? You weren't thinking with your head at all, were you, girl? How old are you again?"

I sulked on her sofa, slumping into its brown corduroy comfort. Despite my hangover, I'd managed to get to Bunny's and even remembered to pick up bagels on the way over. Cal was out at rehearsal for at least another hour, so I had my friend alone for a bit. I'd been hoping for a little commiseration from my usually gentle friend.

"He's smart. He's an artist. You'll like him," I countered, wondering if I had the energy to drink the orange juice she'd poured for me. "You *would* like him, if I ever see him again. What got into that cat? Do you think she's one of those psycho ferals who just can't stand any male of any species? Has she just decided that I'm her property?"

Bunny looked pointedly at the juice. She had the coffee pot in her hand, but withheld from pouring it. I sighed and pulled myself upright in the deep cushions. I drank. My stomach accepted the liquid. With an approving nod, she poured the coffee.

"I've heard of cats like that. I don't know, maybe she was abused as a kitten. But I am not going to end up single and abstinent because of a cat. As soon as I find a good home for it, that kitten is gone."

"You need a good cat," she started her familiar refrain.

"I know, I know, Bunny. But I'd like a good man, too. And if I have to choose…." I left my statement open, but Bunny looked at me, eyebrows raised over her cats'-eye glasses.

"What's gotten into you?" She put the bagels out on a plate and went back into the kitchen for a knife. "You're acting like this man is the last one on earth. Don't forget: cute boys know they're cute. This man probably has you figured. He's playing you like a harpsichord."

"I know, Bunny, I know. And he is cute, but, well, maybe he's more than that as well. I just felt we really connected. He understood the whole writing thing. He's an artist, too, did I tell you?"

"Several times," she said, as she sliced two bagels open. I pointed to the poppyseed. "Though I haven't heard that you've seen any of his paintings, girl. Do you miss Rick that much? Cal and I never really figured you two for a lasting couple."

"We weren't, I don't think. I mean, I don't regret not moving to Arizona with him." I slouched back into the couch cushions and tried to rev up my brain. "Maybe it's going freelance and leaving the everyday of the office. I feel less connected to everything. Maybe it's being in my thirties. Maybe it's losing James."

"Which brings me back to this kitten."

"I don't know, Bunny. Even aside from the weird man-thing, I don't think I'm ready. I've got to look at this as a fostering situation. Maybe it will be my job to train her not to attack men."

"Where'd this kitten come from, anyway?" Bunny spread cream cheese on the open half of poppyseed bagel and layered lox on it, then handed the plate over to me, holding it over the head of her small, agile black-and-white shorthair, Astarte. I took a bite and found I was hungry.

"Oh, this is good. Is this Nova?" I devoured the bagel half and reached for another. Astarte gave up and began washing.

"Did she come from that cat hoarder you were writing about?

"Hmm? Oh yeah." I was busily prepping two more lox and cream cheese open-faced sandwiches, and got my hand slapped reaching for the red onion that Bunny was still slicing. "I picked her up the morning I found Lillian's body. I didn't want Animal Control to get her."

"What? Theda, wait till I'm done. This is sharp. What did you say? A body?"

That's when I realized. I'd been so busy and so distracted by Connor that I hadn't kept Bunny up to date on all that was happening with Lillian, with her death—or murder—or Violet and Patti and the house full of cats who were even now waiting in the shelter for new homes or death.

I did so now as my horrified friend stared at me and our coffee cooled.

"So, it probably was an accident," I yelled back from the kitchen in conclusion. I had removed the knife from her hand a while ago, but she still sat there frozen. "That's what the cops think, anyway. But I'm beginning to wonder, myself." I poured a hot, fresh cup for Bunny, who seemed oblivious, and more for me. I took a sip.

"Ow, hot. Anyway," I continued, gingerly replacing the mug on the table. "I'm really getting to like Violet, but I wish she'd give me some straight answers. She just refuses to have anything to do with the cops and she keeps going back to that house to rummage around, when she knows that she could get in serious trouble. There's something off there. I don't like to think she's stealing, but what she's told me about looking for clues just doesn't all make sense. Plus, I know she's pretty broke and maybe now that her friend is dead…

"Then there's this neighbor. Did I tell you about her?"

Bunny's big marmalade lad, Pangur Ban, claimed my lap and I let him lick some cream cheese from my fingers. "She really hates cats and she wasn't too fond of Lillian either. She's a realtor, and she's applied to be the administrator of the estate. She really wants the property. Needs it, really. I gather she's going broke, and she's not the type to suffer poverty gladly.

"And then there's Lillian's son, Dougie. He's got schizophrenia, lives in a group home out in Western Mass. And from what I hear, he's had some trouble staying on his meds. I wanted to talk to him at the memorial service, but he kind of slipped away. I should really follow up on that."

"Theda. Shut up. Just—just be quiet for a second." Bunny put her hand up for silence, staring at me with a look that could have pinned a butterfly to a board. Pangur Ban jumped down. "Do you hear yourself? A woman has died. A woman you had only just met. And on the urging of some little punkette you've got yourself halfway to believing that her death was caused by somebody who wished her harm. And that you're the one to solve it."

"No, I don't think I'm going to solve it. Violet thinks she will. I just want to ask…."

"Wait, wait, Theda. Listen to yourself. Last week at this time, you hadn't even thought about a cat hoarder in Cambridgeport. You certainly wouldn't have gotten involved in second-guessing the police. This is crazy talk, and I don't like it. You've got to call the police and give them that plastic thing you found and get yourself out of this."

She was right, at least as far as turning over the personal alarm pendant. "I know. I was going to call Bill on Monday."

"Bill?"

"Bill Sherman. He's the detective who showed up at the scene. I ended up hanging out with him last Wednesday. That's when he told me that the cops were going to rule

Lillian's death as accidental. He explained everything about head wounds to me. Nice guy, actually."

"Theda, I don't believe you." She was laughing now, the color coming back into her face, so I felt better. Or at least slightly off the hook. I dipped my finger in the cream cheese and let my arm drop surreptitiously toward the floor. Pangur's rough tongue made quick work of the treat. "Cut that out. He's fat enough." I was caught, but the evidence had been destroyed. Bunny turned back to me. "You're picking up cops now? I don't know. People who hang around crime can pick up some very bad karma. I mean, at the very least you get used to seeing people who've been hurt."

"And maybe seeing crime and death also teaches you to appreciate life. I mean 'carpe diem' and all that, right?" She was missing the point. "And besides, I'm not going out with him. We just ran into each other at Central Café over in JP." I was glad the tension had broken. I could eat again. "But I will call him and I will give him Lillian's pendant." I bit into another bagel half, the lox just salty and greasy enough to ease my aching head. "Though how I'm going to explain being in her house in the first place will be a bit tough."

"I'm sure you'll find a way, Theda." Bunny sighed and reached for another bagel too. Pangur Ban jumped into her lap and began kneading. "You always do."

"HMMM, KITTEN ATTACK." Cal seemed to be taking my problem seriously. "That would be a buzzkill." He reached for the peanut butter to spread on a bagel, knocking Astarte off the counter with a small shove. Despite our best intentions, Bunny and I had finished the lox long before he got home. "Though it could be the test of a man. I remember a certain feline reaction to a certain new beau that almost put the new beau off."

"That's not fair," retorted Bunny, jumping in as Cal chewed

his sticky concoction. "Pangur Ban had been taken by surprise. Suddenly there was another person in the bed, and he didn't know what to make of you."

"True enough, true enough." Cal wiped his mouth and poured us all more coffee. "I'm just saying that cats can have adverse reactions. I had to throw those sneakers out, eventually. Couldn't get the smell off them."

"But Pangur got used to you eventually, right?" I was looking for reassurance with my coffee, even though the offending kitty now lay curled on the sofa, a picture of domestic bliss.

"Yeah, and I got used to him. Which leads us to the big question. You're not asking about the kitten, right? You want to know if you'll see this guy again."

"I don't know if she should," Bunny interrupted. "He's too smooth."

"Not smooth enough in the face of an attack kitty, sweetie." Cal was used to her mother-hen tendencies. "But what does Theda want?"

"I don't know." I was still feeling sorry for myself. But I had to admit the food and the friendship had done much to repair my mood. "No, I'm lying. I do know. I really like this guy. I really, really like him. I'm just worried that the night went from no-holds-barred to claws out and, well, what's he going to think of me? That I'm some lust-maddened crazy cat lady."

Neither of them responded.

"Thanks, guys. I needed that this morning."

Cal broke out in a grin. "You set yourself up for that one, darling. But why not relax a little? If he's worth all the fuss, he'll call you again."

By now even Bunny's fur had been smoothed. "Cal's right, Theda. This time, you've got all the more reason to wait and see what he does."

I didn't necessarily agree, being more of a fix-the-damage

rather than a let-time-heal type, but there really didn't seem like much I could do. Not that afternoon, anyway. So I settled back and enjoyed the gentle comfort of my friends, letting the afternoon turn into evening, our bagels to Chinese take-out, and my hangover into an unpleasant, but vague memory.

THAT NIGHT, upon returning home, I found Musetta as affectionate as before, twining around my ankles like a well-upholstered serpent.

"What is it with you, kitty?" I asked, lifting her in my arms so I could stare into those round, green eyes. "Do you have something against men? Or is it just that you want me for yourself?" The off-center white blaze on her nose gave her a goofy look, making her eyes appear slightly too close set. The overall impression was of innocence. She was, after all, simply a kitten. "Did some man do you wrong?" She wasn't talking, although the paws that pressed against my chest let me know she'd rather be on the floor. I set her down and watched her speed toward my tiny kitchen. I followed and reached for a can to open, succumbing to the routine that my small feline houseguest already accepted as her due.

FOURTEEN

MONDAY DAWNED, as it always does, full of good resolutions. I tumbled out of bed the first time the alarm rang, dislodging the cat, and reached for my sneakers as the horrible buzzing faded in my ears. Shorts, sports bra, tee shirt, keys. I was still tying my hair back, doubling up the fabric-covered elastic that contained the bulk of my unbrushed curls, as I descended the stairs. Stretching against the stoop—left leg, reach, then right—I realized that resolutions should go more than muscle deep. Today, I thought, I would finish up some of my outstanding projects. Send them in, and write up and mail the story invoices, too. Paper in the mail meant money coming in at some point, and I'd been getting way too lax on the billing front.

I'd also call Bill Sherman and arrange to get him the pendant I'd found at Lillian's house. I'd promised Bunny, and Cal too, that I wouldn't mess any more in Lillian's death; they'd kept after me until I stopped calling it murder. But, as I started off at a brisk trot, I did let myself muse on the idea of talking to Violet, even if just to clear up some of my own questions. What I would not do, I vowed as I turned the corner and picked up speed, was call Connor. After Saturday's passion and his later rapid retreat, he really had to be the one to make the next contact. I paused at a light, running in place as my muscles warmed up, but when it changed, I didn't cross, obviously startling the little tan Hyundai that stood waiting for me. I waved it on, squinting into the sun, and turned left instead.

In light of my promises to Bunny and Cal, I wouldn't let myself run by Lillian's house, "just to look." Instead, I'd head toward the river, joining the pack who marked off miles by counting bridges. A footpath along the Cambridgeside bank meant cars were no threat, and even the occasional bicyclist knew to give ground to the city's rabid runners. The scenery— the meandering river, the occasional sculler, and the university's regal Georgian graduate school on the opposite bank—made a refreshing change from my beloved urban streetscape. And the dappled shade path through the overhanging willows would be sufficient reward for keeping at least two of my resolutions. I queued up the CD in my Discman, an upbeat new zydeco band with a rocking rubboard, and headed out. A whole new week lay before me.

My muscles, sadly, remembered Saturday's debauch, and it was quite a while before I was able to relax into the trancelike stride of a real run. But I pushed myself, imagining all the toxins draining out as I sweated, and gave in to a good, long walk much of the way back. Still feeling virtuous, I called Bill Sherman as soon as I got in, picking up his card as I reached for a towel and wiping my face as the precinct phone rang. Voice mail answered, even though my clock read nine-thirty. Did cops work odd hours? I laughed at my own question. One trouble with freelance was that it isolated you, made you think that everyone else held down nine-to-five jobs, when in reality the world was much more fluid. No matter. I left a message, explaining that I'd found something I thought he should know about, and treated myself to a long, steamy shower. My workday hadn't even started yet, but I'd met three of my resolutions already.

Time to start on a fourth. My notes on the acoustic café had sat long enough to feel cold and dull, so I put on some Patricia Barber piano blues to get back into the mood and found myself thinking of Bill Sherman. He'd been awfully friendly that night, more than mere courtesy called for, and he'd followed up by phone, letting me know what was happening with the investigation into Lillian's death, even though the news was that there was no news. Barber's smoky voice broke, freeing her jazzy piano to wander into that intriguing almost-dissonance that keeps blues fresh, and I let myself listen and, to be honest, daydream. Then the song ended and I looked back at the computer screen. Get a grip on yourself, girl. You're acting like you're in heat. A man can still be polite, can't he? I forced myself to concentrate on the words in front of me. Ninety minutes later I hit "send," and the story landed in the *Mail*'s features queue. A phone call to one of Tim's harried assistant editors confirmed its arrival, and I followed it up with one to the photo department. One down, one to go.

Finishing up the bookshelf story wasn't going to be fun, no matter how I looked at it, so I toyed with the idea of taking a break. Wasn't it time for lunch? Musetta, snoozing on the chair behind me, had nothing to say on the matter, so I turned my computer off. Standing alerted me to a return of last week's stiffness, and I congratulated myself on the long cooldown walk that had ended my workout. I was barely limping as I made my way down the stairs and out into the growing heat of midday.

"Warm, isn't it?" Greg, my postman, was dragging his little cart of mail up the sidewalk. He was already in the gray regulation shorts that distinguished his summer uniform.

"Boston," I nodded in agreement. "Spring's over, summer is already here."

"Gotta love it," he said without much conviction, and reached into the cart's canvas pouch. He leafed through a stack of envelopes held together with a rubber band. "Here."

I looked at what he'd given me. Two bills, one renewal

notice for a magazine, and an offer to buy into a timeshare on the Cape, which promised to develop into "a money-making opportunity." Not likely. I would have to finish that shelving story today. Under these was an envelope with a return address that had "Memorils" as part of its name. It was about James' ashes, I realized with a start. This was the notice to pick them up. When he'd been euthanized, I'd arranged to have him cremated and paid extra to have his ashes—his cremains, as they called them—kept separate from those of other peoples' deceased pets, and returned to me. The service had agreed to deliver them to the vet's office, I now recalled, and to notify me when the remains, in the personalized urn I had ordered, were ready for pickup. I'd forgotten that this step was still pending, and the polite, careful wording of the condolence letter inside made the finality of it all—and my failure to remember—the more dreadful. How could so much personality be contained in a still, silent urn? How could I have been distracted from thinking about him?

The bright day no longer seemed so glowing as I made my way into Central Square. Was I even hungry? For comfort, I realized, not food. Comfort and maybe a brownie. Walking past the Mexican place with the great salads, I found myself pulling up a stool at the Mug Shot.

"Hey stranger." Violet was all smiles in a vintage Disco Sucks tee shirt. "Latte with extra foam?"

"And a brownie. One of the big ones, with nuts." I was in no mood to be consoled, but they were awfully good sweets. She came back with a small glass plate overflowing with several large pieces.

"These were broken, so I'm charging you for one." They looked very freshly broken, I could have pointed out, but held my tongue.

"Thanks."

"Bad day?"

I really didn't want to talk, so I handed her the letter about James' remains. She started to read it, biting on her thumbnail, and I started to rouse from my funk. What was I doing, handing her a letter about a dead pet when she had just lost a human friend? I almost reached for it back, ready to apologize, when she looked up.

"This must be horrible," she said. Her eyes were filled with tears. "Too many people don't understand. They say, 'Oh, it's just a cat.' I hate that. I mean, we love them like our family and they love us, right? Love is love, right?"

I could have kissed her then but settled for a weak smile.

"Thanks for understanding." Someone called "Latte up!" and she went over to fetch my drink, a tall glass of comfort in a pint glass. I raised it in salute. "I really do appreciate it."

"Hey, I know grief," said Violet, leaning on her side of the tall bar. "Even before Lillian." She looked down at the blond wood bar and began to pick at a rough edge in the finish.

"Did you lose someone?" My words sounded trite, but clearly she wanted to talk.

"Yeah, first love. First loss. You know how it is." She looked up into my startled face. "Oh, not dead. Sorry, I didn't mean that. Just, you know, the usual. Heartbreak."

"I can sympathize with that."

"That's how I ended up in the practice space. We'd lived together, oh, almost two years." She was misting up again, so I pushed the plate of brownie bits toward her. She took one, but only picked out the nuts. "I moved out. I mean, I couldn't keep living there afterward. That's when I started helping Lillian out. Kept me busy, you know? Gave me somewhere to go. And she'd listen. Man, she was a good listener."

"I gather from everything I heard at the memorial that she'd been through a lot of her own hard times."

"Yeah." Violet picked up another piece of brownie and this time ate it, which I took as a good sign. "She was a really tough woman. Hard to believe she's really dead."

"You think that's why you're so sure it's murder?" I didn't want to push Violet too much, not when she'd just been so kind to me. But there did seem to be some reality checks in what she'd told me so far.

"No, I'm sure because I'm sure." I looked in her face expecting anger or the stubborn set of jaw that shows that confidence is beginning to crumble. Instead, I saw calm resolution. "I just haven't figured out why anyone would want to hurt her yet."

"But the police didn't see any reason to rule her death as anything other than accidental. Even with the medic-alert necklace." I hadn't told her what I'd found, but it seemed immaterial to my basic argument.

"There you go with the cops again." She was smiling at me, like I was a child.

"Okay, then, tell me, Violet. Tell me why you don't trust the cops."

"Hang on." She went to help a customer, and I watched as she measured out a pound of beans and poured a French roast into a large cardboard to-go cup. Was she stalling or concocting a story? I'd have to be on my toes.

"Okay." She pulled up a stool behind the bar and leaned toward me. "About three years ago, when I first came to town, I was really into hardcore. That was when there were all these all-ages shows, not just in clubs but in VFW halls, college dorms, places like that, remember?" I'd been a little old for the hardcore scene when it hit its zenith, but I did recall the popularity of the loud, fast music and the teenage subcultures it spawned.

"Well, the band I was in then, Right Life, was really hooked up. We were playing around at all the colleges. We were *it—*

the hot band for the parties, particularly on a certain frat house circuit. Which was kind of funny, right? Because we were straight-edge." She looked at me to see if I got it.

"Straight-edge," I repeated. "So none of you drank or did drugs."

"We didn't eat meat or dairy products either." She nodded. "We were clean, sober, and vegan. Well, I thought we were."

"Wasn't it hard to play the parties?"

"No, not really. I never had much of a head for alcohol, and those frat boys did nothing to make keg beer look good. What I missed more was the occasional burger, the really thick, greasy ones. Like the Cheeseburger King platter at Charlie's. I used to dream about ordering one of those. But drugs, booze, no, no loss. And the money at these parties was great. They'd offer us five, six hundred for a four-hour party, and half the time they'd throw in another c-note just for an encore. We were playing all over New England, even in Albany. And all originals, too. Things were really happening for us."

"And?" She'd paused and I couldn't help wondering if she too was trying to figure out what happened next.

"And the cops fucked us up. That's what. One night, real late, maybe three, we were pulled over driving back from Portland. A taillight was out, I think, but the cop took one look at us—my hair was green then—and had us out of the van. He had us all spread-eagled and leaning against the side while his partner went through our pockets, our instrument cases, everything. For a while, I thought he was really going to hurt us. He made Jemma, the bassist, fall on the pavement cause he kept kicking her feet farther back and farther apart. He groped her, too; she's got more meat on her than I do. And he wasn't too gentle with me either, running his hands up my legs with a bit more force than necessary, all the time he was talking really nasty. 'So, you ever been in jail? You know what it gets like at night?' That kind of thing. Finally his partner found something in a baggie and they hauled us all in. That's when I was really scared, but there was a police woman on duty and she must have known about those jerks. She was rough, but she kept us out of their hands. It was still a very long night." She paused, obviously remembering details she didn't care to share. With a deep sigh, she continued.

"Turns out Neal, the drummer, was sneaking a little toke in between the tofu burgers and seitan. He owned up to it, finally, and tried to get us all clear, but the cops weren't listening. They were in hog heaven and we spent the night in some shithole on the North Shore and we lost our van. I don't think Neal did any time. There was barely enough pot for a possession charge. But without the van the band was history. For a bud and a few seeds, history."

A small line of customers had formed by then, and Violet went to help her colleague, filling mugs and teapots with a grim look on her face. Finally, the mini rush died down again and she came over. I'd finished the brownie and she picked up my plate and the empty, foam-glazed glass.

"So you want to know why I don't like cops? The van and my band and one incredibly shitty night in jail, that's why." She wiped the counter where my plate had been and turned to walk away.

"Violet, wait." I stood and walked over to where she was stacking the dirties. "I didn't mean to pry, I just didn't understand."

"That's cool, Theda. I never meant to be so mysterious about it." She turned toward me and the anger had gone from her eyes. "Just pisses me off, you know?"

"Yeah, I do. I do now." Her story made sense, and made me feel a little guilty about my desire to dismiss her suspicions. Maybe she'd been right all along about Lillian's death. Maybe once again I was withdrawing from people. I remembered my resolutions. If not now, when? "Violet, one more thing."

She looked up from the rack again, ready to hoist the glassware into the washing machine in the back. "Yeah?"

"Dougie. Do you know him well?" I wanted to ask her about his relapses, about whether he was ever violent toward his mother, but I didn't dare. Violet's feelings about authority were clear, and she might be one of those who supported the rights of the mentally ill to refuse medication. I liked her too much to fight right now.

"As well as anyone, I guess. Why?" She heaved the wide tray to her knee and then up to rest on the counter.

"I wanted to talk to him, get a feeling for what his role might be in, well, in everything. His inheritance and all," I added hastily, before she could accuse me of looking to place blame.

"Well, let's go talk to him, shall we?" She disappeared into the kitchen area, and I could feel the blast of steam from the open washer. In a moment she was back, wiping her face on a dishtowel. "I've been meaning to visit him, now that Lillian won't be. Let's take him out to lunch tomorrow."

"Lunch?" I remembered those bills, and a few others I had at home.

"Don't sweat it, Theda. Dougie's idea of the high life is a Happy Meal with extra fries. I'll call the house tonight, but I know he'll be thrilled. I'll open tomorrow," she looked at her colleague, who nodded and reached for the scheduling sheet. "It's going to be another warm one, just like today, and it'll be good to get out of the city. Come by at ten and pick me up. We'll be in Northurst by noon."

THE PHONE WAS RINGING as I unlocked my door, and I nearly booted the cat as I lunged for it. "Hello?" I tried to catch my breath.

"Theda, are you all right?" It wasn't Connor, and I silently apologized to Musetta, who had taken refuge under a chair.

"Uh, yeah." I grabbed the receiver and stood up. It was easier to breathe without the sofa back bisecting my middle. "Sorry, I just came in and ran for the phone."

"It's Bill, Bill Sherman." I silently kicked myself for not recognizing his voice. "You left a message on my machine?"

"Yeah." I paused. How to give him the pendant without admitting that I'd been in Lillian's house? "It's about Lillian Helmhold." I tried to think of what to say next.

"I'm glad you called. I was thinking of touching base myself." That was nice. His voice was nice, too, warm and friendly. "We've had some complaints." A thought, not yet formed, evaporated. "Theda, are you listening?"

"Yes, Bill." If he was going with first names, I wasn't going to give him his title either.

"We've been hearing from a neighbor that someone has been snooping around Lillian Helmhold's house. There'd been a strange car, a Hyundai, parked in front of her house—the neighbor's, that is—and that made her curious, she says. Each time, she thinks she saw someone through the windows. If that's true, and I have no reason to doubt the report, that means someone is guilty of criminal trespass."

"Someone? You mean Violet, don't you? You want me to tell her to keep out."

"I don't see any reason to come down hard on a grief-stricken girl, but yeah, it does seem likely that it is her, from what you've said."

"And you're just taking the word of the neighbor that she noticed a suspicious car? Hasn't she heard what parking is like in this city?" He paused, and I saw an opportunity to drive home my point. "Besides, Violet doesn't have a car." I remembered what she'd said about the band van. That wasn't a car, right?

"She told you this?"

"Hey, she's bummed rides off me."

"And you've given her rides." I heard a sigh. "Well, she should stay away from that place. It's a safety risk, if nothing else."

"Safety risk!" Disappointment had turned to fuel for my temper. "Right, as if Patti Wright cared about Violet or the house or the cats, or even Lillian for that matter. She just doesn't want the property damaged until she can get her own hands on it."

"Now, Theda, that's not fair, and I'm not saying the report came from Ms. Wright. Any neighbor would care. A vacant house is at a much greater risk for fire and other forms of vandalism, even if it's just from kids hanging out. You don't have to assume any ulterior motive here."

"Maybe I do. Violet's told me about her history with the police, about how she gets hassled just because of the way she looks."

"You can't think…." Bill sounded resigned, rather than defensive, but I wasn't stopping for anything.

"Why not? I can't think that here, in our liberal city, someone would be hassled for having purple hair?"

There was quiet on the other end of the line. I'd gone too far. "Bill?"

"I'm here, Theda. And whatever this girl has told you, I can't say whether or not it's true. I can't speak for everyone on the force. But you might take it with a grain of salt, at least till you hear the whole story. At any rate, I'm not the enemy. Really I'm not."

"I know, I'm sorry. It's been a weird few days." What had gotten into me? Time to fess up. "I've been meaning to confess a little trespassing of my own."

"Oh?" That had taken him by surprise.

"It wasn't what you think, I mean, what I think you'd think.

And anyway, my car's a Toyota." This wasn't helping my case any. "I was over by Lillian's house and there was a cat who looked like he was starving and really wanted to be let in, so I opened the door…."

"You opened the door."

"Yeah, Violet had told me there was a key under one of the stones in the path." He started to say something, but I knew if I stopped now, I'd never get it all out. "Anyway, I found some cans and fed the cat but then on the way out, he bolted and hid in a corner. And when I picked him up, there it was."

"Theda, you're not making sense."

"The medic-alert pendant, the little alarm necklace that Lillian wore? The cat had found it for me, and there it was in the corner of the porch. So I took it."

"You took it?" He sounded like I do, when I have a bad headache coming on.

"Yeah, I took the pendant. I got the cat to come out, too, and I locked the house up tight. So I wanted to call and let you know that I had Lillian's alarm pendant, just in case you needed to check it out for clues or fingerprints or anything."

"After a cat had been playing with it and you picked it up, right?"

"Well, I guess I wasn't thinking too clearly." Why hadn't I scooped it up with one of those old magazines? "But I do have it here. I mean, I could bring it by the station and leave it for you."

"Why don't you do that, Theda." He sounded very tired. "And Theda?"

"Yes, Bill?"

"The key. Why don't you bring me the key to Lillian's house as well."

PLACING THE RECEIVER DOWN as gently as I could didn't help. The call from Bill left me with one of those cringing feelings that lets you know you've screwed up, and good. I looked to Musetta for help, but she was still sleeping, and just when I thought I'd wake her for a pet, she rolled over. "Nuff," she muttered, deep in a dream, and sighed. I couldn't compound my crime.

Instead I did penance on the keyboard, finally filling in the blanks on that damned bookshelf story and sending it off to the Home Section editor. If I were really good, I thought, I'd call Sally Hudson and give her a heads-up. I knew the story was slated to run the week after next, and I had a strange feeling she'd want to alert all her friends. But the idea of trying to make civil contact with another human being right now just didn't seem worth the effort, so instead I typed out a bunch of invoices and tucked them into envelopes. If I had any other work to do, I'd have done it, but I really wasn't up to pitching new stories. Instead, I grabbed an extra envelope, dropped the pendant in, and headed out to the street once more. I'd mail the invoices and pick up the hidden key at Lillian's. With any luck, Bill wouldn't be at the police station. I could stick the key in with the pendant in the envelope, leave them there for him, and never talk to the man again.

The fresh air revived me a bit, and the growing home-bound traffic reminded me that I wasn't the only awkward soul in the world. I made a circle back through Central Square, telling myself I wanted to drop the invoices off at the post office, but really just to enjoy the crowd. Over by the bank, a violinist was busking for quarters, an urban sign of spring as welcome as the first robin. I gave him what silver was in my pockets and wondered briefly if economics obeyed karma. No matter, the invoices were in the mail, and I turned back into the residential streets of Cambridgeport, on my way to Lillian's.

There was a car out front, but it was a late model Acura that showed a bit of wear and tear. I stopped to examine the dark blue sedan, a bit upscale for this area, and as I stood there,

it beeped. Patti Wright was coming down Lillian's overgrown front path. In her hands was a pile of circulars and restaurant menus that she'd probably just picked up from in front of the locked front door. Leafing through them, she didn't see me until we were almost nose to nose.

"Oh, you startled me!" In her heels and a lime-colored suit she was almost as tall as I was, and considerably brighter colored.

"Hi," I said, brilliantly. I doubted that she knew about the key that I'd come to collect, and I wasn't sure what to tell her.

"Can I help you?" She still had on her perky realtor voice, although her lipstick had been largely bitten away. Then I remembered.

"Well, yes, actually. I wanted to ask you about your applying to control the estate."

"What?" Her blue-rimmed eyes opened wide.

"Your application to be the administrator of Lillian's property, Dougie's inheritance. It's a matter of public record, you know."

"I know, I guess I know." She had the grace to look flustered. "But that just came through today so I didn't realize that word had, I don't know…." She waved her hands, and Lillian's junk mail, in the air. "That word had gotten out so fast."

"It didn't," I explained. "I'd just gone to look up some probate records and saw your application. But I was wondering. From all I've heard, you weren't close to Lillian, and you're not close to Dougie. Why do you want control of the estate?"

"Well, I understand how to handle such an asset." She half turned and gestured to the sagging structure behind her with both hands, using a Mary Chung's menu as a pointer. "Property values are highly fluid, particularly in this kind of neighborhood, and it takes special knowledge and training to know what to do with such a grand property. It's quite a structure, you know. We're calling it a heritage property." She talked as if she'd made up the term, or at least this use of it, and was awaiting applause.

"So that's the phrase for a big, old house now?" I couldn't resist needling her, not when she stood there in that game show pose: displaying the prize to the contestant. "A heritage property? It sounds like you already have brochures printed up."

"Well, you have to move quickly in this market. And it's not doing anyone any good just sitting here empty. In fact, the value depreciates...."

"Wait a minute." Her sales pitch had gone too far. "Doing good? Is that what you're doing, as the administrator?"

"Well, I am a registered notary public and a licensed realtor."

"But are you a friend of the family? Do you give a damn about Dougie?" She stood silent, her mouth slightly open. "To hear you talk, you've already got the listing for this property and the luxury condos I have no doubt you'll develop here. But you didn't like Lillian any when she was alive, and I doubt you give a damn about her son. Credentials aside, isn't the point of an administrator to make sure that the estate is used for the best interests of the heir?"

"Now, just a moment, young lady." Her voice had dropped from its birdlike twitter, but even her stern new tone couldn't stop me.

"I know you're hard up, Patti, so give it up. I know you're failing in the real estate biz"—she gasped at that—"and that you jumped too soon into this neighborhood. This 'mixed' neighborhood." I stressed the word to show her my disdain. "But maybe you haven't noticed what makes up a neighborhood. We're people, Patti, and this is where we live. Yeah, maybe we don't have much money, but we're certainly not trying to make a buck by selling each other out, or by pricing each other off our own streets, and I'm not going to sit back and just watch you trample all over that."

"Now look who's talking." Her little mouth pinched up and

turned pale, the last of the lipstick gone. "Look who's talking about diversity."

I stared at her, not sure what she meant. "I know who you are, Theda Krakow. I can hear who you are every time you open your mouth. You're a college-educated white girl, probably went to school right across town. And here you are slumming in Cambridgeport, pretending to be a punk rocker, and congratulating yourself on your low-rent neighbors and your low-budget clothes." I was, I realized as her eyes raked over me, wearing a stained Slash tee shirt with my jeans and worn sneakers. "Well, that's your little game and that's fine, but don't pretend any different to me, Miss Boho. You're not like that punk girl I see you with. You're not some rock and roller, living in an illegal squat." She spit out the word as if it tasted sour. "No, you're a little long in the tooth for that. But unlike you, I'll give a person the benefit of the doubt. I'd guess you're just trying to make a living, build a career, define yourself without a man to give you a name." She stamped her little shoe for emphasis with each declaration. "Just. Like. Me."

With that she veered around me and off the path, heels digging into the soft turf as she stormed back to her car and drove off, a little too fast for the street. I stood there, aghast and embarrassed for the second time in the afternoon. She was yuppie scum, I had no doubt of it. But also, at least a little, she was right.

I tried breathing deeply in through my mouth and out my nose as I waited for my heart to stop racing and my face to cool down. Despite the crowds up in the square, I didn't see anyone around, but I imagined a snickering face behind every curtained window. No matter, I was here for a reason. I walked back to the edge of the property and peeked down the street. There was no sign of Patti returning. Acting as nonchalant as a scarlet-faced redhead can, I walked around back, very conscious with each step of looking as sneaky as I felt. One more glance around and I knelt, lifting the loose slate out of its bed of damp earth. I'd just grab the key and be gone. I'd never have to see Patti Wright again. But my fingers confirmed what my eyes didn't want to believe. I lifted the slate entirely out of the damp depression it had created, and then the one behind it, and the one behind that. It didn't matter if I pulled up the entire path. Once again, the hidden key to Lillian's house was gone.

FIFTEEN

"WHAT AM I doing these days? Where am I going with my life?" These were the questions that rumbled through my head as I woke, tangled in the throw on my sofa. My life was in disarray. Patti Wright was right. I was a faker, a poseur, my rock-scene lifestyle as outdated a costume as her neon power suit. My writing career, which had seemed such a good idea only a few days ago, wasn't really developing along the lines I wanted, unless I was aiming for a job at Home Depot. The only story I cared about had died with Lillian Helmhold. Even though I'd held my own with Patti, the barbs in her words had found some tender spots.

Add in that I was becoming a grump, so quick to judge others that I couldn't be trusted in human company. Look at all the evidence: I'd dropped all my friends over the winter, and I wasn't being that great now about keeping in touch. But that was because so much else had been going on then, my waking brain argued with itself. And besides, I was trying to make things up. Bad train of thought: I hadn't done much better with new people either, I realized ruefully. Bill Sherman wasn't likely to call again. Not in such a friendly way, anyway, seeing as how I'd dropped off the pendant with only a quick note—"key gone, sorry!"—the night before. And Connor? Would I ever hear from him again? The memory of my one date in months only served to prove the case that few humans, no men anyway, would want to spend much time with me.

I was in a funk, no doubt about it. To top it off, I could feel a throbbing headache coming on. Musetta, who had muttered and snored on her chair so adorably all afternoon, had become frenetically playful once I wanted to call it a night, pouncing on my feet as they moved under the covers each time I was ready to drop off. After one particularly successful attack—she actually bit me through the blanket—I finally gave up and kicked her off the bed, only to be awakened what seemed like minutes later as I heard her rolling some noisy toy—an earring? a button?—around on the floor.

"What are you doing, kitten?" I had yelled in frustration as I threw off the covers and got out of bed. The clock had read three-something. "Are you trying to ruin my life?" She'd taken my actions as an invitation to play and scampered down the hall. I'd followed, feeling guilty for my outburst, and found a cork for her to play with instead, tossing it for her to bat until sleep had returned and I crashed on the sofa sometime after four.

Sunlight streaming into the living room had woken me, and with the one sane part of me I let it flood me as well with the determination to get my life back on track. The physical portion of it, at least, I decided as I reached for my sneakers. Everything would look better after a run, and as I completed my stretches and started an easy lope toward the river, I began to see my way toward surviving the morning. Beyond that, I just didn't know. Was I too old for the club scene? I hadn't felt so, until Patti Wright suggested it, though I couldn't stop thinking of the night when Violet's band had played and all the fans had looked so young. But that was an anomaly, the exception that showed the scene was still vibrant and growing, wasn't it? And hadn't I still loved every minute of her set? Besides, for me, being hip to the latest thing or fitting in with the entire crowd wasn't my reason for going out. I went for the camaraderie. No matter how many younger music lovers joined us, the Casbah and its like were still where I met my peers. Where we gathered. Such clubs and bars offered the perfect "third place," neither home nor work, where I could go to unwind and socialize. I wasn't ready to give that up.

Nor did I feel that old anymore. As my mind had wrestled with its issues, my feet had gotten into a rhythm. As I breathed the damp morning air, the band of pain around my forehead began to evaporate. Running was good for me, I realized. Maybe that would be what would keep me going as my thirties progressed. And for the rest? Not this morning, not yet. I hit the footpath and turned toward Weeks Bridge, speeding up until I could hear my heart pounding and the sun on the river glittered like a tray of gems.

ASPIRIN AND a large mug of my own dark brew cleared the rest of the fog away, and I actually managed to make some pitch calls before it was time to pick up Violet. Not that I reached anyone or even really expected to; no editor I knew started work before ten, or if they did they weren't answering their phones. I couldn't blame them. My own time on the *Mail* copy desk had shown me how quickly paperwork could pile up, and how precious a few minutes of quiet could be. No matter, when they did check their voice mail, I'd be there with a brief, catchy pitch and my phone number repeated twice, along with the assurance that I'd touch base again later. I still had a few minutes to play with Musetta before heading out, and I amused us both with a balled-up rejection letter from one of the better women's magazine and cries of "Kill, kitty, kill!"

"WHAT IS THAT?" Violet looked as fierce as the kitten, staring at my dashboard. I popped the tape, a compilation of traditional Cajun fiddle tunes, and let her examine it as I pulled into traffic.

"Oh, it's in French, that's cool." She put the tape back in, but turned the volume down, and handed me a bag. "Muffin pieces. If I eat any more of the unsalable ones I'll burst."

"Thanks." I swallowed a handful of lemon and poppyseed bits, before getting down to business. "So, you know how to get there, right? I'm assuming we take the turnpike out to Northurst."

"Yeah, I called yesterday and got exact directions. But basically, yeah, stay on the pike until you see apple blossoms."

It was probably too early for the Western Massachusetts orchards to be flowering, but I liked the image and sighed as I picked up my toll ticket and we blended into westbound traffic.

"You okay?" Violet looked over at me. My sigh must have been audible over the music. "I can spell you on the driving, if you want."

"No, I'm good," I told her, and I was. "I think I needed to get out of the city for a bit. Even just for a day. Things have been crazy."

"Tell me about it." She looked lost in her own thoughts, feet up on the dashboard, eyes hidden by her bangs. Then she looked up. "But what's going on? What's up with you?"

Where to start? "It's just the usual life issues stuff. I had a date on Saturday that was, well, confusing. And then yesterday I got into a fight with that neighbor, Patti Wright."

"Wright? I hope you tore her a new one. What was that about?"

"Actually, she got to me." I knew I should say something to Violet about the missing key and the cops' interest, but I wasn't up to a confrontation at the very start of a two-hour drive. "It was, well, I did ask her about applying for control of Lillian's estate, Dougie's property. She accused me of being a snob and I think she had a point."

"Wait, back up." Violet was sitting up straight now. "Wright is getting control of Lillian's house? How's that possible?"

"It's all legal. I did some poking around in probate court last week. Legally, Dougie isn't competent. The lawyers on the board of his group home serve as his conservators. It's not a big deal, really, it's less control than if they were legal guardians. But they're supposed to oversee complicated matters for him, and an inheritance counts. They're out in Northurst, though, and it sounds like they do most of this pro bono. So they were looking for someone to actually administer the estate and Patti Wright applied."

"Is that normal? That doesn't sound right."

"The woman I spoke with in the courthouse said it was all pretty standard. Most cases, with someone who has a mental illness, maybe a parent or guardian would have set this up already, arranged for her passing. But I guess Lillian didn't expect to die."

"Didn't expect to be murdered, certainly." Violet sunk back down in her seat, brooding over something. "You don't think she did it, did you? I mean she's got awful taste and I don't trust her anywhere near a cat, but a murderer?"

I shrugged, no longer sure about my own suspicions, and she continued. "So, can that woman actually do anything to Dougie's house? And what can we do to stop her?"

"Everything and nothing." I didn't know what else to say. "What's likely is that she'll sell the house and Dougie will inherit the proceeds. It's been bothering me because it seemed like a conflict of interest, her being a realtor and all. Plus, well, you know what she's like. I don't trust *how* she's going to sell it. I mean, Cambridgeport has lost enough affordable homes with everything on the market being converted to condos. But it's all above board."

"Damn, I've been too slow." I thought she was talking to herself rather than me. "I've got to get moving."

"There's nothing either of us can do, I'm afraid. In the eyes of the law, she's doing everything right."

"Just wait, Theda. Just you wait." She looked over at me and I dared a glance back. "There's something going on, I know it. And I'm going to get to the bottom of it."

"Are you planning something?" I hadn't liked the look on Violet's face, a stare of intense concentration shot with anger. Would she torch the old building for revenge, turn it into some sort of feminist cat-hair funeral pyre in her friend's memory? "You know, the cops have gotten reports that someone has been in Lillian's house." I wanted to warn her. "They're on the alert, now, and they'll arrest you if they catch you there."

"They won't catch me. And I've got to keep searching. I know the answer is in there somewhere."

"Is that why you took the spare key?"

"What? No. I mean, I took it to make a copy, but I put the hidden one back days ago. I figure anyone who knows about it should have the right to use it. I just wanted my own."

"You put it back? Oh, tell me another one!" My exasperation was only partly faked. She was growing on me, sure, but she still wasn't being straight with me. "Violet, what am I going to do with you?"

"You sound like my mother." She was changing the subject, but I couldn't force answers from her. Not while driving.

"You've got a mother?"

"Hmmm, two really. My dad passed away when I was a kid and Mom and Alice have lived together since I went off to college."

"What college?" It wasn't the question she expected.

"Bay State Arts," she said, and I could hear the pride in her voice. The private art school drew international talent in all media to teach, and the gifted students went through a rigorous jury system for a place in each class.

"Impressive." It was. "Did you graduate?"

"No." Her voice dropped, and now it was her turn to sigh. "Mom got sick and it was all Alice could do to take care of her. I transferred to the state school, started taking biology classes. I thought maybe I'd end up a vet. But then even that got too pricey, so here I am, the punk-rock barrista. Maybe I can make some money as a cat sitter."

"Oh hell." I suddenly remembered Lillian's cats.

"What?" Violet sat up fast and looked around.

"Cats. I just remembered. Isn't tomorrow?" I didn't know how to say it.

"Yeah, D-day. I've been thinking about it all morning. But I know the shelter. They'll give them all day tomorrow in the hope of getting just one more placed. But then, it's the shot."

"Damn."

"Yeah," she said. "Damn."

We rode in silence for a while then, watching the budding and still bare trees go by. And when we started to talk again, it was about less pressing matters. She'd grown up in a rural area in upstate New York, not unlike the farming country around Northurst. She still had cousins there, people who would welcome her if things ever got too tough.

"But I'm a city kid now, you know?" I did.

In turn, I told her about my own upbringing. In comparison, my comfortable suburban life, decent public schools and private college sounded pretty easy. But neither of us had any siblings, so when I told her about losing both my parents within a year of each other almost ten years before, we were on common ground.

"It's weird, knowing that it's just you now, isn't it?" she asked.

"Yeah, that's it. The sense that you could walk off the face of the earth and nobody would know."

"Until rent was due, anyway." We laughed.

"I think that's what I get out of the scene, in a sense." I was trying to put into words the series of disconnected thoughts I'd had during my run that morning. "It's not family. I don't even know how many people I know that well. And I do see my close friends outside of bar hours, but…." I let the thoughts trail off.

"It's family of choice."

"Exactly."

"But, well…." Now it was Violet's turn to stop in the middle of a thought.

"What?"

"You've got to be careful."

"Yeah, Mom? Anything specific?"

"I told you the other night, when you wanted to know why I stalked off, that I saw this creep, right?"

"Uh-huh." I remembered.

"Well, he was more than creepy. He was dangerous. He tried to rape me."

"In the Casbah?" I was appalled.

"No, no, it was at Lillian's actually. About a week before she died."

"Back up, what happened? And do you know this guy?"

"No, I don't. I've never seen him with anyone I know, either, or I'd get the word out. Just some—some real creep. What happened was one night, after rehearsal, I went over to Lillian's. She'd gone out to visit Dougie that day, and she didn't always get the bus back. So I thought I'd swing by, see how the cats were doing. You know, feed them, scoop out the litter if it needed it. It was around midnight, but I can be quiet. I figured, worst case, Lillian wakes up and finds her litter-boxes have been cleaned.

"So, anyway, I let myself in and was being as quiet as I

could be, when I heard a noise. I started to turn around, when suddenly this bastard grabs me. He had his hand over my mouth and I tried to bite him, but he just laughed. He laughed! He said something horrible, something creepy, like, 'Well, what's this little bonus prize?' and pressed me up against the wall. He had his hands all over me. I was trying to kick him— he had my arms sort of wedged against the wall—but he'd caught me totally off guard. And then a light came on in the next room. It was Lillian. She'd heard something and she must have known somehow that something was wrong. She started yelling, 'Who's there? Who's there?' She said something about having a gun, though I know she didn't. Then she yelled, 'I'm calling the police!' and for a moment everything was still. I think she would've, too, if she really had to— despite all her old fears. But just for a minute there was silence. He was staring at me. God, he was creepy. Then he dropped me and ran. I kind of had the wind knocked out of me or I would've gone for him, then. I swear I would've. I'd have been able to take him, too. But he was gone."

"Damn, that's awful, Violet. I'm so sorry. But why didn't you let Lillian call the cops?"

"*Let* her? Are you serious? After dealing with storm troopers, she wasn't comfortable with anyone in authority. And I wasn't going to press her. I'd been through that once already and, believe me, the cops are no better than that jerk was! I wasn't going to put myself in their hands again."

"Not all of them are bad." I thought of Bill Sherman. My cop.

"You're not a street girl with purple hair. They see me, they see 'fair game' written on my forehead. Besides, the guy was gone. And I could've taken care of myself—could've taken care of him, I mean—it's just that he startled me. Lillian scared him, but if she hadn't I would've been able to fight him off. I was just waiting for my opening."

"'She may be little, but she is fierce,'" I quoted at her, unsure whether to laugh or start lecturing.

"Huh?" Violet looked up at me. I shook my head, amazed at her spirit if nothing else, and she continued. "So when I saw him in the Casbah the other night, it made sense."

"What?" I wasn't following.

"He must know about me. Maybe he'd seen my band or something." I shook my head. I didn't understand. "A lot of guys, well, no, that's not fair—*some* guys think that if you're gay you're a threat to them, to their manhood. Or a challenge. You just need to get worked in or something."

"Oh." Of course. Violet was lesbian. I'd just never put it together.

"You know I'm queer, right?"

"I do now." I laughed. "Sorry, I just never really thought about your sexuality."

"That's okay, Theda. You're not my type either." I shot her a look and she smiled back. "But that's one of the things that was so great about Lillian. You'd think that her generation, they'd be more traditional, be full of the stereotypes and crap. Well, she knew and she didn't care. Hell, she was always asking me if I couldn't meet a nice girl and settle down! After that night, she wanted me to move in. Not to help her out, but so she could keep an eye on me. But I loved her too much for that. It would've felt like I was taking advantage. Now I wish I had."

"Damn!" She slapped the dashboard and sat up straight. "Maybe it wasn't about me. I'd figured he'd been waiting for me, knew my habits. Or maybe he'd heard the rumor that Lillian has some kind of treasure trove buried in among the old magazines and kitty litter she kept. That one keeps coming back. Or he was just a local jerk. But maybe he wasn't after me. Maybe it wasn't a simple break-in or random or anything. Maybe that creep was out for her—and then he came back and hurt Lillian. But why?" She bit her lip. "Damn, damn, damn. I should've confronted him when I saw him at the Casbah. I should have grabbed his skanky ass the other night when I saw him walking through the club. But, you know, Theda? I was afraid. Me! I saw him and I just wanted to get away."

"That's human, Violet. And, you know, you might have been right the first time. It might have been gay-bashing." I paused, silently cursing her secretiveness. "But why didn't you tell me this? I mean, did you tell anyone?"

"I can take care of myself, Theda." She stared straight ahead, trying for tough. All I could think was how young she looked, how vulnerable. I wanted to argue with her, to point out how her assumption had helped a criminal go free. How it might have led to Lillian's murder. But she looked so fragile just then, and besides it was too late.

Instead, I asked as gently as I could, "You never called the cops about the break-in, about the rapist, did you?"

She shot me a look. "You have to ask?"

No, I didn't.

WE MADE THE REST of the trip in a silence that gradually grew more comfortable. Violet took charge of switching tapes, I tried to think of a way to pass along all this new information to Bill without involving her. I couldn't quite see how to do this, not yet, and was grateful for her occasional interruptions to give me directions. Worcester sped by, and the day continued bright and clear. But about a half hour later, once we'd taken the exit for Northurst, I realized that our easy mood was changing again. It was me: I was growing more tense rather than less. Something other than Violet's story was weighing on me.

"It's coming up, right on the left," said Violet, and I caught myself clutching the steering wheel hard. There didn't seem to be anything around us to make me nervous. In fact, everything looked better than normal. Idyllic even. As we cruised down Dougie's street on the outskirts of Northurst, what I saw was an old and settled community, with newer ranch-style houses interspersed between their tall, older neighbors. At Violet's prompting, I pulled up in front of one of the big, original houses, three stories topped with eaves and flanked by towering oaks that had just begun to bud. A wheelchair ramp curved around to the porch, and the fresh, flawless paint job—light lavender, with darker purple and black for the trim and shutters—marked it as slightly different from its neighbors, but only in the sense that it looked better cared for. Clearly, despite the money stolen, Greenleaf House had its supporters.

Dougie was waiting by the steps, smoking a cigarette, as I pulled up to the house. Dwarfed by the huge old building and the shadow of two tall trees, wearing the beat-up cardigan he'd had on at his mother's funeral, he looked vulnerable rather than threatening. But that didn't mean he couldn't have had a psychotic episode, especially if his treatment had been disrupted. It didn't mean he hadn't accidentally caused his mother's death, I reminded myself as he looked up, waved, and stubbed out the cigarette with slow, deliberate movements.

"It's because of the fire they had out here," Violet was explaining. "No smoking indoors." He started toward us, and as he got closer, I saw how big he was. Even plump and out of shape, he would easily be a match for an old woman. Violet waved at him. "Plus, they've all become extra careful about disposing of their butts."

"But wasn't it arson?"

She shrugged. "Yeah, I guess so. But, hey, everyone is so quick to blame these guys anyway, it can't hurt for any of them to be extra careful."

Feeling vaguely ashamed of my own suspicions, I managed

a smile as Dougie reached the car. Violet got out to greet him and they exchanged a brief hug. She pulled her seat forward so he could squeeze his considerable bulk into my back seat, and then introduced us.

"Dougie, do you remember Theda? She was at your mother's memorial."

"No, I don't remember," he said quietly, his voice a monotone. "But thank you. Thank you for coming to my mother's memorial service."

"You're welcome. I'm sorry for your loss." He looked up and nodded, then went back to hunting for the backseat seatbelt. My rearview mirror showed the top of his balding head, the remaining hair curly like his mother's. Suddenly an intense face stared up at me and I started.

"Found it!" I heard the seatbelt snap.

"Shall we?" I sighed and started the car.

Violet answered for us all "I'm starving!" and gave me directions back to the village we'd passed by. A few blocks out, toward the local community college, we found a strip mall anchored by two fast-food joints that disrupted the almost rural calm of the town. Dougie started bouncing in his seat, and I realized one of these was our destination.

"I'm not really sure how to talk to him," I confessed to Violet, once we had parked. "I've written about mental illness before, but I've never really spent time with someone who was, well, this disturbed." Dougie had gone straight in to one of the garish outlets and stood in line, studying the illuminated menu overhead with rapt concentration. I'd delayed a bit, looking for the break to confess my fears to Violet. I felt as out of place as the restaurant's big plastic signs.

"Just talk," she said, as we followed him in. "He's okay when he's on his meds. He's just a little stiff, a little formal."

She looked back at me and saw my hesitation, the awkwardness I wasn't sure how to overcome.

"Theda, he's basically a very shy guy." She pulled close to me so we wouldn't be overheard by any of the lunch crowd who were filing past us. "Just keep in mind that he's sort of fragile. Don't yell at him, or even talk too loud. And, well, you know, keep your voice steady if you can. He doesn't like loud noises or anyone he doesn't know getting too close. It's only been the last two visits that I made with Lillian that he let me hug him. I think he's more embarrassed by his illness than anything else sometimes."

What qualified as a loud noise? Could something have startled him that night at Lillian's? I didn't see how I could ask Violet, she seemed so attached to the guy. Nor could I tell anymore what was a legitimate suspicion—and what was really just my own discomfort with Dougie. Instead I asked, "Does he know?" I wasn't sure how to phrase it. "I mean, does he know *I* know about his schizophrenia?"

"I think he assumes everyone does. Sometimes he gets sort of preachy, you know, saying he wants to raise awareness and that he's a client not a patient, that kind of thing. Some days he seems more vulnerable. Play it by ear."

We'd pushed through the door and Dougie had turned back to look at us, so we broke off.

"Shall we order?" His voice, though low, was polite and modulated now.

"Yes, let's." I was falling into his somewhat courtly style.

"Three cheeseburgers with fries, right?" Even Violet seemed a bit subdued, in volume if not spirit. "And sodas? Or coffee?"

"Diet for me." I was relaxing.

"Soda," said Dougie. "And extra fries. Don't forget the fries!"

"As if I would," she chided him and went up to order. I

reached for my wallet, but she waved me away. "My treat, you guys. Go find us a table."

I followed Dougie, who had quickly turned and headed out to the restaurant's wing. Large floor to ceiling windows gave the alcove the feel of a greenhouse, despite the plastic chairs and tables, and I began to see how this could be a pleasant outing. But then we sat, and we were alone. My nervousness returned, and I did my best to swallow it. It was time to ask some questions.

"Dougie. May I call you Dougie?"

"Sure. You're a friend of Violet's. And everybody calls me Dougie." The big windows made the alcove ring with echoes, and his low voice was barely audible. I leaned forward without thinking. He drew back, and I made myself do the same.

"Thank you." How to begin? "I wanted to ask you about the trouble at Greenleaf House a few months back, when you left for a while." I didn't really care about the fire or the theft, but if it had prompted a relapse on his part, it seemed like a good place to start.

"I lost my job." I wasn't sure I'd heard him, but resisted the temptation to lean forward.

"Your job?"

"I had a job in the office at Greenleaf. Three hours a day." He'd picked up the salt shaker in what I now saw were yellow-stained fingers and started turning it around.

"What did you do?"

"Filing mostly. I was in charge of some mailing, too. Whatever the counselors needed." The salt shaker went round and round.

"I'm sorry about that. Did you lose it because of the fire? Or because you left Greenleaf House?"

"He said I was bad. That I wasn't telling him the truth." The fingers holding the salt began to tremble and he clamped them hard around the shaker. I didn't know if he needed another smoke or if my questioning was getting to him, but it seemed time to back off. Besides, Violet had just shown up with a tray from which rose a surprisingly delicious smell.

"I got extra ketchups. You've got salt, I see." She looked from Dougie to me and raised her eyebrows. I didn't respond. "So, whatcha been up to, Dougie?"

We all reached for the paper-covered burgers and drinks, and the tension subsided. Maybe hunger had been a factor for both of us, I thought, as I tried not to wolf the thin, dry, but amazingly tasty burger.

He proceeded to tell her, between bites, about the day program he was in and how he hoped to get into a job-skills class soon.

"I don't know if I'm ready." He paused and put his burger down. "I'd like to try. I liked having a job."

"I bet you'll do great," said Violet, eating the cheeseburger with the gusto of a former vegetarian. She licked her fingers. "But only if you want to. Do you really want to work outside Greenleaf House? That's what those classes are for, right?"

"I don't know." Dougie looked down at his burger. For a moment, I felt we had lost him to his thoughts and wondered what we'd see next.

"What are you thinking about, Dougie?" Clearly Violet had some concerns as well, her voice becoming softer and gentler as she called him back to the present.

He looked up, recalled himself, and started to eat again. I thought he had forgotten the question, if he'd heard it at all. But after finishing his fries and starting on the fourth serving that Violet had bought for the table, he responded, his voice even, if low, once again.

"I think I may have to get a job now, another job. I liked working, even if what I did was very simple. But I don't want to fail again. My mother took care of everything. She always said everything was taken care of, but now I don't know."

"Dougie, your mom did what she could for you and I know you'll miss her." Violet was trying to sound reassuring, despite her own sadness. "But you're still getting your Social Security, your SSDI, right?" I recognized the initials for the disability payments that were the main support of Dougie and his fellow Greenleaf residents.

"I get my SSDI. But now I don't know. I always thought Mother took care of everything."

He looked up and just for that moment, I saw the huge sadness there. Poor man, so lost in his own mind. Seeing him like this, my nervousness evaporated. Instead, I wanted to reassure him. I wanted to tell him that it would all be all right. Even explain about the possible sale of the house, about Patti Wright's probable disposal of the estate. No matter what she did with it or the neighborhood, he'd be the recipient of a good deal of money. But I didn't fully understand the timetable for when anything would happen, or even the legalities of the matter. Wouldn't he lose the Social Security payments if he came into a large cash inheritance? Might it not be worse to be waiting for the sale, anticipating a windfall that might never come? And would money in any form ever make up for the doting parent that he'd lost?

Besides, I couldn't let my sudden sympathy interfere with my reasoning. I had never suspected Lillian's son of intentionally harming her. My sadness didn't change the facts of his illness. Violet and I exchanged a look as Dougie polished off the fries.

"Dougie, what happened after the fire? Why did you take off?" I had to bring up the subject. We were almost done with our food. It was now or never.

"I tried to keep everything in order." He was picking at the cardboard container, stabbing at crumbs and salt crystals with a thick, stubby finger. His nails looked bitten; several were lined with raw red flesh. "I told him everything I could. I wanted to explain, to show him. But he said I was holding back. Disorganized. Disorganized thinking."

"So you took off?" He seemed absorbed in his quest for the last salty bits and didn't answer, so I tried another tack. "Who told you that you'd done a bad job, Dougie? Was it the police or the firemen who came after the fire? Was it one of the counselors you worked with?"

"Disorganized thinking." His voice had sunk to a whisper; those large hands had dropped to his side. From the way he hung his head, I suspected that he was quoting someone else's hurtful words, phrases either actually spoken or lobbed at him by the demons in his head. I made one more attempt.

"Did you go to visit your mother last week? On Monday?"

"I wanted to show him." Dougie looked up. "He was my friend." For a moment, his eyes met mine, and if Violet hadn't warned me, I'd have reached to embrace him. He looked so lost, so sad, so alone. The moment passed and he looked back down, staring at the empty wrappers on the table as if they held the future or could explain the past. "Dougie and Davey." He'd begun to rock a little in his seat, much as he had at Lillian's memorial. "Dougie and Davey," he repeated. "Dougie and Davey."

SIXTEEN

"WHAT WAS THAT ABOUT?" Violet positively hissed at me once we were outside. Dougie had excused himself to smoke a cigarette and stood at the end of the concrete walk, while we waited by the car.

I didn't pretend not to understand her.

"You want to know what happened to Lillian, right? Well, you've got to consider all the possibilities." She looked at me hard, waiting. "Violet, Dougie's a sick man. He might have caused his mother's death. Face it, he's not completely there even with the drug treatment. If he were off his meds, isn't it possible he might have done something to Lillian?"

"He'd never hurt his mother." Her whisper grew louder. I raised my hands to quiet her and she nearly spit back at me. "He loved her."

"I don't doubt that, but it could have been an accident. Maybe she startled him and he reacted." I had to watch to keep my own voice from growing louder. "Hell, he could have started yelling and maybe that caused her to fall back and hit her head. I'm just trying to look at all the angles here."

"How do you know he was even in Cambridge?"

"I don't, but he doesn't always come home at night, right?" She stared at me, then nodded once. "And he knows how to get out to the city. He's got money for bus fare, right?"

"But he's never been violent. He's never hurt anyone."

"After the fire, when he disappeared, didn't the police pick him up?"

"Yeah, but that was because he was sitting outside. It was early March. He was talking to himself, freaking people out, and it was like zero degrees out. They took him in cause they thought he'd freeze to death, and that's how they got Lillian's name and number and she picked him up and got him into a hospital. She got him stabilized and he was fine."

"But where did they find him?" I suspected I already knew the answer, but I wanted to hear her say it.

"In Cambridge. He was sitting on a bench in Central Square, why?"

"Cause he was in Cambridge and he was incoherent, and he feels someone has done him wrong. Seems like reason to lash out to me."

"You're wrong. I know you're wrong." She kicked at the dirt. My reasoning was getting to her.

"Prove it to me, then. Find out if he was here, in Northurst, last Monday night." A thought had occurred to me. "Seriously, you want to spend more time with him, right? Well, I'm going over to the local newspaper. There's a reporter there I want to speak with."

"I'll do it, but you're wrong, Theda." She glared up at me, and we both looked over at Dougie. He was done with his cigarette, and we watched as he carefully ground it out with his heel and then picked up the dead butt to carry it to a trash can. I unlocked the car for our trip back.

"I hope you're right, Violet." I didn't want this gentle man to have made his own life worse. "I really hope so."

DOUGIE SEEMED to have regained his composure with the nicotine fix, and we had a jolly ride back to Greenleaf. Violet was telling Dougie the latest news about her band, and he looked happy for her, though the mention of a sold-out crowd in a packed club made him wince. I dropped the pair off, telling Violet I'd come back in two hours, at most. Dougie seemed to have forgiven me my intrusive questions and once more thanked me politely for my visit in his quiet, courtly manner.

Finding the *Northurst Eagle* wasn't hard. A slow cruise down the town's main street didn't turn up its offices, but it did bring me to a newsstand. A copy of the paper gave me the address, and the vendor was kind enough to direct me, once I'd paid my fifty cents. Investigative journalism, I reassured myself, sometimes meant bribing sources.

Of course, I hadn't called ahead, so I had no idea if Jim Brett would be working today, or if he'd be free to talk if he was. But I was counting on professional courtesy—journalist to journalist—to get me into the morgue, the paper's archives, if not.

"Hold on." Unlike the lackadaisical security at the *Mail,* the *Northurst Eagle* had a real security guard, one who wasn't going to let me into their second-floor offices without the word from someone inside.

"Jim, there's a lady here to see you?" He'd picked up a phone and someone must have answered. "A Thea something?"

"Theda, Theda Krakow."

"Oh, it's Theda something. She's from the *Boston Mail?* Okay, will do." He hung up and grabbed a clipboard for me to sign in on. "He said he'd come get you. Let me write you out a badge. You've got to keep this on while you're in the building."

I clipped the plastic ID to my shirt and looked around the lobby. Tiny, really just an alcove at the top of the stairs, separated by a glass wall, it had a flash of color from a few framed prints. Through the glass front, a picture window looked out across the stairwell, too, letting in more daylight than most of my old newsroom ever saw.

"Theda Krakow?" I turned and looked up. The man who addressed me was tall, way over six feet, with a shock of Dennis the Menace brown hair that seemed in danger of falling in his eyes. I recognized his voice even before he introduced himself. "I'm Jim Brett."

"Hi." We shook. "I'm really sorry to barge in like this. I was out here and thought I'd see if you were in."

"Doug Helmhold and the Greenleaf House fire, right?" I must have looked surprised. "I have a memory for conversations. Comes in handy when the tape recorder fails at interviews."

We both smiled at that and he led me through the door behind security into the workings of the paper.

"It's so quiet!" I couldn't help myself. Despite the necessity of concentration for both writing and editing, the newsroom at the *Mail* always seemed to be operating at a low roar. This office hummed, if anything, with a pleasant mellow buzz. I could hear keyboards clicking and somewhere a low voice making polite conversation on the phone. As Brett led me past row after row of carpeted cubicles, I had to stop myself before I blurted out, "And it's so clean!" The gray-carpeted cubicles were kept from sterility by the personal touches: photos and posters had been thumbtacked everywhere, as well as the usual official notices and circulars about everything from early deadlines to someone's '64 Impala being for sale. But the carpeting showed no dark stains, at least to my eyes, the trash cans weren't overflowing. I couldn't smell any burnt coffee or forgotten lunches. "It's so nice," I said instead.

"It's a very nice maze," agreed Brett. "We're very nice little mice."

"Oh, come on now." I was tempted to explain the comparison and then stopped myself. A lot of the people working here probably dreamed about getting onto a big city paper.

Anything I said comparing the two would seem disingenuous, or even insulting.

"You don't have to say it. I know what you mean." Brett led me down one little hallway to a cubicle that held a desk and a tall, padded chair. He folded himself into that one, reached across into the empty cube opposite and rolled another chair in for me. "We may be mice in a maze, but at least there are no rats and no roaches like some newsrooms have. Have a seat." I did, surprised once again by his perceptiveness. "I spent eight years in Hartford, four more in New Haven," he continued. "I know what those city newsrooms can be like."

I hoped my face didn't register my surprise.

"What am I doing here?" I guess it had. "Quality of life. That and our third kid, my little girl." He plucked a framed photo off the top shelf of three, and I saw two brown-haired boys with their father's cowlick and a Buddha-like infant in the arms of a smiling mom. "When we had Renee we decided we really wanted to get out of the city, have a place with a yard and trees. So when this opened up, I grabbed it. Less money, but I still find some interesting stories. And as you noticed, I've got a quiet place where I can actually think about what I'm writing."

"Impressive." I found myself nodding and wondering about the possibility myself. No, I was too much of a city person to ever give that up.

"So, tell me what brings you out here. You're looking into some kind of bigger story, aren't you?"

"Newspaper instincts?"

"Something like," he nodded. "Also, we got a phone call from a cop, someone from your neck of the woods. He also wanted to hear what I could tell him about Doug Helmhold." A wave of relief washed over me. I wasn't the only one thinking about Lillian's son! My thoughts must have shown on my face, because Brett pushed his chair back and sat for a moment, looking at me. "So, spill."

I had been the one counting on professional courtesy and it only seemed fair, so I did. From the first visit with Lillian through finding her body up to my lunch with Dougie. I kept out some of the details, of course, like the fact that Violet was routinely illegally entering the now-vacant house. But I did share her suspicion that the death was not accidental, and my own growing fear that her son may have somehow been involved.

"Violence against family members, the last taboo." He nodded, when I was done, considering the option.

"I know people don't like to talk about it, but…."

"Yeah, I know." He reached for a fat green book off one of the shelves and found a reference. "What's the risk factor? Something like ten percent of family members reported some violence, according to one National Alliance for the Mentally Ill study." I remembered the cousin he'd mentioned. "And that ten percent is pretty much the folks who go off their treatment plans, or who have never been diagnosed or treated."

"Dougie was supposedly never violent before, but he did have a history of going off his meds, right?"

"Hmmm." He replaced the book and tapped his pen. "Yeah, he did." Clearly he was thinking through the chain of events. "So the big question now is whether Doug Helmhold was at Greenleaf last Monday or had he gone AWOL, right?"

"Right. I've got a friend trying to dig that up this afternoon."

"Well, let me see what I have in my files, see if anything rings a bell." He rooted around on his desk and then bent himself almost double to open a file cabinet drawer. I held my breath in hope.

"No," he said, leafing through it. "Nothing new. Nothing since the local cops gave up on tracking that lost money."

Damn, I was disappointed. "You might talk to one of our freelancers, though. Guy named Ethan Reinhardt?"

Ethan! He'd never gotten in touch. Well, I'd offered. "Yeah, I've met him. He did some of your coverage?"

"A lot of it, actually. He spent the most time with Doug, went back a couple of times for follow-up interviews, drove all over the county collecting background."

"That's right." I remembered an in-depth story on the halfway house. "I read the story."

"It was good. He can write, but I think he was disappointed with the play it got. Ethan's ambitious. He was, well, he was noticeably peeved when he didn't get offered a staff job on the basis of that series. But who knows? He did so much work, maybe he can sell a magazine piece on the whole affair."

That was always the staff writer's take on things: in their eyes, we had an infinite number of markets. They didn't understand the insecurity, or the frustration of being passed over. "You wouldn't know how to contact Ethan, would you? I've run into him a few times, but I didn't get his info."

"Hold on." Brett flipped through a Rolodex and came up with a card. "I think he's trying to get into your market. The last few times I called, I got his answering machine. He had said something about spending time in Boston, and he hasn't called back. I really was sorry about that staff job." He paused, and I decided to cut him some emotional slack. Maybe he did understand what we dealt with. "The powers that be felt he was a little too, I don't know, intense. I think he's just too smart for our little burg, and got frustrated. With reason! He sure knows how to put a story together. Hey, try him anyway. He's got no reason not to talk to you." He copied down the number, a local one, and handed it to me.

"There was one other thing," I said, thinking aloud about what Dougie had said at lunch. "The counselor who went missing, Doug seemed to have been really attached to him. Do you have anything on him, even a name?"

Brett pored through the file, pulling out papers. "You mean Anna Nussbaum? Here, did I give you her number?" He handed me a page. I put it on his desk.

"You did. This was a guy, though, a Davey something?"

"Davey? Oh yeah, hold on, here it is." Brett pulled a yellow loose-leaf page out of his file and began to read down it. "Yeah, I remember him. Davey, David, Dave Sullivan? Fitzgerald? Whatever, he was a real charmer. Smooth talker and he had those Irish looks that you gals always seem to fall for."

"Blonde hair, freckles?" I asked, feeling superior. That had never been my type.

"Tall, pale, no freckles. Ah, here it is." He stopped, with his finger halfway down a page. "David Connolly. Knew it was something like that. And no, not blonde. This guy looked more like a gypsy. Dark hair, lean, but he had these really weird blue eyes, and something with his tooth." He motioned to the front of his mouth, and I froze, thinking of Connor's similar gesture as he explained the chip in his perfect grin. Connor, who had just shown up in town, right around the time this Davey must have gone missing.

It couldn't be, I told myself. The world is full of dark, handsome men, many of them wanderers, and some of them even complete with dental problems. I was just feeling silly, realizing that I was one of those "gals" who went for a particular type. Still....

"You wouldn't have a picture of him, would you?" I tried to sound nonchalant as I asked, but I could hear my voice rising.

"Hang on. We should." He didn't seem to notice how closely I was following as he made his way over to a tall file cabinet. "There was a group shot of everyone in the home, the counselors and all." I looked over his shoulder as he flipped through folders, trying not to dive into the drawer myself. He pulled one out and leafed through it. "Funny, it's not here. Someone must have checked it out."

"If it shows up, could you fax me a copy?"

"Sure. And I'm sure it will. We're pretty good about who we allow access to—these files are our life!" I smiled at that, but without putting my heart into it. The chipped tooth, the missing photo: this was getting to be too much to be coincidence. I copied out my phone numbers, and the one for the *Mail* fax, and waited while he Xeroxed some more of his files for me. I wasn't sure I needed to read anything. I had a lot of questions that needed answering, but they were the kind of questions that I had to ask in person, where I could look into a certain pair of deep blue eyes and gauge the reaction. In the meantime, it was time to pick up Violet and head back to town.

She was waiting on the curb when I pulled up to Greenleaf House, more than ready to go.

"Theda, thank the goddess. Boy, do I have news for you. First, Dougie was here! He was here, Theda. He was at the house last Monday, for all of last week. He couldn't have done it."

I'd almost forgotten that I'd sent her to check the home's sign-in sheet.

"So, he signed in?"

"He didn't sign out, actually. That's how they do it. So he never left that night." She looked at me, as I pulled into traffic. Northurst's main street had its own little rush hour. "What?"

She must have seen something on my face. "Don't tell me you don't trust that? I mean, it's not the greatest security system in the world, but I trust him."

"You trust him?"

"Yeah, I asked him about it, about where he'd been. Well, you wanted to know." Her chin pushed forward as if to make her point. "I asked him when he had last seen his mother,

actually. I made it sound like I was sympathizing with him."
No wonder she was acting so touchy; she felt guilty. "I asked
when she'd last visited him and it was, like, two weeks ago.
That makes sense; that was the night that creep jumped me.
Lillian had gone out to see him that day. Then I asked again
a little later, when the last time he saw her was. Just in case
he'd gone to visit her since then." She looked away from me,
out the window. "He knew something was up, that I wasn't
just asking to be nice. He said, 'I told you, Violet. She visited
me two weeks ago.'"

"I'm sorry, I didn't mean to turn you into a spy." I did feel
bad, but I wasn't as convinced as she was. "And you checked
the book, right?"

"I did. I snuck into the office and flipped back to last week.
I know that's not conclusive, but I believe him, Theda. He's disturbed, but he's not stupid and he does care. Even if—big *if*—
something did happen, he blew up at her or something? He
wouldn't have walked off and left her there. Even if he didn't
have it together to call 911, he'd probably have just stayed with
her until morning. You saw how he gets, he turns inward."

"You're right, it was probably nothing. I just had to check."
What she said had made sense. Dougie might have hurt
someone, but the man I had met didn't seem like he'd abandon
his mother, no matter what. Plus, I couldn't help wondering
now what role, if any, Violet's attacker had played, or if my
wild ideas about Connor had any weight to them. Still, it
didn't make sense to put complete faith in my instincts or in
Violet's, either. No matter what my young friend thought,
another call to Bill Sherman was in order. I remembered what
Brett had told me about Cambridge cops requesting information, and wondered if my friendly neighborhood detective
was already aware of Dougie, and maybe the missing counselor, too. I really didn't want to make myself sound like a

fool again: a conspiracy theorist or amateur detective. I sighed, knowing I couldn't share any of this with Violet. "Thanks for following through."

"I'm glad I did it, glad I could help and also hang with Dougie some. But spending time with him can get exhausting, you know? I mean, for both of us."

"Yeah, I do. I mean, I think I do." I knew I sounded distracted, but I didn't want her blowing up at me, if I pressed the case about Dougie. And now there was a new factor, unless of course I was just being paranoid. Or pissed—a man doesn't call and the next thing, he's an arsonist or a thief? Besides, there was traffic. "So what did you guys do, after I left?"

"Well, we talked and I got him to go out for a walk. I don't think he gets much exercise and it's good for him to get outside. I wanted to ask him how he felt, you know, give him a chance to talk about his mom?" She looked up at me and I nodded. "But he was too raw. You touched a nerve over lunch, I think. And I can't always tell how much it's good for him to air, and how much is just too stressful, so that was sort of tense. Finally, I just asked him about what he did during the day."

I wasn't really listening, but I could tell Violet needed to unload a bit, so I let her go on about the day program and the fellow residents, whose every quirk, endearing or annoying, Dougie had described to her. We were on the turnpike, half an hour back toward town when she began to slow up, and I tuned in again.

"So, Theda, solvents?"

"Huh? I'm sorry. My mind was wandering."

"I noticed. You're going nearly eighty by the way."

She was right and I eased off. I wanted to get back to Cambridge as soon as possible, but I also wanted to do it in one piece. We passed the first signs for Worcester. Civilization, I thought. Hallelujah.

"Now, what were you asking? Something about solvents?"

"Yeah, I feel like a fool. Two years of art school and I still can't mix colors without making a mess. I was wondering if you have any turpentine or any other kind of paint thinner, something to get this gunk out of jeans."

I glanced over and saw what she meant. A particularly hideous dead-flesh pink was splashed across her thigh like a fake bruise. Any other color and maybe she'd have gotten away with it.

"Wow, that's a real Patti Wright hue, isn't it?" I couldn't help laughing.

"Oh, great, thanks." She laughed too and examined the spot. "No, it's not bright enough, is it? I could say it's a fashion statement: baby-puke puce, or something. Market these as one-of-a-kind designer pants. But they're my favorite pair."

"And that won't wash out?" The splotch did look awfully thick.

"No, it's oil paint." She picked at the spot, and I could see that not much was coming loose.

Someone had been talking about oil paint recently. Connor again. I couldn't think about him and tried, instead to remember what he'd said. All I could recall was that you needed particular solvents to remove it. "Well, I don't have any paint thinner on hand, but Pearl Paint will still be open when we get back."

She sat there silent and I understood. "And I can spring for some turpentine."

"Thanks, Theda. You've been great. If I could just borrow about three bucks, I'd be grateful. I don't mean to be such a mooch. In fact, I was going to offer to chip in for the gas but then lunch actually came to more than I expected."

"Don't worry about it. That lunch was great, especially the fries." I was still chuckling over "baby-puke puce" and pulled out my wallet. She fished out a few singles and handed it back. "One more assignment about wedding budgets and I'll almost be in the black for this month!"

"Wedding budgets?"

"Oh, yeah." I gave her the rundown about my glamorous freelance assignments. I couldn't believe I hadn't before. She was a great audience, laughing at my impersonation of my editor Tim and sympathizing with my woes.

"The worst part is that most of this stuff just seems to belong to another life, you know?" I'd gotten onto some of the home renovation stories that I covered. "I mean, do you know anyone who has a budget of thirty-thou just to redo their bathroom?"

"Ask me if I know anyone who has thirty thou, period." She sighed and sunk back into her seat. The splash of paint on her leg caught my eye again as she rested her knees up on the dashboard.

"So how did that happen?" The image of the tree-shaded house where we'd left Dougie came into my mind. "They're not painting Greenleaf House in that awful color, are they?"

"No, no. The restoration work is totally done now." She continued worrying at the spot with her thumbnail. The paint was dry and hard. "This was from Dougie's personal set of paints. Some of his stuff is actually pretty powerful. Some of it's really disturbing."

"They let him work with oils?"

"Yeah, he's not a kid. He's just messed up."

"I know, I know, I'm sorry. I guess I was just surprised that there wouldn't be a house rule about 'watercolors only' or something. Besides, those paints are expensive, aren't they?"

"Tell me about it." She sighed. "No, these are the ones that his old counselor left. They were in some closet that the fire didn't touch. Dougie got them when he got out of the hospital."

When his counselor left? Had Dougie's counselor been the

one to go missing, or was this some more benign job change? Was this another Connor connection?

"Theda, what is it?" Violet looked over and I realized my foot was pressing down once more on the accelerator.

"It may be nothing, Violet. It may be nothing. I've got some things to think through."

Connor. All I could think of was Connor. But it didn't seem fair to accuse anyone, not yet. Especially when he might be on my mind for other reasons. Still, I couldn't leave Violet entirely in the dark. "I think—I'm not sure, but I do have a suspicion— that I might know who ripped off Greenleaf House."

"You do?" She leaned toward me, almost pushing herself out of her seat. "Theda, if you know something—well, those guys are really hurting without that money."

I waved her back. "Sit down, Violet, sit down. I don't know anything. I have some suspicions, but I might also be completely off base." I really didn't want to explain what could sound like an obsession. "I need to think about it."

The whole truth was that I needed to sit down in some quiet place and try to reason through everything I'd heard, try to put it in context with my own emotions, but Violet accepted my excuse. We rode on without speaking, each lost in our thoughts as the miles whipped by. Soon Violet was able to get a Boston college station on the radio and we caught a local music show that ended just as I pulled off for the Cambridge-Allston exit. The next DJ up started a reggae tune, and Violet started flipping around, searching for more rock. At some point a lyric seemed to spark a memory and she'd started to tell me something. She was so excited, all I had to do was nod assent, and that let me stay lost in thought. I wanted to see Connor, as soon as I could. I wanted him to have an explanation for his ready money. For his oil paints and for where he came from. For everything.

"So, do you think you can come by?" Violet must have been going on for about twenty minutes, all twisted up in her seat like she was ready to jump out, when I tuned her in again.

"What? I'm sorry. What did you say?"

"To the house tonight. I figure we've got not quite twenty-four hours."

"The house? I'm sorry, Violet, I've been in a whole other world."

"I should have known when you didn't interrupt me to tell me about the danger, how I was going to be busted." She was smiling. For the first time I noticed that she looked happy. Triumphant almost.

"Wait, start at the beginning." We were pulling into Central Square.

"Hey, drop me at the Mug, okay?" I nodded, waiting for her to continue. "I knew there was a second thing I had to tell you." We pulled up in front of the coffee shop and I turned to her. She had my full attention.

"Well, a couple of things Dougie said made me think. You know how he kept saying his mom took care of everything?" She was looking me full in the face, making sure I was listening this time. I was, and nodded again. "Well, he didn't just mean in the past. He meant in the future, too. I asked him, Theda. And he remembers! He remembers her telling him, making him repeat it so he'd get it right. Lillian wrote a will, Theda. She wrote a will that will take care of Dougie, the house, and all the cats, too. And that will is in the house somewhere. It's got to be. And before those cats are put to sleep tomorrow, I'm going to find it."

"Wait a minute." I wasn't following her logic, and the cars honking at my stopped vehicle didn't help. "He just told you this now?" She nodded. Had she mentioned this on the drive? If so, I'd been too distracted to hear. "He'd always told me she'd made plans for him," Violet went on. "And I'll confess, I'd been hoping there was something like this, in all that mess of an old house."

"So now you're saying you weren't looking for clues?" I was finding it hard to credit her changing stories.

She shrugged. "That too. I still think the answer has to be there, somewhere." I remembered the medic-alert pendant. I'd never told Violet about finding it, I realized with a flash of guilt. She'd been right about that one thing at least, and deserved to be heard out.

The excited girl hadn't noticed my thoughtful pause. "You didn't get to know Lillian. I did. She always said that everything was in there, that if anything happened to her I'd find the answer at her place. Then today, when I was talking to Dougie about his mom, it all came out. It was like he'd just remembered the word: will. He said it like I should have known what he meant before. I don't know, maybe I just hadn't been listening to him."

Her words echoed my own thoughts so closely I turned to stare at her. "Are you sure we're not being taken up by wishful thinking here?" I had to ask.

She shook her head. "He was really clear on that. I mean, clear for him."

Knowing Dougie's tenuous connection with reality, I still couldn't discount the wish factor. "If she really did write a will, wouldn't it be filed with the city or something?" Violet raised her one pierced eyebrow. "Oh yeah, Lillian didn't trust the state."

Someone honked behind me and I started, almost plowing into the car in front of me. I shifted into Park as Violet got out and reached for her bag. So that's why she'd been so happy all the way back. I didn't dare point out the obvious: that Lillian's unease with authority might have extended to whatever rigamarole you have to go through to make documents legal. Or that Dougie's connection to reality could have taken a big detour through wishful thinking. Nor any of the other options, that any will might have gone the way of all trash or been shredded by one of her feline wards, or might just never be found. What she'd posed was at best a slim chance. But she'd become a friend, and I was done with letting my friendships slide. I'd help her if I could.

"So you're going over there now?"

She shook her head. "You really have been out of it, haven't you?" I smiled back and shrugged, guilt acknowledged. "No, I've got that fund raiser at Goddess Books to play. Wish it wasn't too late to cop out, but that will just be two sets, a few hours. And first I've got to check in with Laurel, the manager." She motioned to the coffeehouse behind her. "I may not make it in for my shift tomorrow. But I'll be at Lillian's by midnight latest—if you want to help."

"Yeah, I do." I thought of those cats, caged and waiting. "I've got a few things of my own to take care of, so, yeah, that'll work."

I was wondering where Connor would be right now. "Midnight sounds fine. I'll be there. If there's a will, we'll find it."

"There is a will." She stepped back, a broad grin on her face as she waved me on. "And we'll find the way!"

SEVENTEEN

SEVERAL MESSAGES and one rather upset cat greeted me upon my return. A plant, the last of my slow-dying succulents, had been overturned, its ceramic pot shattered and its mica-flecked soil scattered all over my living room rug. Musetta seemed to know she'd done something wrong and kept darting back and forth, unsure whether to make nice by rubbing against my shins or to try to hide the damage. I picked her up and rubbed her neck to console her. That plant had been on its way out for months, but the pot had probably made a fearsome crash. She rewarded me with a hearty purr as I turned my back on the mess of shards and soil and hit the message replay button.

"Hi girl! It's Tess." I scrambled for a pen to write down her new number. "There's a party tonight over in the South End. If you wanna come, let me know?" I knew I wouldn't make it, but I made a mental note to call her as soon as I came up for air. I was glad she was back in town.

"Theda? This is Bill Sherman. Would you call me, please?" I should've known that one was coming. Well, I'd dropped off the pendant and had some new information for him next time we touched base. Of course, it would've been easier to deliver it if I had also had the missing key he'd requested.

"Hey, Theda. This is Shel on the copy desk. We've got a few questions in your Central Café piece." I groaned and put the cat down, reaching instead for a pencil to record the *Mail* extension that Shelly, one of my old desk colleagues, had left.

I didn't have time for this, not now. But I'd spent too long on the desk myself to duck a call. Tracking down writers was a thankless task when deadline loomed and questions or inconsistencies—like a name spelled two different ways, neither of which could be verified—meant the difference between clean copy and a sloppy section.

"Miss Krakow? This is Sally Hudson. Would you call me? I need to talk to you about something." Just my luck. I'd filed that story yesterday and I'd bet anything the Tory Row matron was calling to change her mind about it. She'd say she was wrong about half the prices or the kind of wood, or that she'd decided she'd rather not have any photos run after all. According to every rule of journalism I'd ever learned, once you identify yourself to a source and that person agrees to an interview, everything the source tells you is on the record. Nothing can be recanted. But with service features and other "soft" stories, we tended to be more courteous. We weren't going to force our way into some tony house to photograph cherry-wood shelves over the objections of the homeowner. We weren't serving the public good by insisting that a price quoted for satin-finish paint not be altered. But such easing of the rules, especially for people who did not understand or respect the concept of deadlines—or working journalists, for that matter—had made more than one story like this unnecessarily complicated. Well, that call could wait for tomorrow, too.

I found my printout of the café story and dialed Shelly's extension. She was up against deadline—her section had to ship by six-thirty—so we kept the usual chitchat to a minimum.

"Okay, I've got it," I found myself telling her. "The pianist's last name was definitely Burch, with a 'u,' and the instrument she took out was a kalimba. That's with a 'k.' So are you playing out these days?"

"Kalimba with a 'k,' got it. Isn't that some kind of thumb

piano? Oh, never mind. And yeah, I'm just doing my songs
solo now. I may have a Wednesday night residency coming
up, maybe for a month at the Friar, maybe at Amphibian.
Maybe I should call Carole, too. This acoustic café thing
sounds just my speed. Anyway, I'll let you know."

"Do, I'll try to make it, wherever you are. And, yeah, here
it is." I found the answer to her last question in my notes.
"Cover is three dollars. All of the door goes to pay the performers. That it?"

"That's it, Theda. Thanks and see you around."

I hung up and tried to collect my thoughts. Violet's discov-
eries rattled around my head, and I wanted to get back to what
I'd been thinking about before we'd headed home. When I'd
left the *Eagle,* the similarities linking Connor and the mysterious Davey had seemed too numerous to be pure coincidence. I'd decided then that I had to track Connor down and
suss out the truth. But I was going on little sleep and lots of
caffeine, and a vague ringing in my ears reminded me just how
zonked I was. In my hypercaffeinated state, was I merely
creating an excuse to talk to Connor, to see him face to face
and find out if the electricity I had felt on Saturday was
mutual? Wasn't it possible, even likely, that in this state my
imagination had gotten away from me? I tried to think the
links through—the oil paints, the ready money, the mysterious past, the dark Irish good looks marred only by a chipped
tooth. In the quiet calm of my apartment, none of them held
up. How expensive were oil paints, and how common? I didn't
know. Had I ever followed up with Connor about his roots?
No, I'd been too busy telling him about mine. And as for
ready money, well, we had been on a date. Maybe he'd been
living on ramen noodles all week to be able to pay my way
on a Saturday night. As for tall, dark ladykillers, why was I
swallowing the opinion of a married man? Davey could

resemble Rumpelstiltskin more than he did Connor. The truth was that all the links were vague, just fuel to my overtired, overheated imagination. I'd just ask him, next time I saw him, what his last day job had been. That's all I had to do.

Musetta jumped on the sofa next to me and started purring again. Leaning against me with her solid little bulk, she seemed to be willing me to stay. Warm, comfortable, and with a living backrest, she soon quieted into sleep. How could I disturb her? I'd just rest my eyes for a minute, my hand right by the soft rise and fall of her back.

The room was dark when I sat back up, the long shadows of twilight stretching to cover the street outside. How long had I been asleep? More than an hour, obviously, and longer than I had to spare. But the nap had done me good—I felt sharper, more alert. And still suspicious. I tested the idea as if it were a broken tooth of my own. Yup, there were still too many similarities between the missing mystery man and Connor for me to be completely comfortable. Besides—ah, here was a sore spot!—I really did want to talk to him, face to face.

I checked the clock. If I were going to meet Violet by midnight, I'd need to find Connor soon. He'd probably be in one of Ralph's usual haunts. Then, I'd be able to go over to Lillian's and help Violet with a clear purpose. Briefly, I considered calling Bill Sherman back, but it was too late for office hours. Besides, I had no doubt that he would keep after me about that missing key, and he certainly wouldn't condone my rummaging through the old house with Violet. I didn't think it likely that any will would surface, not in time to rescue those poor cats anyway. But Violet had become a friend, and I owed it to her to help, even if the search proved to be futile. I'd call Bill back first thing tomorrow.

No reason not to do some of my legwork via Ma Bell though. I reached for the phone, disturbing Musetta, who peeped in protest, found Ralph's number and dialed. He wasn't there, and I didn't want to leave a message for Connor on his voice mail, so I started thinking. Where would either of them be on a Tuesday night? What was happening?

The Goddess Bookstore happening didn't seem likely, not given what I knew about those guys. Then it hit me: Tuesday's Blues. The Tuesday open blues jam, a weekly happening at the Keg, might be a place to start. It wasn't particularly hip, but Kate, the current owner, had begun to draw a crowd thanks to the chicken wing and spare-rib barbecue she offered for the three-dollar cover. If Connor really was a broke artist, he'd probably have heard about it, and I knew Ralph was partial to barbecue. At any rate, someone there might know something. I stood up, stretched and reached for my boots, only to be tackled by Musetta.

"Yow, that hurts!" She had thrown her paws around my ankle and although she hadn't used her claws, she had then bitten me, just hard enough to break the skin. "You're feeling frisky." I reached for a pencil and waggled it enticingly. She eyed it for a moment, then jumped for my hand. At least this time she didn't bite.

"You want to play, don't you?" She'd scampered away a few feet and then run back to bat at my boot, which I'd slipped over my vulnerable toes. "You don't want me to go out, do you little one?" She looked up at me eloquently and I picked her up for one more quick cuddle. "Momma's got some investigating to do, kitty. But don't worry, we'll have a good game of kill the cork when I return."

FIRST STOP, if I was going to make a night of it, was the Mug Shot. Violet had been and gone, but her replacement set me up with a double-shot latte to go. With it I got another surprise: Ethan was sitting at one of the tables, staring out the front window. "Hey, I didn't know you were an addict, too!" I smiled.

I must have broken into his reverie. He looked up, distracted, but managed a smile. "Nice place. Just found out about it. You're a regular?"

I held up the tall, warm carry-out cup in confirmation, and he motioned for me to join him.

"Welcome to the neighborhood," I said, taking a seat. It seemed churlish to run off. "So are you settling in around here?"

"I'm looking around." Catching my glance at the empty mug in front of him and a plastic stirrer that seemed to have been bent and knotted more than pure utility allowed, he must have realized that this answer didn't suffice. "I'm at the Y, living there and out of my car," he confessed, folding the stirrer into a napkin. "Trying to figure out what to do next."

"Trying to get out of news, right?" Mentally, I kicked myself for not taking the initiative to get in touch. I knew how difficult breaking in could be.

"I guess so, I guess so." He looked past me, out the window. "I'm fed up with everything. But I want to be careful about what I do next. Maybe I just need a good story to follow. Like, whatever happened with that old lady whose body you found?" He turned to me suddenly, and I found myself drawing back.

"Lillian, the cat lady?" He nodded. I was being selfish; he knew Lillian was my story. But I had to be honest. "I'd just met her. I'd been planning on a feature, you know, because of all her cats. But I don't write about murder."

His eyes narrowed. "Murder?"

"Well, to be strictly accurate, I can't really say." Time to backtrack to reality. "The cops are still calling it an accidental death, but my friend Violet is convinced that there was some foul play."

"Now why would she think that?" Ethan's eyes shone. Maybe he was a natural born newshound. "What can you tell me? Why does anyone think it's murder?"

I really didn't want to revisit that day. "You should talk to Violet. She knew the woman who died much better than I did, and she works here."

He paused, waiting.

"You can't miss her. Five-one, bright purple hair. Hard to miss."

"Oh, yeah. I was wondering about her. She's in a band, right? I thought I saw her at the memorial service."

I vaguely recalled seeing him that morning, seeing his glasses actually. Poor guy, that's probably all anyone ever saw. "You were there?"

He nodded. "Yeah, I didn't want to bother you. I mean, we'd just met. I remembered thinking she was in charge. I really wanted to talk to her afterward, but everyone took off."

The trip to the shelter had been open to all, but maybe he'd felt overwhelmed: a bunch of kids, folks from the neighborhood who already knew each other. Then it struck me. He'd wanted to talk to Violet alone. She was cute. Maybe he didn't realize she wasn't into guys. How could I tell him? "Um, may I ask why you're interested?"

"It's a good story," he shrugged, and pushed back his chair. Stared at the ground, like a little kid telling a fib. I must have hit a nerve. "I mean, I wasn't sure then if you were going to do anything with it. And there was obviously a lot of feeling there. She sounded like an interesting personality. Hey, from what you're saying now, well, maybe it's a real murder mystery with tons of local color." I was off the hook from meddling into his private life. "Do you think they've found anything yet?" He picked up the stirrer again, worked on tying one more knot. "Old enemies? Abandoned lovers? Whatever?"

"Fifty-year-old crime of passion? I doubt it. In fact, I don't think there's even going to be any official follow-up at all unless Violet can convince everyone that there even was a crime."

His hands were still again. "What's her stake in it?"

He was staring at me, and I had to remind myself: this is a guy who has spent most of his life ferreting out facts. Plus, he's desperate for a meaty story. But Violet's secrets weren't mine to share. "I'm not sure, really. It could just be that she liked the old lady too much to let go, and she knows the family." What was the word Jim Brett had used? Ethan was definitely "intense." I smiled, trying to lighten the mood. "For a guy who wants to leave hard news behind, you seem very focused on this."

He shrugged, and I remembered the rest of my conversation with the staff writer.

"Sorry about the Northurst job."

"You heard about that?" He was suddenly transfixed by a small coffee stain on the table. He had to be embarrassed.

I sympathized. "Yeah, editors! They love it when they get our work and don't have to pay benefits, or a regular salary for that matter."

"There was more than that going on out there, Theda. I deserved that position. Earned it. Bastards!" He spit out the word, and I realized he was angry rather than ashamed. "I was digging up more on each story than their regular staff guy ever dreamed of. Not that he'd bother even trying."

Jim Brett had seemed nice enough to me. "He actually said good things about you. Maybe it was just a personality conflict—"

"Yeah, I have one. Not that they ever gave me any respect." He was still staring at the Formica tabletop, but I could see the tension, the knot of muscle, working along his cheek. Well, often enough I'd gotten steamed about Ralph, mulled over how much better I would do if I had the position of the

Mail's staff music critic. Such resentment went with the territory. As freelancers, we had to work harder for our stories than the staffers. We had to hit a home run every time, and we received neither the perks nor the security. But Ethan wasn't letting it go.

"Brett and those editors. They're all humps. I was getting them stories they never would have found themselves, and they knew it. They had it out for me."

"I can relate." I couldn't really—his anger seemed a little too extreme—but the gesture worked. He looked up at me, as if seeing me again suddenly, and for a moment he smiled. I did, too, and became aware of a foam mustache on my upper lip. I reached for a napkin, and a way out of a touchy subject. "I read your stories—at least some of them." I continued, wiping away the milky residue. "The in-depth on the halfway house? Great piece."

He nodded, accepting the compliment. "There was more that I couldn't put in. Nothing solid yet, but at least one of those guys was very bad."

"The counselor who went missing?" I wasn't ready to share my suspicions about Connor being that guy, not yet. But he nodded in assent. "Sounds like you have your story."

"Not for the Northurst guys. I want to write—really write—but I have no desire to go back to that particular hole."

"Well, maybe you won't have to." He was silent, staring out the window again. I'd lost him.

"If you're waiting for Violet, she's not working tonight."

"No?"

"She's playing a benefit over at Goddess Books. I'll be seeing her later though. Shall I tell her you're looking for her?" I drained the rest of my latte. Time to get to work.

"No, no." He waved me away, once more in another world. "I'll catch up with her. Don't worry."

"THEDA! LONG TIME, no see!"

"I know, I know, I hibernated this winter." Kate crushed me to her ample bosom in a hug, and I patted her back till she released me. Exuberant as she always was, I didn't want to explain the whole season of loss, from Rick to James. We'd need a full day and boxes of tissues for that.

"What's up with you?" I tried to deflect her attention.

"Same old same old." She gestured around the bar and restaurant she'd inherited and, despite her modesty, turned into a thriving business. Her uncle's bar might have lost some of its former regulars, the nurse-a-beer-for-three-hours crowd, but these days the Keg was packed almost every night. This early I saw two old-timers up by the long oval bar, too, so I gathered her policy of not charging a cover before nine had staunched the alienation of the older crowd.

"You're too modest. This place looks great." It did. The paneled walls of the big, main room had given way to paint, with framed black-and-white photos of musicians lending the high-ceilinged space the feel of a gallery.

"My little touches." Kate blushed, clearly pleased, and led me over to one of the newer photos. "Shot right here, three weeks ago."

"It's amazing." I was being honest. The way the photographer had captured the light shining on the guitarist's face put his straining mouth and neck muscles in high relief, emphasizing the passion of his playing. His hands, curled around the neck of his instrument and the pick he held, came forward in the composition as well, making a second almost as expressive focus for the eye. "Who shot it?"

"Connor Davies. He's new in town. Didn't even have any fancy equipment."

I froze for a moment, and Kate continued.

"Very sweet guy." That smile and the twinkle in her eye showed that his charm had worked on her, too.

"I know him," I managed to stutter out. "I didn't realize he did photography."

"I think he also paints. A renaissance man, you know? He wants to set up his own studio; says he's just trying to raise some funds. He said I was his first sale in town."

I didn't know what to say; the emotion in the photograph seemed so honest, so direct. Could someone this sensitive really have ripped off a bunch of mentally ill people? I had to see him, to see his face, in order to judge for myself. But when I did, would I be able to ask the hard questions?

Kate had continued talking and I caught the tail end of a sentence. "He didn't want much, so I gave him trade."

I looked over at her rosy, smiling face. My mouth must have dropped open.

"Barbecue, Theda, barbecue." She patted my shoulder and started to laugh." What did you think? Plus, he's on my permanent house list. I want that boy around. He's good for business!"

I regathered my wits. "Tonight. Has he been here tonight?"

"Not yet, honey, but maybe he'll show. Joey's putting the food out now. Why don't you get a plate of ribs and settle down? The first band's about to start. Nice kids, South Shore, but the harp player really kicks."

THE RIBS WERE a little sticky, with one of those ketchup-based sauces that are a bit too sweet for my taste. That didn't stop me from polishing off two plates' worth by the time the first set by the talented suburbanites wound to a close. Maybe I was eating so much because I was nervous, but I need not have worried. Although I recognized a few faces in the crowd, neither Ralph nor Connor showed. The buffet ended at ten, so I drained my Diet Coke, the third of the night—I wanted to stay sharp—and left a few bucks on the table. Was I being silly? Wasn't this a wild goose chase? I called Ralph's number again, and this time left a message, asking either of them to call my cell. But I had two hours before it would be time to meet Violet, so I decided I might as well continue. Waving goodbye to Kate, I retrieved my car and headed over to the Casbah.

The difference between the clubs could be counted by degrees. I'd left the house with a sweater on, worn it during my hour at Kate's, and hadn't thought to leave it in the car. I should have. The Casbah was warm and damp with flesh.

"Hey, Theda!" Mark, a drummer with the regulation tattoos all over his thickly muscled arms, waved to me. I'd written about his band a few months before. He was sitting with his girlfriend and another couple as I walked over.

"Hi, Mark, Susan." Nods all around. "Do you know Ralph from the *Mail* or his friend Connor?"

"I know Ralph, why?"

"Have you seen him tonight?"

"No, sorry." The three other faces looking up at me smiled, but clearly none of them had anything to add. There were no extra chairs, and besides I hadn't been invited. I thanked them and walked on through the club.

"Nick, hey. Where's Lucy?" My garage-loving friend had emerged from the men's room and twirled me around in a hug.

"She's in the music room." He released me. "You coming in?"

"I'm actually looking for someone." He paused, waiting. "You know Ralph, the critic from the *Mail?* I'm trying to get in touch with his friend Connor—tall guy, thin, dark hair?"

"Sorry I can't help you, love. Come in later if you want to dance."

I didn't, and he was gone. I squeezed into the bar to order my fourth Diet Coke of the night and caught myself tapping the bar with my fingernails. My skin was crawling, as if someone was watching me. The caffeine was beginning to make me jittery; without all those greasy ribs, my ears would probably be ringing from the buzz. I put the thick bar mug down, pushed it away. Time to move on, at least to free up the bar space.

"Suze, hey, what's up?" I was happy to see my old roommate standing in line for the bathroom.

"Theda! Oh, hey, not much. How's Rick?" It had been a while.

"We broke up." Saying that didn't hurt anymore. "He moved to Arizona, actually. Can you believe it?"

"Wow, sorry." A stall opened up and she took it. I grabbed the next and when I came out, she was gone. A quick perusal of the room revealed a few more familiar faces, but none was the one I was looking for. Could that be Ethan over there? I cringed and closed my eyes, realizing that I didn't want to hear more stories of how he'd been screwed over. But when I opened them, the sullen writer was nowhere in sight. Suddenly I felt very tired. I was imagining things, and that feeling that someone was looking at me returned. Fatigue, age, and now paranoia? What did I expect, cruising the rock clubs, anyway, at thirty-three, looking for a guy I'd made out with once? What kind of connection could I have made with someone based primarily on volume and beer?

That way madness lies, I told myself. Besides, I had legitimate questions for Connor, in addition to my romantic longings. Pushing off the wall, I made my way through to the back room, where Ted the bouncer waved me in.

"Arr-arr-arr-arr-arr." Okay, that wasn't what the band was shouting, but that's how it hit me, the volume amped up strong enough to blow my hair back. "Arr-arr-arr!"

Through the crowd I could make out Nick and Lucy, both jumping in the peculiar head-bouncing dance they'd made their own. It wasn't pretty, but I knew if I could see their faces, they'd both be beaming. Somehow they'd found each other. They'd bonded in a way Rick and I never had. Maybe it was because Rick would never dance. Maybe I should have known from that. I went up to the bar.

"Diet—no, club soda."

Kelly, the back bartender, raised her eyebrows. I nodded. It was too loud to explain fatigue, age, and a pointless quest. She garnished my plastic cup with a wedge of lime and I tipped gratefully, glad to have something in my hand as I continued on through the room. I couldn't shake the feeling that eyes were following me, and turned around. A tall figure over by the soundboard looked familiar, and I headed over.

"Hey!"

"Sorry." At least it was only club soda, I thought as I shook my drink off my hand and arm. The hulking shape bounding past me had already disappeared into the dancing mob. I looked back to where I'd thought I'd seen something, but the tall figure had disappeared.

"Was there a tall guy here, black hair, like a minute ago?" I yelled into the ear of the band's manager, pushing one of her braids out of the way to get through.

"What?" She was standing behind a table of merchandise—tee shirts, CDs, bumper stickers—at the far back of the club, but the volume was still deafening.

"Tall guy? Dark hair?"

"Sorry!" I didn't know if that meant she hadn't heard me or hadn't seen anyone like that, but I didn't think I'd get anything else from her. I smiled and made my escape.

"Loud, huh?" Ted the doorman didn't look surprised to see me emerge so soon.

"Oh man, and I forgot my earplugs! Who are they?" I stood to the side as he collected five-dollar bills from a steady stream of black-clad patrons.

"Noise Toy, from Rochester. Not your thing?"

"I'm too old, Ted." He didn't contradict me, and I made my way back to the bar.

"Risa! What's up?" I actually found a seat. "No, no beer tonight. Just club soda."

"You on the wagon?" She put a clear mug in front of me, but waved away my money.

"Just tired. I'm actually looking for someone. You seen Ralph's friend Connor here tonight?"

She wiped the bar. "I thought I did, earlier. Did you check the music room?" So that had been him!

"He's not there anymore."

"Can't help you then, hon. Gotta work." She moved off down the bar, leaving me to my unwanted soda, looking out over a room of strangers.

"You know, you might try Iggy's." I looked up. Risa had returned to my end of the bar. "I shouldn't be saying this." She shot a glance over at Lou, the manager, who held court about five feet away. "But they've got a killer bill tonight. That's where all the over-thirty crowd is probably hanging."

So it wasn't just me. I thanked her and grabbed my sweater from where I'd stashed it, behind a pillar. Next stop, Iggy's.

IF I'D THOUGHT the Casbah was crowded, I'd obviously not been out in a while. Not at the right places, anyway. Iggy's was so packed, I'd had to park three blocks away despite the emptiness of the Financial District neighborhood at this hour. The sounds emanating from the club served as a sort of wavering beacon, growing loud as the door opened, then muffled again as it shut.

"Seven dollars." Iggy's had come up in the scene since this winter, and I wasn't known here as a writer. I forked over the cover and offered the back of my hand for its third stamp of the night. I'd remembered to leave my sweater behind, and was grateful. The room I stepped into was as hot as a sauna, packed nearly to capacity as far back as the bar. It was going to take me a while to work through this crowd, and my eyes were already gritty from cigarette smoke and lack of sleep. Time for more caffeine.

"Diet Coke?"

The bartender filled a plastic cup without looking up, and I pushed a few singles over the wet wood. The cool helped, and I held the sweating plastic to my brow. The band didn't hurt either. Unlike the Cashbah's hardcore attack, this trio had more of a slow grind going, its punk roots made deliberate and weighty as a sledgehammer. I leaned against the bar and closed my eyes. No chance of falling asleep here, not standing up anyway, but the music washed over me. This is what drew me back, I realized as one song gave way to another.

My reverie was broken by a sharp jab. I caught my drink from falling and looked over to where the knock had come from. The couple necking next to me had grabbed each other, and a flying elbow was oblivious to my bare arm. Love, that's right, I thought. Careless love. But I took my cue to begin working through the room, starting down the bar and then weaving through the crowd.

"Hey, watch out." I'd stumbled, too tired to keep up with the heaving crowd, and this time it was me who spilled my drink, all over a young guy in leather and his goth-looking girl.

"Sorry, man. Sorry." I made feeble brushing motions at the wet spot on his biker jacket.

"Bitch." I could read the word in the sneer of his girlfriend's lip rings, but what could I say in response?

"Sorry," I repeated, to the space they'd left. Not wanting to repeat the mishap, I finished what remained in my cup and maneuvered over to the side bar to leave it. There it was, a glint of light. A flash as if someone was shining a lens on me. But when I looked up, it was just the mirror that ran along the back of the bar. Sunken eyes, floating on huge bags, stringy hair curling every which way, no wonder I was spooked. I placed my cup down and turned away. The music seemed to have lost its power.

"Theda, hey babe. Whatcha doing?" Like a vision, Tess appeared before me, as cool and calm as a young tree at an oasis. "You want to hit that party later?"

"Oh, Tess, I can't. You wouldn't believe everything that's been happening." I almost threw myself against her.

"Come here, girlfriend." She wrapped one arm around my shoulder and led me over to a corner. Somehow it seemed quiet in her presence. "Okay, what's wrong?" Her dark brown eyes looked straight into mine. "What's going on?"

I wanted to tell her, wanted to get the whole damned mess off my mind. But what would make a complicated story over coffee would be incomprehensible in a club. So instead I just said I was looking for someone.

"That guy Connor. You met him the other night, at the Casbah? Was he around here tonight?"

"Why are you looking for this man—and looking so wrought up about it? I don't like the feel of this, Theda." She put her long fingers under my chin and raised my face up to hers. "What does this man have on you? Why are you so hung up on him?"

"No, no." I shook my head. If I hadn't have been so tired, I would have laughed. Her questions were the same ones I'd been asking only a day before. Now such different ones were crowding them out of my head. But there was no time, and I lacked the energy. Instead, I pulled away. "I don't know him well enough for that." At some point later I'd tell her about our one date, time enough if all worked out and he was innocent of my paranoid suspicions. "I need to talk to him about something else. Something about a story I'm working on." I hated lying to Tess, but it was the quickest explanation I could come up with.

"Well, I haven't seen him, girlfriend. Not here."

"What about Ralph? They hang together a lot."

She looked at me for another moment, considering. "No, not that scumbag either. Look, I don't like the sound of this and I don't like the way you're looking. But if you're set on finding either one of those guys, they might be at that party, the one I called you about. It's happening over on Thayer Street. One of the old lofts that's going condo. I think it started soon after dark, and I know it'll go on till dawn. That's Ralph's scene, at least it was the last time I was in town. You might check that out. But maybe you'll wait for me? I've got to talk to these guys after their set. It might mean a gig, but I could head out right after."

"Thanks, Tess." The idea was appealing, but I didn't have the time. "I can't wait." She took my shoulders and looked once more into my face, but I shook her off with a smile. "I'll probably be there and gone by the time you show up. Home asleep. But we'll do something soon, I promise." With one last appraising glance and a hug, she let me go. I wanted nothing more than to go home to bed. Or, if I couldn't, to hang with her in this calm corner, and let the music soothe me. But I had questions I needed answers to, and so I made my way to the door, out into the relative quiet of the city at night.

I HADN'T ASKED TESS for the loft's street address, but I didn't really need one. The area had changed a lot since I first started clubbing, the industrial bearing works and paint wholesalers giving way to galleries and high-priced housing. But the big brick buildings still had a style of their own, evoking the

Boston of a century before, when industry and shipping more
than high tech or higher education had been the city's claim
to fame. This end of Thayer still grew quiet at night, at least
during the week, and once I parked it was easy to locate the
party from the sound and light that drifted down four stories
to the street.

There was an elevator, a huge one for loading machinery, but
I opted for the stairs that wouldn't announce my arrival in such
a grand manner. Two flights up, I started to regret the decision,
but then I was there and a door opened onto red light and music,
the sound of laughter and in the distance a bottle breaking.

"Hey."

"Hey." I nodded to the slumped figure that leaned against
the wall. A large plastic mayonnaise jar by his side was
labeled "Donations," so I shoved a few bucks through its wide
neck and walked on by.

The wall he was supporting was a fake one, I noticed,
erected as a baffle to subdivide the room. It ended as soon as
I turned the corner and entered the loft's dim main space, lit
as much by the continuous highway construction outside as
by the few red bulbs someone had plugged into a standing
lamp. Over by the windows, a wall of glass divided into small
dirty panes, a couch covered by a tattered chenille throw
invited me to sit, or even sleep. But the real action was farther
back, where I could see the silhouettes of dancers. They were
illuminated by a primitive stage spot, red again, focused on
the two blues women I'd seen on Saturday. The music they
were grinding out was intimate and low, a sexier, lazier sound
than they'd been working on the weekend, and all the dancers
were moving slowly. Tuesday, in the middle of the city, but
there had to be forty people here at least. After midnight I
knew the crowd would double.

I listened for a while, enjoying the seductive ebb and flow

of reverb, and realized I was drifting off on my feet. I started walking to the makeshift bandstand, the better to view the assembled throng. Dark hair, but—no, in the moving spot I saw the reflection of glasses. Not Connor.

"Excuse me. Excuse me." I seemed to have two left feet, tripping over dancers and earning myself some hard glares. Nobody looked familiar anymore; nobody looked up at my voice. I reached the end of the room and turned around. From the edge of the stage, caught in those red spotlights, everyone's face seemed flat. The warm blood-tint made them all appear strangely cold, their eyes dead. But someone somewhere was alive. Again, I felt eyes on me, like a butterfly pinned to a mat. I turned away.

"Beer?" I looked up and saw Ralph. Dear old Ralph. I could have hugged him.

"Ralph! Oh, no thanks. Do they have soda?" He shrugged and I looked past him, to where two large plastic garbage cans were filled with ice and cans. I found something with sugar and caffeine and snapped the pop top. The cold alone was refreshing.

"What brings you here?" I was watching Ralph, but he was looking elsewhere.

"Oh nothing. Not much." He was watching the dancers, though I couldn't tell if he'd picked out his prey for the evening.

"Is Connor here?" I tried to sound casual and followed my question with a large swallow of soda.

"He was, somewhere." Ralph looked at me. "You know, you should really let him pursue you, Theda."

I choked on my drink and coughed, and he had the graciousness to pat my back. "Here, put that down." He took my can and placed it on the speaker behind us and turned back to me. "Now breathe."

"I'm breathing. I'm breathing." I bent over, my hands on

my knees, the air returning to my lungs. "But what did you mean by that?"

"We were out at some other clubs earlier, knew this wasn't really going to heat up until midnight, and someone—that bartender at the Casbah maybe?—said you were looking for him. No man wants to be chased, Theda."

"Thanks, Ralph. It's not what you think." He shot me a look and I reached back for my drink. I needed to cool the hot blush that had risen up my chest. I took a long swallow. "But anyway, is he here?"

"Can't help you if I don't know," said Ralph, his attention clearly elsewhere. I saw him eye a single woman gyrating in front of the band, and with a muttered farewell he left to make his move.

What was I doing? For the umpteenth time that night I asked myself the question, and the answers that surfaced weren't ones I liked. I was clutching at straws, seeing conspiracies that leaped social boundaries and linked people who lived hundreds of miles apart. I was out of it, weaving an identity out of imaginary crimes and half-forgotten acquaintances. I was lonely, I should face it, and had let thoughts of one bad date grow to assume nightmare proportions. Maybe it was time to throw in the towel and go home, take a shower and go help Violet. But first, one more circuit around the room. If I could only find Connor, it would put so many questions to rest.

I turned back toward the speaker, thinking to leave my empty can there. It was only about a foot away, but as I turned it seemed to waver, to ripple in the stage light, and I couldn't quite reach it. Funny thing about those lights, those flat red lights. I took a step closer, but the floor started bucking and heaving from all the dancers and all the movement. I stretched out my arm to reach for the wall and then it too seemed to weave up and down and down again as the can grew too heavy to hold. I heard rather than felt my hand release the empty as it dropped to the floor with a bang that echoed and echoed, and from a great distance I saw it start to roll away and swim and whirl. I opened my mouth to yell at it but my mouth was too dry, and all that left was my breath. With great effort, I looked up, at the red light, which pulsed and glowed and grew till it covered the stage and the ceiling that swam to meet it. Until it turned to black.

EIGHTEEN

I WOKE UP TO the rasp of a warm tongue and the feel of fur in my mouth.

"Musetta? Whoa, kitty." I removed the small beast, who had been carefully washing my face, and sat up. From the pounding of my head, it seemed not all of that fuzzy mouth could be blamed on the kitten. "What happened?" I was on top of my bed, fully clothed, though my shoes were off. The clock said 7 a.m. I had no memory of how I had gotten here, or where the rest of the night had gone.

"Ah, she lives!" I heard a voice from my bathroom and jumped. Tess stood in my doorway, one of my towels wrapped around her lean body.

"I don't know what you were into last night, girl, but I didn't think you could drive home. I wasn't going to leave you there, either, the way you were," she said, wrapping another towel around her long wet curls. "I was worried about you, Theda. No offense, darling, but you looked bad and you were sounding crazy. I rushed over to that party as soon as I could. You couldn't have been there for that long but already you were staggering into the walls, like a zombie. Looked like you'd fallen in something, too. I wanted to just bring you over to my place, but you were going on and on, something about cats, so I found your keys and drove you back here. Glad you woke up, though. I wanted to make sure you were okay, but I've got to get to work."

"Thanks, Tess." I put my hand to my aching head. What had happened? "The last thing I remember was that loft party. I must've blacked out. But Tess, I wasn't drinking."

"Nothing?" She looked at me with her thin brows raised in disbelief.

"Nothing. I was too tired and I needed to think. I mean, I had a can of Coke."

"Did you leave it anywhere? I mean, once you'd started drinking it?"

"Maybe, for a moment." I remembered choking and putting the can down on the speaker, as Ralph patted my back. "Just for a second or two."

"That's all it takes, girl. Someone slipped you a roufy or some other fun new date-rape drug. I'm glad I followed you. I knew something was up."

"Rohypnol? Wow, maybe. Unless it was fatigue or caffeine or something." I couldn't clear my head of that horrible trapped feeling. I remembered not being able to move, like I was frozen in my own body, but that was all. Why didn't I remember anything? "You said I was going on about the cat?"

"Cats—plural—though all I've seen is this little kitten here." Musetta had been twining around her tanned ankles and now stopped to lick at a drop of water on her foot. "I don't think I let any other cats out."

"No, she's all there is." It didn't make sense. "Cats, you say?"

"Cats. Look, I've got to run. Are you okay?"

"Yeah, I need coffee, but I'm fine." I hoped I would be. Who would do this to me? Could Ralph have been that desperate? Was there a real streak of meanness hidden beneath his buffoonery? I was trying to recount every interaction I'd ever had with him, drunk or sober, when Tess interrupted me.

"You sure you're fine, girl?" I nodded, and immediately regretted it. She was looking at me hard. "When I get home later,

I want to hear this story from the beginning. The real story, Theda." With one more stare, she walked past me into the living room and I could hear her slipping into her clothes.

I wasn't ready to stand yet but I looked up as she ducked back into the bedroom to say goodbye.

"Your keys are by the door, and your car's out front. Before you do anything else, you might want to check in with a doctor, too. Some of those designer drugs are nasty."

"Yeah, I promise. Uh, thanks, Tess. Thanks."

"No problem, babe. Paying into the karmic debt. You take care."

THE BETTER PART of me wanted nothing more than sleep, but I didn't quite trust that urge, so slowly, slowly I stood up and made my way into the kitchen. Drinking from the tap, I must have inhaled a quart of cool water, and slowly my head returned to my shoulders and the floor stopped flopping around.

"Mew." I looked down at an upturned face.

"Musetta, that was a perfect little mew!" In my sensitized state, I found this thrilling.

"Mew," she repeated, with a head butt for emphasis.

"Ah, food. Of course." When was the last time I'd fed her? Luckily cats don't hold grudges. I opened a can and heard the purr start up in anticipation. What is more satisfying than feeding a cat? I leaned back against my refrigerator and watched her lap and chew.

The cats! Of course, today was the last day to place Lillian's cats, before they'd be euthanized. My mood came crashing down to earth, and then I remembered Violet. I'd said I'd meet her at Lillian's and help her search for the will. Had she been there all night? Had she found anything? There was nothing for it but to go see. Her quest might be futile, but I owed it to her. It might not be quite as profound as rescuing a buddy who'd been slipped a mickey, but it was what I could offer. This is what friends did for each other.

I WAS STILL A BIT SHAKY when I drove over to Lillian's, but a couple of temporary No Parking signs out front forced me to walk a block. They were for the next day, but the walk did me some good. The back door to the old house was open when I got there.

"Violet?" Even my voice felt stronger.

"Up here." I followed the sounds of thudding and grunts through the living room and up a set of creaky stairs. "What kept you?"

The Violet who rose to greet me, wiping her hands on filthy jeans, looked like she hadn't slept all night. Or bathed for a week, either, though I knew she'd been bright and fresh just the day before.

"It's complicated. I was looking for someone, and things happened." I didn't have the energy to explain.

"Did you find him?"

"No. And, I'm sorry."

I offered her one of the two travel mugs I'd brought as a peace offering, and she took a deep draught of the dark brew. "Wow, strong stuff," she gasped. "Laurel's brew, right?" I nodded and she settled into the desk's rolling chair.

The taste of my own Mug Shot house blend reminded me. "Did a guy named Ethan find you?" She looked blank. "Writer, curly hair, glasses?"

"No. Did he come to the gig?"

"I told him about it." Strange. He seemed so eager.

"Well, I got a lot done here." Violet broke into my thoughts. "The will is definitely not in any of the boxes downstairs, and I've moved on to her bedroom. There's an old desk that seems promising." She pointed to a scarred, but classic rolltop, set against the wall. "And those of course." More cardboard boxes, piled in towering columns, filled half the large room. "But I could use a break."

"Did you sleep at all?" I settled on the floor, still not entirely steady.

"Yeah, for a few hours. I got here by eleven-thirty or so last night, worked for a while, but by four-ish my flashlight battery was going dead and I was beat. I curled up on Lillian's bed over there." She nodded toward a king-size bed, crowned by a carved oak headboard. It was almost dwarfed by the boxes. "Made me really feel her presence. I still can't believe she's gone."

We drank in silence for a few minutes and I felt my own coffee, liberally laced with milk and sugar, waking up my drugged body.

"So what are we looking for? I mean, what should I be on the alert for?" I was ready to go to work.

"Any sheet of paper with writing on it. I'm betting that it's a holographic will, written out in her hand. That's legal, as long as she got witnesses, and I'm sure she did. All we have to do is find it." She paused and stood, wiping her mouth with the back of her hand. "Which we will." I suspected that last bit was added to cheer herself on, but I wouldn't contradict it. In response, I pulled one of the big cardboard boxes toward me and opened it, removing first newspapers and then old issues of the *New Yorker* from the 1950s.

"Was she still dancing in 1952?" I asked, just to make conversation.

"I bet she was. Let's see, how old is Dougie?" We both fell into our own calculations as I went through more memorabilia. Lillian had saved everything from her brilliant, if brief, career.

"Wait a minute." I looked up at Violet, who had gotten to the bottom of one of the desk's deep side drawers. "No, no,

sorry. Camp inventory for one of Dougie's summer outings."
We went back to work.

An hour must have passed before we heard the door,
followed by the tap-tap-tap of high heels on stairs.

"What are you doing here?" We looked up to see Patti
Wright, the shocked look on her face set off by the bright
peach-pink of her ensemble.

"There's a will, Patti." I started to explain, but she was
having none of it.

"You're trespassers, both of you. And that tatty cat." I remembered the frayed-ear feline I'd fed days before. Was he
still hanging around, or were there others? "I don't know
what you think you're doing here, but it's got to stop. In my
book you're no better than common thieves!" I suspected that
I now looked as grimy as Violet, but this was too much.

"Now, Patti, listen." I reached for her arm, but she recoiled.

"Don't touch me. You're filthy!" She backed toward the
stairs. "I'm calling the cops. I'm warning you. And then I'm
changing the locks. I'm the administrator here. I'm having this
place cleaned out tomorrow, and I won't have you trespassing. I'm getting rid of those feline vermin, too. I'll give you
fifteen minutes to get out." She stormed back down the stairs
and we heard the door slam as she left.

"Can she do that? Clean the place out?" Absently putting
down the pile of papers she'd just taken up, Violet looked at
me, worried.

"I don't have the faintest. But it doesn't matter to us, does
it? The cats at the shelter only have till the end of today." I
reached for another box, and thought about the one ragged
feline I'd seen here, the one who'd found Lillian's pendant.
Were there others? Violet had mentioned some ferals. "And
any cats that are still hanging around will be okay, probably.
If they've survived this far, they'll know how to stay clear of

the wrong people. Plus, if she calls the cops, well, we are trespassing."

"She won't do it," said Violet, focusing once more on the papers. I didn't know if she meant that Patti wouldn't call Animal Control back or the cops; nor did I know which would make her more upset. "She's all bark, that one. But I'm going to lock the door behind her, just to give us a heads-up in case she comes back to check."

I wasn't so sure. But in for a penny, in for a pound. I opened the box before me and began lifting out what looked like photo albums. Violet scooted down the stairs and I heard her secure the door, shaking it to make sure the lock held. She joined me a moment later, and in silence we both went back to work.

FIFTEEN MINUTES PASSED and I relaxed. Another hour and we were chatting a bit, remarking on the finds Lillian had squirreled away. The work was slow; Violet had only finished one side of the desk, and piles of sagging cardboard boxes stacked almost to the ceiling remained by the window. But even as we lapsed again into silence we buoyed each others' spirits. It was good to have company. If there was a will, we'd find it. Then, in the midst of our searching, we both stopped and turned toward each other. Down below the unmistakable click of a key in a lock was followed by the opening of a door.

"It's gotta be that woman, Patti," hissed Violet.

I wondered if she'd returned with the cops. Maybe she'd give us one more warning. "Let's hide," I said. "Maybe she'll go away."

We ducked behind the two remaining towers of unopened boxes as we heard a tread upon the stairs. The steps sounded heavy for the bird-thin realtor, and I peeked my head out from behind my box.

"Connor!" Despite everything, my heart leapt and I stepped

out to greet him. After so many hours of fruitless searching, here he had found me.

"You know this bastard?" Beside me, Violet had come forward too, but with arms slightly raised and fists clenched.

"Violet, what's going on?"

"This is the guy who broke in and attacked me. He's the creep!"

"Connor?" Of all the crimes I'd considered him guilty of, this was a new one. I looked at my onetime suitor for an explanation. But the man who looked back no longer resembled the charming artist I had desired. The planes of his face, once so sculpted, now seemed machine-like, repellent. Those stunning blue eyes stared back hard. And in those long, sensitive artist's fingers, he held a matting knife.

"The two of you." He was nodding, the knife resting loosely in his hand. "Well, that explains a lot. When I saw that kitten at your place, I should've known you were after the same thing I was."

"Connor, what are you talking about?" He wasn't making sense.

"The treasure, Theda. The old lady's treasure. That's why we're all here."

"You're crazy, Connor. There's no treasure. That's a kids' tale."

"Don't talk to me about crazy. Didn't I spend long enough cleaning up after those psychos? Didn't I count out pills and hold their hands long enough before I got a payoff? I'm an artist, Theda. I'm sick and tired of having stupid day jobs. I deserve better."

"But Connor…" I noticed Violet edging slightly away from me. I didn't know what she was planning, but I had to keep his attention. "What treasure are you talking about?"

"Don't play dumb, darling. It's not becoming." He smiled,

revealing that chipped front tooth, but the charm was gone. "You talked to that schizo Dougie, too. He must've told you. His mom was as loony as he is, but she was never locked up. She kept enough stuff here to survive another war, he said. Yeah, most of it's junk—papers, books, those damned cats— but there's gold here, too, somewhere. Gold, cash, who knows what else? I'd have had my prize and cleared out of this little city weeks ago, if it weren't for all of you interfering. First this one." He turned toward Violet and gestured with his knife. She froze, and he turned back to me. "And then that damned kitten. I'd have been in and out of this dump if that pesky cat hadn't tripped me up. Yeah, I kicked it. I'd have had the treasure already if it weren't for that mangy beast."

"So, Lillian interrupted you and you killed her?" I looked at the knife, more of a razor blade, actually, and tried to think: there were two of us. It was a short blade. What was possible? I backed up and found myself hard against a stack of boxes.

"I should have." He stepped closer to me, his eyes menacing, and I scooted a few inches to my right. He was still between me and Violet and the door, but I felt the window sill against my leg and ventured a peek. Where was Patti? Where were the cops she'd threatened to call? Down on the street I saw the car, a tan Hyundai.

"But you don't have a car!" I could hear the hysteria in my own voice. He raised the knife.

"What are you on about?" He grabbed a box from one of the low piles and slit it open, the sharp blade of the matting knife cutting through the cardboard easily. Violet and I exhaled in unison. "No, I didn't kill the old lady. That kitten's yowl woke her up, though, and I had to scram before she could set off that alarm thing she wore."

He dumped a box of papers on the floor and kicked through them. "Hey, hand me another one. You must've seen the parking permits out on the street—that neighbor's getting a Dumpster delivered and cleaning everything out. This is my last chance to go through this mess. So, all in all darling, it doesn't matter what you're on about, I'm not leaving here till I find it."

"You're not leaving here, period." I looked up. Connor must have spun around, too, because I heard his quick intake of breath. "Drop the knife." It was Ethan, standing in the doorway with a gun in one hand, a black backpack in the other.

I gasped. "Ethan?"

"I tried to keep you out of this, Theda. I thought you'd take the hint when I never called." He put the pack on the floor and gestured with the gun. Connor stepped a little closer to Violet, who shuffled over toward me. "The knife, Connor? Or should I say Davey?" It made a dull thud as it hit the papers already on the floor.

"Don't remember me, do you Davey?" With the window at my back, I couldn't see Ethan's eyes behind his thick glasses. I remembered the odd flashes of light, the feeling that someone was watching me. The rage that he could barely keep in check. "You were the charmer, the one who seduced everyone at the home—and everyone here, too." He was nodding toward me. "I knew you took that money, that you'd taken the drugs—some of them, anyway. Guys like you have no reason to notice guys like me, do you? But I was around long enough to fit the entire story together, Davey. And I could see where you could come in handy. I'm the reason there are no photos of you in the newspaper file, you know. You owe me."

"You know about the fire?" Connor's voice had dropped to a husky whisper.

"I know about everything, my friend. That's why I grabbed the photos. I thought they might be useful to cover my own tracks. I knew you talked to Dougie, and I figured you for the missing funds. You always did go for the easy score, didn't you?" He glanced at me for a moment, and I winced. "Foolish, really, because what did you get from the halfway house? A couple of grand? That just alerted the cops, and it wasn't enough, was it? When I followed you here that night, I figured you were out for the same thing I was—the big prize. I was watching you. If I hadn't been careful you would have heard me laugh. Scared off by a kitten! I knew then that my planning had paid off, that if anyone had to take the fall, well, you were a suspect in the embezzling and for the fire. I couldn't have written it better! All I had to do was make sure those photos got to our reporter friend here. Turns out I didn't need them, but I didn't want to take the chance that she was so smitten that she couldn't put two and two together." He motioned toward me and smiled.

I wished he hadn't. With the sun reflecting off his glasses he looked like a giant insect, his grin the reflex before a bite. "You were both after the treasure?"

"You don't believe in it, do you? I do." What he had said about crime, about how exposure to violence changes a person, came back to me. He'd felt cheated—angry at the world—and I'd thought maybe he had some reason. But had he ever been different? "I do my research, even if nobody else does. I spent enough time with Dougie to have a good sense of what was true and what was delusion, Davey. Did you? Dougie even told me about his mother's little alarm system. You knew about that, didn't you, Davey? Yes, I saw you that night. You were worried about that little kitten blowing your cover, afraid of that doodad hanging around the old bag's neck."

He was staring at Connor-Davey again. I peeked down at the street. Nothing.

"I wasn't." Ethan continued talking in that same quiet, reasonable tone, the madness held down underneath. "She was fast, though." His arm had to be getting tired, but the gun didn't waver. "She was still awake, that was the problem, Davey. Didn't go back to sleep once you'd run off, even though I waited for an hour after you'd gone. She had her hand on that necklace almost before I could grab it and shove her against the wall. Couldn't be quite sure she hadn't pushed the signal button. Otherwise I'd never have left before turning this place upside down."

"So you killed her." Violet was whispering, but every word was clear. "You left her, not knowing if she was going to die."

"Oh, I knew. See enough bodies, you get a feel for these things. After a while, they don't bother you anymore." He turned that awful grin on Violet, and I felt her stiffen. "Didn't want to wait around to see if the paramedics were going to show up, though. I'd planned to be in and out without any fuss. That's always been the plan. Nobody else involved, nobody else hurt." He turned to me. I wished he hadn't. "That wasn't a lethal dose of Haldol, Theda. I guess it wasn't even enough to keep you out of this. And who thought your friend here would be up and about so early after a gig? But I guess we all saw those signs on the street. It seems like we've got a deadline, folks. Luckily, I've always been great on deadline. So, Davey, why don't you just kick that knife over to me? Gently, please. It'll make my work easier."

Just then we heard the tap-tap-tap of heels on the stairs again.

"The door was unlocked, you people! I called the—" The quick gasp of air that punctuated Patti's sentence told me that she had seen Ethan's gun.

"Another guest for the party. Come in, my dear." Ethan motioned with his head, rather than the weapon, which remained pointed straight at me.

"Theda?" With panic growing in her eyes she stumbled over, shaking visibly.

"The cops? You called…." I couldn't tell if she had it together enough to understand my half whisper. Then it hit me. She hadn't known about Ethan; at most, she'd phoned in another complaint about us. How quickly would the police respond to a report of trespassing? To the kind of call that had been coming in regularly from an irate neighbor of an empty house? They'd think it was a nuisance, nothing more. My hope evaporated.

"That's enough chit chat, folks." Without looking away, Ethan knelt and reached into his pack, pulling out a roll of duct tape. "Davey boy, here." He tossed it. "Tie the ladies together, if you please. Use it liberally. We don't want any accidents."

"Connor?" I looked up into those blue eyes and heard Ethan laugh.

"Don't be fooled, darling. Our Davey has a way with the ladies, but that's just made him soft and lazy. He's not going to risk his own neck for anyone." I stared at my onetime beau, but Connor—Davey—lowered his head and pulled the end of the tape loose.

"Don't worry about fingerprints on that tape, Davey." Ethan looked positively gleeful. "In fact, the more the merrier." With a slight movement of his gun, he motioned for Violet and Patti and me to move closer together.

We shuffled, knowing that we were readying ourselves for slaughter. But as we pulled closer together, something caught my eye. There, down by the street, was another movement. A patrol car. No, an actual uniformed cop—but he was simply standing there, looking at Ethan's tan Hyundai. He had to be waiting for Patti. Without her, the complaint, he'd probably write up the visit and drive on. Even the No Parking sign wasn't in effect till tomorrow.

We were standing side by side now, and Ethan was motioning for us to move closer with his gun, waving it gently to indicate we should stand back to front. For a moment it pointed off to the left. I started to turn. "Duck!" I yelled—hoping Violet and Patti would act fast enough—and smashed my elbow back through the window, breaking through the fragile old pane and the storm window with a crash. Surely the sound if not the shower of glass would catch the cop's attention. Ignoring the wild stab of pain that rushed up my arm, I pushed Patti out of the way and fell on top of Violet, aiming to roll us both over to the shelter of the boxes. I landed hard and felt the wall of cardboard shudder.

"You bitch!" His composure finally broken, Ethan lunged for us. But he didn't fire. Maybe because his set-up wasn't in place or maybe because he wanted to feel himself inflicting pain—there was no loud echoing report. No blackness. Startled, I looked up and saw the heavy weapon's handle right above me, aimed to come down on my head.

"Mrow!" From somewhere I heard an unearthly scream. I ducked, covering my face with my hands, but the blow never came. "Rrrow! Pssst!" I looked up. Out of nowhere, it seemed, a streak of fur and spit descended amid a hail of cardboard and papers. The cat must have been hiding on the top of the boxes, until my heavy landing had prompted it to jump—upsetting the pile. "Aslan!" Violet yelled in recognition, but the shaggy cat was too busy to acknowledge her. In an arc of fury he had landed by chance or choice on Ethan's head. "Damn it!" He dropped the gun and clawed at the furious beast that had attached itself to his face. "Get this animal off of me!"

"The gun! Get the gun," I yelled and dove for it myself. As I did, I heard a loud thud. Ethan went flying. Violet stood beside him, holding the heavy oak chair that went with

Lillian's desk. She'd knocked him flat with one swing. Now
she raised it over his head to deliver a killing blow.

"No, Violet! No!" I jumped over his prone body and
grabbed her, the pain in my elbow shuddering up my arm.
Between me and the weight of the chair she stumbled
backward. "Bastard." She put the chair down.

"I know, Violet, I know." She sat back in the chair and I
stood beside her, cradling my cut arm and looking around. In
all the hubbub, the man I knew as Connor had sunk to a seated
position against the wall, felled by the avalanche of boxes. His
head hung down. Whatever Lillian had hoarded, it had given
her some posthumous revenge.

"Connor?" I asked, softly, but he didn't look up, and so I
turned away to stare at the still body beside him. Had Violet
killed Ethan? No, we heard a groan. And then another, in a
higher voice, from the wall by the door behind us. I turned
and saw Patti sitting upright, her legs splayed out before her,
one peach pump missing. Her eyes unnaturally wide with
shock. In her arms she held the shabby tabby who had saved
our lives. If a cat can smile, this one was grinning ear to
ragged ear.

WE MUST HAVE BEEN frozen like that for only a few minutes,
but it seemed like hours before Ethan groaned again and we
all started.

"What can we tie him up with?" I looked around for the
roll of duct tape. Patti was still staring, and Connor was unconscious or at least dazed. "Where's that tape?"

"Let me hit him again, please?" Violet stood and grabbed
the back of the chair. "I'd love to smack them both."

"No need, Violet." I was holding the gun where Connor
could see it. Ethan, too, if either of them opened his eyes. That
would serve for now. But just as I started to kick at the papers,

hoping to uncover Ethan's roll of tape, I heard another, heavier tread on the stairs.

"Hello?" It was a man's voice, and it sounded vaguely familiar. Bill Sherman.

"It's the cops." I looked at Violet. Patti was still frozen, cat in her arms. Relief washed over me, but common sense followed quickly behind. Here I was holding a gun. None of us belonged here. What were we going to say?

"Are you ladies okay?" Bill entered the room, and I heard his partner and the uniformed patrolman downstairs. "Bill? Bill?"

"Up here," the detective yelled down. We hadn't said a word.

"We were looking for a will." I managed to get that out. It was a start. The pain from my elbow was making me dizzy.

"And he thought there was treasure," I heard Violet chip in, and knew she was using the chair to point to the prone Ethan. Bill was already on his knees. He lifted Ethan's head none too gently by the hair and saw a flicker of life. At that, Bill flipped him over and cuffed him, then turned his attention to Connor,—or Davey as I now knew him—taking him roughly by one arm. The dark head lifted; the blue eyes blinked.

"David Connolly, you're under arrest for arson and embezzlement." Bill pulled him to his feet and held him there. "And, I suspect, for other crimes to be enumerated later."

He proceeded to read my onetime beau and the semi-conscious Ethan their rights, and a few minutes later, an ambulance arrived to bandage me up and take Ethan away. By then, the uniformed cop I'd seen outside had cuffed Connor, that is Davey, and shuttled him down to the patrol car. The detective lingered, looking at the three of us, still frozen in place.

"I don't understand," was all I could say. "Patti called you?"

"Don't you return phone calls?" He countered my question with his own. "But, no, she phoned the station house to report trespassers. I heard the call, and figured there was a good chance that you'd be involved. Besides, I've been trying to reach you since late yesterday. I wanted to tell you that we matched the pendant you found with a line of bruising that had been noted on the back of Lillian Helmhold's neck. The necklace had been torn off her. That and one clear print that didn't match the deceased meant we were reopening the investigation. With the cooperation of the Northurst police and some information from civilian sources, we knew something bigger than simple breaking-and-entering was going on. And then we began to uncover information about that reporter, too." He nodded toward the spot where Ethan had fallen. A small spot of blood still marked the dust. "The Northurst cops said they'd been watching him, before he disappeared. He seemed to take a little too much relish in reporting from crime scenes. And evidence had begun disappearing when he was around, too."

"Jim Brett at the *Eagle*," I said, and Bill nodded. "I'd been meaning to call you." Was that only yesterday?

"We thought Reinhardt and the missing counselor might be working together," he continued. "But we couldn't quite make it all fit. We'd been looking for his car, when I heard the trespassing call."

"We were doing fine." Violet stepped forward. Her spirit had returned.

"Yeah, and I got to stop you before you killed a man."

"Self-defense," countered Violet.

"Not if he was already unconscious," noted Bill, looking at her from under those slightly shaggy eyebrows. "And what brought you ladies here today, anyway?"

"There's a will." I needed to step in before these two came to blows. "Lillian Helmhold left a will. Dougie told Violet, and we've been looking for it. Today is the last day to save her cats, and we were hoping that there would be some provision made to keep them somewhere, keep them alive."

"I'm afraid I can't help you, Theda. Besides, you should get to the hospital. The EMT said he couldn't be sure he got all the glass out. And Violet," he did her the courtesy of a brief nod, "will or no, you've got to go. I'm going to seal this house off now. And put new locks on the doors. This is a crime scene, you know."

"No!" Patti had been so quiet we'd almost forgotten about her. But now we turned to see her holding onto the shaggy cat. "Kitty!" The tabby was struggling, pushing against her peach sweater, and finally he hissed. She dropped him. "Kitty!" The cat bounded to the corner of the room, and Patti threw herself after him. Violet and I reached for her. We both knew you don't grab a cat who wants to be let alone.

But the scrawny tiger wasn't running. With motions as deliberate as the day he had shown me Lillian's pendant, he was sniffing at the floorboards, first one, then another, before finally settling on a spot just by the head of Lillian's bed. He started to paw delicately at the corner and then to scratch.

"Oh no, no kitty. Let's go outside." I reached for the cat before he could commit a bathroom indiscretion. But as I did, I noticed that the board he pawed at was loose. Unlike the other wide hardwood boards, it seemed to have no nails in it. It was held in place simply by warping and wear and time.

"Bill, Violet. Someone hand me that knife." Violet found the weapon where Connor-Davey had dropped it and before Bill could intervene put it in my good hand. Working the short, sharp blade into the space between the board and the wall molding, I managed to lift the floorboard up a bit. The cat sat by me, lashing his tail as if excited. I pushed the blade in further, using both hands and ignoring the shooting pain in my left elbow. Suddenly the whole board came loose. Violet,

Patti, and Bill leaned over me as I raised it from the floor, revealing the space beneath.

"Oh my god." Patti's breathless voice spoke for us all. For in what should have been the dark hollow between floors, we saw a glow. Where there should have been insulation, there was gold. Coins, chains, one large pendant of a bird that looked Russian, with eyes that could only be rubies. Violet reached in, pushing her hand into the cool, glowing treasure.

"There's got to be a couple of pounds of stuff here," she said. "Could this be piled all the way to the wall?" She shifted and ran her hand through the treasure in the other direction. The sound of sliding coins marked her progress as she moved her arm beneath the floorboards, running her hands through the treasure back toward the center of the room and then toward the other wall. No wonder the ceiling below had sagged.

"Wait, what's this?" She ducked in a little deeper, and I could see her concentrating. "Underneath, there's paper." She reached in. "I've got it. Some of it." The sheets she pulled out had fine, old engraving on them. Stocks, they looked like, marked with seals and phrases like "share" and "partnership." Some had the heading BEARER BONDS, and I heard Patti whistle softly.

"Wait, there's something bigger down here. Hold on." Violet was up to her elbow, reaching back toward the wall. What she brought out was an envelope, oversize and of good quality paper. On the front, in spidery but legible handwriting, were the words: *To Whom It May Concern.* Bill reached over and opened the unsealed envelope. He unfolded the single piece of paper inside.

"It's a will," he said. "A holographic will." And seated beside us, the cat began to purr.

EPILOGUE

TWO WEEKS LATER, the dust hadn't even begun to settle. Lawyers were dealing with both defendants, though it seemed likely that neither Ethan nor Connor would be free to bother us anytime soon. Appraisers and contractors were all over Lillian's house, but they had to work with felines underfoot: the terms of the will made that clear.

Lillian had been smart, even if unconventional in her banking techniques. All her treasure from years of touring fame and subsequent savings went to two trust funds, one for Dougie, the other for the care of the cats. The only other question came up when trustees for the funds were named. The Greenleaf House lawyers would manage Dougie's funds, that was clear enough. But the cats—their maintenance and the establishment of the Lillian Helmhold House for Wayward Felines—were handed into the care of one Edith Hayes. That had taken us all by surprise, that morning as we sat around the old house and deciphered the spidery script.

"Edith? Who's Edith?" Patti had asked, slumped against the dirty wall, completely oblivious to the muck staining her suit. She was once again cradling the moth-eaten tabby in her lap and absently scratching behind his one good ear as he purred.

"The Hayes is familiar," I said, though I couldn't place the name.

"Edith Hayes," Bill repeated, reading from the document. Violet cleared her throat. We all looked toward her.

"That's me," she said, and even under the layers of dust and sweat I could see her blush. "My real name. It's not Violet. I'm really Edith."

The rest of that day had gone smoothly. One of Lillian's witnesses was her neighbor, Ruby, who had died of natural causes only a month before her friend. But the other was Lillian's regular pet supplier, a friendly shop owner who drove down from his store in New Hampshire every six weeks or so with a load of food and litter. He hadn't heard that his long-time customer had died, but once he found out he readily agreed to make a statement about the legitimacy of the will. Bill called the shelter, which was happy to transfer the cats to a boarding facility for a few days, while he and his team collected evidence at the house. One of the other detectives was writing down Violet's statement, and a policewoman had wrapped a blanket around Patti—and the cat—when Bill took me aside. I expected a tongue lashing.

"Everything I did I had a reason for," I started to say. My arm was really hurting, too. Then I noticed he was chuckling.

"I'm sure you did, Theda. I'm sure you always do."

"So what are you going to yell at me for?" The aftermath of fear and pain had left me defiant, agitated, and not a little hungry.

"You never answer the phone, woman. What am I supposed to do?" I looked up at his kind gray eyes and saw a sparkle. I couldn't help smiling back.

"I actually read your story today on the Central Café." He seemed to be changing the subject. "I know it's been a hell of a morning, but I thought you might want to go back there tonight and have dinner with me? After you get properly patched up, that is."

"You're asking me out?"

"If it's the only way I can keep an eye on you."

I smiled and agreed. What the hell, a girl needed to eat.

BY THE END OF MAY, we'd all started new lives. Dougie knew about his trust fund. It wouldn't make a big difference in his day-to-day, but he wouldn't have to budget for cigarettes or burgers anymore. The lawyer who was handling probate had made some cash immediately available to him, and also released sufficient funds for Violet to get started on the renovation. She'd left the coffeehouse, and I missed her, but her replacement had my order down already. Through my freelance work, I was also able to put her in touch with several contractors. It was a rather particular job, notably because you had to be willing to work with a dozen cats underfoot and neighbors bringing by new strays every day. Violet seemed to be hitting it off with one of my sources though, a restoration carpentry expert named Caroline, an extremely buff black woman who spoke of the poetry of the wood and sported a sharp fade cut, too. Not all the cats I'd met that first day went back to the Lillian house, as the neighborhood had already dubbed it. Several of the brood had ended up adopted by Lillian's friends and neighbors after the memorial service, when it had seemed that the strays she fostered were everyone's concern.

One, of course, stayed home with me. I'd made my peace with the memory of James, and Musetta had her own bed by my computer now, although she preferred the wine-colored velvet armchair by the window. And Aslan, the ragged tabby whose fighting spirit may have saved our lives, was enjoying the pampered ease of a house pet. I frequently saw him, with his equally shabby sister, when I went for my morning run, sitting like royalty in the window of Patti's house on their own dupioni silk pillows. (I'd recommended Ultrasuede, but Patti wasn't ready to go that far.) Patti herself often waved to me if she saw me go by, though she knew enough not to stop me before I was done. The For Sale sign never went back up. She and her neon outfits were part of the neighborhood now.

I didn't run on weekends, though. Not when I had anything better to do. In fact, I'd been sleeping in when the phone woke me. A lovely, luxurious morning, Musetta and I stretched in unison. I decided to ignore the ringing, and smiled when I remembered the night before.

"That was a Mrs. Hudson for you," said Bill as he walked in with two steaming mugs of coffee. I groaned. That woman! "I told her you were still asleep and I wouldn't wake you." He put one of the mugs down on my night table and gave me a quick kiss, before ducking out of the bedroom again. He returned with the paper and climbed under the covers again. "Do you want to see this?" He handed me the magazine, which boasted a special section on interior design. "She already did. She said she wouldn't bother you for the world but I was to tell you thank you. You captured, and I quote, 'the essence of her art and her home,' and she loves the piece." I took the magazine from him and felt my professional instincts start to click in. Did I want to read it? What would the layout look like? "Forget this," I said, and contemplated the book review section. Then I reached for Bill instead.

On the floor, nestled on the Sunday paper, Musetta purred and purred.